BROKEN PROMISES

MEL SHERRATT

A NOTE FROM MEL

Thank you for downloading your copy of Broken Promises. As it's been several years since Only the Brave, the last Allie Shenton book, was published, I thought I'd provide a recap of the major characters in the series and where they are now. There is a longer explanation in chapter two but these are the main changes.

Allie Shenton, now forty-six, changed roles and became Head of the Community Intelligence Team, working on the estates around the city. However, when Detective Inspector Nick Carter retired in 2020, Allie got his position and is now based at Bethesda Street Police Station again. Allie is married to Mark.

Perry Wright, fifty, was a detective constable and is now Detective Sergeant in the team. He's married to Lisa and has a six-year-old son, Archie.

Sam Markham is a detective constable and the designated office manager. She is living with her partner, Craig, and has a daughter, Emily, who is twelve. Sam is forty-three.

Frankie Higgins is new to this series, but he's been part of the team as a detective constable for the past three years.

He's twenty-eight, married to Lyla and has a son, four-year-old Ben.

DS Grace Allendale mentioned in the book has her own spin-off four book series, starting with Hush Hush. She was seconded to Allie's role as detective sergeant for three years and then worked on the Community Intelligence Team alongside Frankie. She has now moved to the Safer Estates Team, Frankie staying behind on the Major Crimes Team.

PROLOGUE

SUNDAY EVENING

Billy Whitmore lay on the settee, waiting for the effects of the afternoon he'd spent in the pub to disappear. At least he'd managed to sleep some of it off, although he needed to go home soon, or else he might not have a bed for the evening.

'Get me a coffee,' he spoke to the man who was perched on the armchair across the room.

Andrew shot to his feet and into the kitchen.

The sound of running water going into the kettle reached Billy as he checked his phone: no irate messages from his partner yet. It was five past eight. He'd been here four hours. After his drink, it was time to make a move.

A few minutes later, Andrew placed a mug on the coffee table in front of him. He then went back to the armchair, sitting upright, his hands in his lap.

He was a nice enough lad, Billy would give him that. Harmless, more vulnerable than anything, and exploited by them all. His flat was a great base, always clean and tidy, which was a bonus with the people he mixed with. He wasn't particularly fussy where he laid his hat, but he did notice when others made an effort. And there was always plenty of food for when he was peckish.

He stayed another half hour before finally deciding to leave.

'I'd best be off before the dragon sends out a search party for me.' He laughed.

Andrew gave a faint nod.

'Oh, chill out, man. I'll be out of your hair in a few minutes. Have you got my cash?'

Andrew scuttled over to a side unit, pulled out some notes from an envelope, and gave them to Billy.

He counted it out and then passed one back to Andrew.

'Out of the goodness of my heart.' He sniggered. 'Get yourself something nice. A good bottle of whisky will do the trick.'

'I don't like whisky.'

'Well, get something you do like.' Billy sighed in exasperation. 'Unless you don't want it?'

Andrew held on to it, his eyes dropping to the floor to avoid further confrontation.

'Clever move.' Billy pushed himself to his feet, groaning with the effort. He was more wasted than he'd realised. Fiona was not going to be impressed.

Outside, he trod carefully up the steps to the pavement. Across the road, the old Red Lion stood empty and forlorn. The pub had been closed for three years now. Luckily for Billy, it was an ideal place to deal from.

Occasionally, he got raided by the police or a rival gang. Other times the neighbours had a go at him and told him to shift himself before he'd got rid of his gear. Still, it was better now the days were shorter, the darker evenings keeping him hidden from prying eyes.

Billy glanced around to see if anyone was watching, waiting in the shadows for him. He'd been keeping a low profile since Danny Burton had taken a beating last month. Danny must have been doing wrong for Kenny Webb to have dished out such a fierce punishment.

February's bleak weather wasn't cold enough for a frost, but even so there was a bitter wind that made it feel that way. Billy thrust his hands into the pockets of his thin jacket to keep warm. He staggered with the effort, cursing himself for finishing off a stash he'd had from the day before, taking two lots within a few hours.

He was a fool to still be dealing at his age. He should have quit when he last came out of prison. But Kenny had got on to him the minute he'd been back on the estate. He hadn't had much choice but to be drawn into the fold once more.

It had taken a matter of days for him to be hooked on the brown stuff again. Since then, it had been luck that had kept him out of jail. To be fair, he was surprised he hadn't been used as collateral damage, taking the rap for someone else's misdemeanour. Maybe that was because he wasn't reliable anymore since the drugs had addled his brain.

Billy swivelled when a noise sounded behind him and turned to see a man in a dark coat and trousers. A black woollen hat covered his head, strands of curly grey hair coming out at the sides. Billy peered at him. There was no light for him to recognise who he was.

'What's up, fella?' he asked. Perhaps he'd know his voice if he spoke.

'I need a fix.'

'Not tonight, mate,' Billy muttered, shoving his hands in his pockets, and walking on. 'I'm all out.'

'I – wait!' The man grabbed his arm. 'I need something.'

'Get off me.' Billy shrugged his hand away.

'Please. I have money.' He pointed to the disused pub and pushed himself through the gap in the chain-link fencing.

'Who told you about me?' Billy shouted after him.

The man disappeared. When he didn't reply, Billy followed him, curious to see what was in it for him. Maybe he could do a deal to get him something for tomorrow. 'Hey, I'm talking to you!'

He watched his step but, before his eyes had adjusted to the dark, a knife was thrust into his stomach. He grunted, hunching up at the pain.

The man came at him again, several times; the knife slicing through the air, the gleam of the blade catching the moonlight. It caught him on his hands, his arms through his jacket, until finally the fight left him, and he fell to the ground.

Rolling over onto his back, resting for a moment before trying to pull himself up, he groaned. Nausea washed over him, a warmth in his torso that he didn't recognise. He flopped back to the ground, pressing a hand to his stomach, feeling the wetness of his blood seeping through his fingers.

'Hey.'

Billy's shout came out as a whisper. Then he watched as the man walked away, leaving him there with no means of getting help.

He wasn't sure how long he lay there but, all at once, a complete sense of calm engulfed him. He tried to focus on the stars, twinkling in the black void, pointing at them with a shaky hand.

It was the last thing Billy saw. His arm dropped to his side as he took his final breath.

CHAPTER ONE

MONDAY

Detective Inspector Allie Shenton sat at her desk, her hands wrapped around a mug of tea. The night before, she and the team had been celebrating Sam's birthday with a meal at Chimneys, the local watering hole next door to Bethesda Police Station. On the spur of the moment, they'd decided to stay a while longer. More drinks had been ordered and it had been great fun.

Until she'd been unable to sleep once she was home. That had led to her and husband, Mark, having words that morning. He'd stormed off in a huff and she'd pulled a face at his disappearing back, even though she hated leaving the house on a sour note. Still, at least she had a quiet day ahead of her. There was a meeting with the Staffordshire Stay Safe team marked in for eleven and she was determined to tackle some of her backlog of paperwork.

A knock on the doorframe, her door always open, made

her look up. Allie's office wasn't much bigger than the six-by-six bathroom she and Mark had extended when they'd moved into their home. Anyone in her team could come and speak to her whenever they felt the need, but there was no room for everyone to gather, hence she spent a lot of time with them on the main floor.

'Hiding, boss?' DS Perry Wright came in and sat across from her.

She leaned back in her chair. 'I think I'm too old to party on a school night.'

Perry sniggered. 'You're forty-six, not ninety-six.'

'Insomnia.' She grimaced. 'I've barely had a wink of sleep.'

'I slept like a baby until Alfie bounced on me just after six.'

Alfie was Perry's six-year-old son, a wonderful bundle of excitement and mischief whenever she saw him.

'I hate you,' she replied with affection.

In the open-plan office, people were arriving for the day. Allie spotted the other members of her immediate team, DCs Sam Markham and Frankie Higgins.

'Morning,' she greeted them as she perched on Perry's desk. 'Everyone good?'

'Yes, boss.' Frankie yawned, stretching his arms into the air. 'Great do last night.'

'The next one will be Grace's hen party,' Perry said. 'Will us blokes be invited to that?'

'You'd never get an invite, old man.' Frankie laughed.

'For that, you can make a brew.' Perry passed him his mug.

Frankie exhaled and stood up. 'Anyone else want one?'

Several mugs were held in the air, and he collected them all.

'It was a great birthday.' Sam picked up a card that she'd left on her desk, showing a large cuddly bear. 'But I wish I didn't add a kilo in weight year on year.'

'Get off with you,' Allie replied. 'You're beautiful as you are.'

'Flabby at forty-odd was not my intention, though.' Sam pointed to the parting in her blonde hair. 'Nor having to die my roots every eight weeks to hide the grey.'

'Behave! You look amazing for your age.'

As Sam gave her a high-five, Allie glanced around her team. Changing roles had served its purpose for Allie once her sister, Karen, had died and her attacker was finally caught. She'd needed a break from the stress of what had happened.

And although Allie had enjoyed working in another team, she'd much preferred being part of the Major Crimes Team. All police officers to a certain point became investigators, but she loved getting justice for victims of hard-hitting crimes.

There had been recent changes now too and, despite being worried about the dynamics altering once DS Grace Allendale had left, so far things had been better than she'd expected. Grace had moved to work in the city centre, almost a year ago now, based in an office in Stafford Street. Allie had been stationed there herself for a couple of years when she'd been head of the Community Intelligence Team.

When DI Nick Carter had retired in 2020, Allie got his position and Grace got hers, although as a detective sergeant and with a smaller team. Frankie had joined her as a rookie detective, but they'd worked from the station.

During that time, Grace had been involved in breaking up and convicting a large grooming gang. Several of the people involved had gone to prison, and she'd got to know a lot of the girls in the city as she collected their evidence and witness statements, as well as working in the local community.

When CIT had been disbanded due to cutbacks, Grace had transferred to SET, the Safer Estates Team, a multi-agency initiative. Frankie had stayed on with the Major

Crimes Team, so they were back to four again. There was a position for another detective, but it hadn't been filled yet.

Allie's desk phone rang. 'Oh, that'll be for me,' she stated the obvious, jogging across to pick it up. 'DI Shenton.' She listened. 'Right? How long? Yes. Okay, we'll be there soon.' She replaced the phone, grabbing her coat on the way.

'There's been a suspicious death. Uniform have ID'd him as Billy Whitmore.'

'Billy Whitmore?' Perry parroted.

'Looks like he's finally had his comeuppance. A rival hit?' Sam suggested.

'He's been stabbed multiple times, so more than likely. Let's hope it isn't something brewing on the estate.' Allie looked over at Frankie walking towards them with four full mugs. 'Speaking of brews, leave the tea, fella. You're with us.' Her eyes went back to Sam, who was the designated office manager. 'You know what to do here. I'll leave you to it.'

'Sure thing, boss.' Sam grinned. 'At least I get to drink my tea. Now where are those ginger biscuits?'

CHAPTER TWO

Once she'd signed out a pool car, Allie threw a key with a fob to Perry.

'Your turn to drive,' she said, pushing the door out to the car park.

They climbed into the vehicle, Frankie in the rear, and were out of the station heading around Potteries Way towards the A500 within minutes. It was quarter past eight, and traffic was a nightmare. Morning rush hour was at its busiest, but vehicles moved over for them to pass. Pretty soon they were in Burslem.

The Limekiln Estate was off Hamil Road in the north of Stoke-on-Trent and comprised of a few hundred pre-war properties. On foot, or any kind of bike, it was easy for suspects to escape the police. In a car, it was much harder. There were lots of dead ends and narrow roads.

Both Allie and Perry knew of Billy Whitmore, having worked together for so long. Billy had been in his late forties, but as big a troublemaker lately as he had been in his teens. A known drug dealer, one step from the bottom of the rung and the head of a group of runners. Perhaps he could have done more with his life had he not used more than he sold, landing him in trouble with the ones higher in the chain, plus several stays in prison.

'I can't recall when we last had strife from Billy.' Allie grasped on to the handrail above the car door as Perry raced over a roundabout. 'It must be a year at least. I thought he'd calmed down a little now he was getting on a bit.'

Perry slowed for a bread lorry to get out of the way. He revved up again when he could. 'I've nicked him for stolen goods, no drugs for a while. But I bet he was still dealing.'

Halfway down Hamil Road, they took a sharp left onto the estate, past a row of shops that served the area and less than a minute later, Perry turned right into Redmond Street. Already there were two marked police vehicles with lights flashing, and crime scene tape had been erected across the front of the building.

As soon as they were out of their car, they rooted out latex gloves and foot coverings from the rear of their vehicle. A uniformed officer jogged over to them. He was broad and menacing with a shaven head, but he had a baby face to go with it, which didn't quite fit the picture. Allie reckoned he was mid-thirties at a push and remembered seeing him around the station.

'PC Rogers, Ma'am,' he introduced himself.

'DI Shenton, DCs Wright and Higgins. It's Pete, isn't it?' Allie always liked to remember a name if she could.

'Yes, Ma'am.'

'Allie.' She smiled and then glanced behind. 'Did you call it in?'

'Me and PC Rachel Joy were finishing the night shift when we took the call. The body was spotted by a neighbour whose bedroom window looks directly into the car park. We secured the scene as quickly and as much as we could.'

'Thanks.' Allie nodded her appreciation. Saving evidence

would be even more crucial if this was a targeted hit. 'Frankie, you stay here and help out while we go round the back.'

'Yes, boss.'

The building was a rectangle of discoloured bricks and peeling paint. Allie had stopped a fair few fights and arguments in, and outside, the Red Lion when she'd been in uniform. She recalled one where half the street had laid into a man. It had been brutal, despite the beating being given because he'd attacked a woman they all knew, and resulted in several arrests and charges, and an atmosphere that had lasted for months afterwards.

In front of the pub was space to park approximately ten cars, the markings worn out and barely visible on the ground. A pile of rubbish had been dumped, almost filling the last one nearest to the wall, and then a small overgrown rectangle of grass led onto the pavement. The area at the rear wasn't much bigger and was a known dark corner with no CCTV and lighting that had given up the ghost.

Officers kept an eye on it as much as they could, but the temporary metal fencing put there to keep people out was often getting vandalised. They stepped through a gap and went round to the back of the building.

Being first on scene, Allie scanned the area, checking for evidence of what had gone on. Five rows of paving slabs lay on the ground before a metre-high wall held up a lawned area, rising steeply to a fence.

The houses directly behind caught her attention and she wondered where the call had come from. At her reckoning, it was easy to see from one of four homes, although two had curtains drawn.

A female police officer in her twenties stood next to the body, her long blonde hair tied out of the way. She looked a tad sickly, keeping her back to the body. Allie saw why: there was a pool of blood coming from the victim's torso.

When she spotted Allie, her shoulders rose, and she immediately came back on duty.

'Hi, Rachel. Are you okay?'

'Yes, Ma'am.' Rachel stepped aside for them to see more. 'We haven't touched the body except to see if life was extinct. No pulse was detected, but it's clear he's been dead for some hours.'

'Have you left the body during that time and now?'

'No, Ma'am. I had a quick scan around, but there isn't a weapon I can see.'

'And is this the first deceased person you've come across?'

'First murder victim, Ma'am.'

'Well, make sure you look after yourself once you've finished your report. It's not a nice thing to stumble on. Perhaps have a bit of down time with Pete before you go home.'

'I will, thanks.'

Allie watched her rush off pretty sharpish. Then she moved closer with Perry, wary not to trample all over the crime scene.

CHAPTER THREE

Despite knowing Billy Whitmore had been a woman-beater, a violent drunk, and a drug user who would do anything for a hit, Allie saw a man lying dead when he had no need to be. No matter who the victim was, she would always treat them with respect.

Billy was on his back, head to the left, his brown eyes staring right at them. His jeans and dark jacket were soaked due to the overnight rain. Expensive boots were still on his feet, a watch on his wrist, so a robbery might not have been the motive.

Due to his lifestyle, he had never been a good-looking bloke, and death had ravished Billy more. His skin was already sallow, the blood pooling round him a sign of how long he'd been there.

Someone had taken a knife to him.

She wondered if they'd meant to kill him, or to warn him and it had gone horribly wrong. Allie would estimate he'd been attacked last night. There was no bruising on his face, indicating he might not have had time or energy to put up a fight. Had he been too high?

Questions ran through her mind. Where had Billy last been seen? Was he alone or with someone? Had he come here with supplies to sell or to buy something for personal use?

Had he stepped on someone's toes? Who lived in the vicinity that she could recall? Was someone moving in on his patch? Was it even drug-related?

'Billy still lives in Forest Avenue according to the PNC, boss,' Perry said, coming off the phone.

Allie had almost forgotten he was with her, glad that he was doing the research she required. Forest Avenue was a couple of minutes away by foot. There was a cut-through at the top of the street that would take them to the cul-de-sac.

'It doesn't get any easier when you know them, no matter how many bodies we see,' he went on.

'And so it shouldn't, I suppose.' Allie let out a deep sigh. It was tough when they recognised victims. It had happened several times over the years, and in some ways, it *was* harder, more personal for them to investigate.

Still, they would have a heads-up with his cronies who might know more about what had happened. They would start with the crew Billy mixed with.

Most bodies they found were after people had been reported missing and then found by members of the public out walking. Occasionally, like today, a crime was stumbled upon. She wondered if the killer had chosen this place because Billy might not be found straightaway, not thinking of the properties above.

'We'll walk there soon before word gets out,' she added. 'No doubt Billy will have a list of enemies a mile long for us to work through. Same old, same old.' She pointed to the derelict building. 'That needs checking inside. There's a boarded-up window that's been jemmied open. I doubt we'll be lucky enough that our killer threw the knife in there, but possibly someone might have been in panic mode.'

More services arrived and they went around to the front of the building. Allie kept her eyes peeled as they removed the shoe covers and gloves. Across the street were council-owned maisonettes, two blocks of four. The rest of the properties in the street were semi-detached houses. From memory, she couldn't recall anyone residing in them who had been causing trouble for them lately.

'I'll contact Sam to give her the details so far.' She glanced at Perry. 'Can you cordon off a larger area and get uniform to co-ordinate the residents' exit and entry points and stop the gawpers? House-to-house, then.'

'Will do.'

'Thanks.' Allie glanced at a group of people gathering to watch. 'I'll go to Forest Avenue. Tell Frankie to join me when he's finished talking to that woman. I'm going to speak to Simon.'

Simon Cole was crime editor for the local newspaper, *Stoke News*. Allie had known him since forever and had a good relationship with him. He never overstepped the mark, unlike some of the rabble arriving by his side.

Before there were too many reporters from the media, she wanted to give him the rundown of the basics she could supply. She knew a lot of the press hated how she gave him preference. But trust was a big word in their circles, and she didn't give a toss if any of them didn't like it.

Simon waved as he saw her coming towards him. She pointed along the pavement, away from flapping ears, and he walked to meet her. She dipped under the crime scene tape.

A reporter in a duffel coat and red scarf more suitable for a four-year-old, scowled at her. She resisted giving him the finger. Will Lawrence from the *Staffordshire Post & Times* would always be an arrogant tosser she wouldn't give the time of day to. Although he was in his mid-thirties, with receding blond hair, he spiked it at the front in a way that Allie thought looked ridiculous rather than hip.

'Billy Whitmore?' Simon asked when she reached him, the shock evident in his tone.

'Where did you hear that?' Allie sighed inwardly. Already it seemed the estate knew too much and Billy had barely been found an hour ago.

'One of the neighbours from the houses at the back recognised him. Couldn't wait to tell us about it.'

She rolled her eyes, then nodded. 'I can neither confirm nor deny.'

It was a code they'd worked out between them when there were a lot of vultures after information. The nod let him know he was right and that she trusted him not to share anything until it was okay to do so.

'Do you know how it happened?' Simon asked, getting his phone out at the same time to take down the details.

'Multiple stab wounds, probably one fatal.'

'Any suspects?'

She raised her eyebrows. 'We're good, but we're not *that* good.'

Simon chuckled. 'I meant, was there anyone else around?'

'We don't know anything yet. I might have more for you later this afternoon. How are the wedding plans going, by the way?'

'Don't ask.' He glared at her. 'There's way too much... detail for my brain. Favours and bridesmaids' gifts are this week's topic though. At least we're nearly there.'

Allie hid a grin. She wished she could laugh along with Simon, especially after what she'd just seen.

But as they turned around to go back to the murder scene, she knew what was about to come.

CHAPTER FOUR

Allie left Simon at the crime cordon, walked along Redmond Street keeping a watchful eye on everything she saw, and into the cut-through that would lead into Forest Avenue. It was a place she was familiar with due to Billy's antics. When she'd been in uniform, he was always up to something or other, and she had arrested him on many occasions. Perry had too.

Allie had always got on with Gladys Whitmore, Billy's mum. By her reckoning, she must be well into her late seventies by now. Billy had been divorced and had an older brother who had died a few years back, and a sister who had tried her best to make good of herself. Sheryl Whitmore had married her childhood sweetheart, and as far as Allie knew was still with him but they lived off the estate.

A noise had her turning to see Frankie jogging towards her, dodging the litter that had congregated on the path. His eyes were as wide as his smile, reminding her of how much she'd resembled an eager puppy when she had first started as a beat bobby.

'Forensics have arrived,' he told her. 'Pathologist too. The new man seems okay on first impression. Everything else is in hand.'

'Good. I want you to come with me while I tell Billy's mother.'

Allie enjoyed having Frankie along with her. He was twenty-eight, married to Lyla, and had a four-year-old son, Ben. His auburn hair was always cut short, his face sprouting the makings of a beard, not an accessory Allie was enamoured with unless they were trim.

His real name was Mick, but he was called Frankie by his colleagues.

'It's not because I'm boring and old,' he'd insisted when Allie had asked him about it. 'More to do with being a chip off the old block. My grandad, Frank Higgins, was in the force for thirty years.'

Even though he'd been a detective constable for two years, there was still so much to learn, and boy did he soak everything up. It was as if he were a sponge at times. He'd ask questions like an inquisitive child but was never overbearing. And he could be a huge calming influence in situations where she'd be delivering bad news, like this one.

They came out into Forest Avenue, a cul-de-sac of approximately thirty privately owned and rented properties. Most of them were respectable, let down by one or two with weeds overgrown from last year, rubbish piled high, and cars parked in the garden.

Lights shone through some windows. Behind closed doors, people would be waking up, starting their day, getting ready, without the knowledge of what was happening in the next street.

A large dog rammed his head through to bark at them and Allie jumped.

'Bloody hell.' She held onto her chest, Frankie beside her roaring with laughter. 'He scared the bejaysus out of me.'

'He obviously doesn't know who the boss is around here,' he cried.

Above them was number twelve, the last known address of Billy Whitmore. As they walked along the path, Allie glanced into the living room, where a woman was sitting in an armchair. It certainly wasn't Gladys Whitmore.

The woman stood as they approached, her phone clasped to her ear. She disappeared for a moment and then opened the front door. In her late thirties, she was small but heavily set with brown curly hair and a round face. Her black leggings hugged her thighs, an oversized cream jumper reaching her knees and fluffy slippers covered her feet.

Allie tried not to show her shock at knowing her.

'Hello, Fiona.' She pointed to Frankie. 'This is DC Frankie Higgins.'

Beside her, Frankie held up his warrant card. There was no need for her to do that today.

'May we come in, please?' she continued.

'It's about Billy, isn't it?' The colour from Fiona's face drained away. 'That was my friend, Shell, on the phone. She says there's a man been found behind the old Red Lion, with his hand chopped off. Is that true?'

'No, it isn't.' Allie stepped inside to hurry things along, annoyed that the estate drums were beating the wrong tunes already.

Allie knew Fiona and her daughters. Riley was eighteen, and her sister, Kelsey, fourteen. She'd met them on numerous occasions when she'd been called out to domestic disturbances at their property. Trevor Ryan, Fiona's previous partner, had regularly beaten her, but she'd been too scared to say anything.

But finally they'd got him on grievous bodily harm when he'd thumped ten barrels of crap out of her, the Crown Prosecution Service going ahead this time anyway.

Ryan got four years for the damage he'd caused. With DS Grace Allendale's help, they'd relocated the three of them into a homeless unit and from there a small flat.

It seemed it hadn't taken Fiona long before she'd shacked up with Billy. Riley and Kelsey probably would have had no choice but to go with her. It wasn't the most stable of upbringings.

They went into the living room, a warm space but with lots of clutter. The red Dralon three-piece suite had seen better days, the carpet threadbare in places too. An overflowing ashtray perched on a coffee table alongside three used mugs. In the corner of the room stood a cheap exercise bike, being used as a clothes rail.

'Is Billy okay?' Fiona asked, the tremor clear in her voice.

It was always hard telling people about deceased loved ones. Now, though, Allie wasn't certain in what capacity Fiona knew Billy.

A young woman popped her head around the kitchen door. Her dark hair was tied out of the way in a ponytail, her makeup as brash as her pink uniform. Flat black shoes and thick tights would make anyone assume she was dressed for work.

She frowned when she saw Allie. 'What's going on?'

'Hi, Riley.' Allie pointed to the settee. 'Can you sit with your mum for a moment?'

Both women did as she asked, she and Frankie following suit.

Allie took a deep breath, knowing, again, how she was going to change their lives in an instant. How their worlds would never be the same again.

There wasn't a sound in the room when she cleared her throat to deliver the news.

'I'm so sorry to inform you that Billy was found dead earlier this morning.'

CHAPTER FIVE

There was silence again as Allie's words sunk in.

'It is him?' Fiona gasped. 'Behind the pub?'

Allie nodded. 'We believe so.'

Fiona's face crumpled, and a loud wail emanated from her. Riley's mouth gaped open as she took in the news.

'Are you living here with Billy now?' Allie asked.

'Yes,' Fiona replied. 'We moved in a few months ago.'

'All of you?'

'Yes. Kelsey has gone to school.'

'Okay.' Still not sure of their relationship, Allie continued. 'I wasn't aware you resided here too. I am sorry for your loss.'

'We'd been seeing each other a while,' Fiona managed to say, after a pause. 'It seemed time to take the next move.'

'Ah, right. When did you last see him?'

'He went out about lunchtime, oneish. Said he was going to the pub.'

'Anywhere else?'

'No. I told him not to be too long but wasn't concerned at first when the day went on.'

'And when he didn't come home last night?'

'I-I thought he was sleeping off a hangover.' Fiona sniffed. 'I tried to contact him. I sent him a few messages during the evening, and then I rang him at half past ten and left a voicemail saying: 'don't bother coming home as the door is locked'.' She stifled a sob. 'I wish I hadn't done that now.'

'There was no way of knowing what was going to happen to him,' Allie sympathised. 'Did he often stay out overnight?'

'Not really. He'd be in a state sometimes, but he mostly came back.'

'How about you, Riley?' Allie turned her attention to the younger woman. 'When did you last see him?'

'It was in the morning too.'

'And how did he seem?' She turned her attention back to Fiona.

'He was okay, actually. He was happy for a change. Mind you, it's benefits day today. He was always happier then.'

Allie gave a faint smile. 'So there was nothing on his mind, anything he'd confided in you that he was worried about?'

'No.'

Okay, thanks. I do need to know if you have contact details for his family – his mum or his sister – so that we can inform them too.'

'Billy hasn't seen Sheryl, his sister, for years. She won't have anything to do with him now. His mother lives in Fisher Grove, number twenty-two. Billy doesn't see her much.' Fiona looked at them before moving to sit with Riley. 'What happened?'

'He was stabbed,' Allie spoke matter-of-factly. Although she couldn't reveal all the details straightaway, she always found it best to be honest and to the point. All most relatives wanted to know was had their loved one suffered. Even if Billy had wronged someone, enough for them to violently attack him, he was still someone's partner, someone's son, someone's brother.

'Have you any idea who might have done this to Billy?' Allie asked finally. By her side, Frankie took notes.

Fiona paused long enough for Allie to realise she was being careful with what she said. Then she shook her head. Riley did too.

'Billy hasn't upset anyone recently?'

'I don't think so.'

'Or been –'

'Why do you blame Billy for everything? He's dead, and you're still having a go at him. Show some fucking respect.'

Allie arched her eyebrows, wondering how anyone could use the last two words of that sentence together. She decided they couldn't really but didn't mention anything. Who was she to question how the grief of losing Billy would cause Fiona to react?

'Billy has two children,' she went on. 'Was he in touch with them?'

'No.' Fiona wiped at tears that finally came, a little sheepish after her outburst. 'Last I knew, Curtis was back at his mum's and Shelby has never left.'

'Okay, thanks for that.' Allie stood. Frankie followed suit but she beckoned for him to sit again.

'Is it okay if I look around? We need to figure out who did this to Billy, and there might be something in here that tells us.'

'Be my guest.' Fiona gave a disgruntled sigh. 'You won't find anything. Me and Billy have nothing to hide.'

'Thanks. I'll send a search team soon after, to go through things in more detail. Of course, you can be present at all times. And then we can allocate a Family Liaison Officer.'

'I don't want any police here.' Fiona folded her arms and just as quickly undid them again. 'I don't need them.'

'It's standard procedure. We won't get in your way.' Allie's tone was firm. She couldn't make them have an officer nearby, but it was always a good call for them. 'You're going to need support.'

'Your lot don't need to listen to everything *I* do.' Fiona prodded herself in the chest.' *I'm* the innocent victim.'

Allie wasn't about to waste time arguing. She needed to go soon, break the news to other members of Billy's family before anyone else did. But she did wonder why Fiona was so cagey.

'I'll just take that quick look around,' she said, moving towards the kitchen.

CHAPTER SIX

Fiona watched from behind the curtains until the detectives were out of sight. Well, that had been the last thing she'd expected when Allie Shenton came knocking on her door. Straightaway, she'd assumed she was in trouble for something and was panicking as to what it would be.

But Billy, dead? She wasn't sure how she felt about it, nothing was sinking in yet. Had he really been murdered?

She sat next to Riley, her hands shaking as she lit a cigarette to calm her nerves.

'Are you okay, duck?' she asked, not really sure how Riley would be taking things. Billy wasn't her father, and they hadn't known him for long, but he was someone they were all fond of.

'It's a bit of a shock,' Riley admitted.

'I know.' Fiona placed an arm around Riley's shoulders and gave her a hug.

Fiona was thirty-eight, and life had been tough for her from the get-go. Riley and Kelsey were the best things that had happened to her and, even though she'd brought them up in a life of hell, moving in with Billy had finally given them a grounding. Okay, he was a criminal, a drug addict, and a petty thief, but he wasn't violent towards her, not like Trevor had been.

Since she'd been there, Fiona had kept Billy out of prison. She hadn't managed to get him completely away from the drugs, but he was taking slightly less before he died. Yet now it seemed all her scheming had been for nothing. Billy had well and truly landed her in it.

Fiona glanced at her daughter. Unlike a lot of her school friends, Riley hadn't got pregnant and had a brood that she'd dragged up alongside herself. She was dating Carlton Stewart, having met him through Billy and, even though Fiona would rather she hadn't got together with him, he looked after her well. He lived on the Limekiln Estate too. Carlton's nan had recently gone into a nursing home and, as Carlton wasn't named on the tenancy, the council had taken the house once she'd moved out.

'What will happen to us, Mum?' Riley nibbled on her thumbnail. 'Are we going to get kicked out of here, like Carlton did?'

'I think we'll be okay,' Fiona replied. Because her name wasn't on the housing association tenancy agreement, she'd had the sense to get some accounts set up from the address – her mobile phone, a few shopping accounts and Amazon – so she might have the proof she needed to say that they'd been cohabiting.

'For now, we need to keep our noses clean so that they don't start delving into other things,' she added. 'I don't want *anything* linking us to Kenny Webb.'

'There's nothing they'll find.' Riley paused. 'Is there?'

'No, because I hid it before I let them in.' Fiona pulled up her jumper, revealing a small black notebook shoved in her waistband.

'What's that?'

'It's Billy's dealing book. Luckily, I spotted the police walking along the path and hid it quickly. Allie would have gone mad if she'd found it.'

Riley pointed at it. 'Is that cash too?'

'Yes, there's a couple of hundred quid. I was thinking of taking it, pretending Billy hadn't done any deals, but I reckon Kenny might realise once it was gone.'

Riley narrowed her eyes. '*You're* working for Kenny Webb?'

'No! Well, yes, with Billy. I was just helping, that's all. And now I need to get this out of here. Ring Carlton and ask him to pick it up.'

Riley baulked. 'What if they find it on him?'

'I have to get it out of here before they send in the search team!'

'But why, if it doesn't have anything to do with you?'

Fiona held in a sigh. Riley could be so naive at times.

'Because I don't want to get into trouble for not being able to return it. If we do that, unless Billy has hidden something without telling me, we have nothing else to worry about,' she explained. 'And I need to earn a living somehow, to top up my social.'

'You could always get a job.'

'Don't be so patronising. With my nerves? I can't work, you know that.'

Riley shook her head in frustration.

'I'm sorry, okay! It was an opportunity for me to make a little on the side. I'll lay low for a couple of weeks until the police are gone, and then I'll start again. I don't earn a lot, but it does make a difference.'

That wasn't enough for Riley. 'Don't you care that Billy is dead?'

'Of course I do! But ever since Trevor attacked me, I swore I would never get too close to another man. I don't trust any of them. Me and Billy were an item, yes, but am I sorry he's dead?' She shrugged. 'Not really.'

Riley groaned. 'You are heartless at times.'

'Well, forgive me for trying to look out for my family. You should be more grateful.'

'*Me?* I'm the one who goes out to work each day and –'

Fiona removed her arm from Riley's shoulder and shuffled forwards. 'Please don't be mad at your old mum.' She tried to play on her daughter's conscience. 'You have to help me, or we could be in trouble.'

'*You* will be. I've done nothing wrong.'

'I know, which is why I want that book away from here. Carlton will know what to do with it.' Fiona smiled to reassure Riley. 'Don't worry, this is only a blip. We're not going anywhere. This is our home now. Well, as long as we get rid of this.' She held up the notebook.

Riley sighed and reached for her phone. 'You owe me.'

'You're an angel.'

Fiona gave Riley another hug, but she brushed her off.

'I'm a mug, more like.'

Fiona sighed. She wasn't sure exactly who the mug was. How had she managed to get herself in this mess again? Reliant on a bloke who let her down, even if Billy hadn't gone out with intentions of not returning.

She wondered if his death would hit her later, or if she actually was the callous cow her daughter thought she was. Had her life been so damaged by Trevor that she didn't dare trust anyone again, although hoping to make amends no matter how much danger she put herself in?

She wasn't about to say that to Riley. She didn't want to worry her any more than necessary. But things could get very difficult for the Abbott family over the next few weeks if she wasn't careful what she said.

CHAPTER SEVEN

Allie had decided to leave the search team to it after a quick scout around the house. They would do a far more thorough job, and there was a lot of crap to look through too.

She walked back to the crime scene with Frankie. The weather seemed as if it was about to turn, thick dark clouds looming, making everything else appear a little greyer than usual.

A tent would have been erected around the body by now to preserve evidence. Allie hoped the area outside wouldn't be contaminated too much if it rained again. It would impede the search that had been started in the surrounding vicinity too.

'I can't make my mind up if Fiona Abbott is grieving or not.' Allie turned to Frankie. 'What did you think?'

'Same.' Frankie stepped to one side to avoid a large puddle. 'I suppose she'll miss having Billy around, but she'll also be able to sleep better at night, knowing he's not going to come home and knock two barrels of shit out of her.'

'I don't think he did that, but I bet there were a fair share of unsavoury visitors to the property. It's a shame Fiona doesn't know more, though. I was hoping we might get a few leads from her. Maybe you could have a word with a few of the neighbours later? See if there has been any fracas recently. And check with Control too. There might have been some disturbances we need to know about in Forest Avenue.'

'Yes, boss.'

They were on Redmond Street again. It was busy, by and large a co-ordinated state of chaos. Allie counted at least twenty people hanging around, knowing someone would probably have seen or heard something. It was a matter of teasing it out over the next few days. Despite wanting to stay aloof, people loved to gossip.

As Frankie went to chat to a uniformed officer, Allie spotted a man waving at her, and she waved back. It was Dave Barnett, the senior crime scene officer. He was talking to another man who then came towards her.

In forensic gear, there wasn't much to see, but he was tall with a thin physique. Harry Potter style glasses showed his laughter lines, and there was a hint of short grey hair at the top of the white hooded suit.

'Hi, Detective Inspector Allie Shenton, senior investigating officer.' Allie didn't hold out her hand as he was still wearing gloves. 'I believe you're our new pathologist.'

'Yes, Christian Willhorn. Pleased to meet you. Sorry it's such sad circumstances straightaway.'

She grinned, then just as quickly straightened her face. It would be her luck to be photographed and the image flashed across social media platforms alluding to her acting insensitively at a crime scene.

'I shall be leaving shortly but thought you might like to see these.' Christian held up the first of two evidence bags. Inside was a small notebook, a wad of cash shoved between its pages. 'Dave Barnett said I should show them to you while I came to say hello.'

'Ah, you've met our friendly senior CSI.'

'Yes. He seems like a nice chap.' Christian gave the notebook to her. 'There are lots of names and addresses with dates and amounts next to them. Dave thought you might want to take a few photos of the pages?'

'Right, thanks. I will.' Allie pointed to the swirl of colours in the other bag. 'And that one?'

Christian held that up too. 'A scarf. It was inside his coat.'

Allie frowned. 'Our killer left it?'

'I think so. There's blood on part of it where it must have caught an open wound, but I'd bet money on it being placed on the victim after death.'

Allie peered at it. 'It looks like a woman's.'

'It does. I'm not sure of its significance, but that's where you come in.'

'I do!'

She got out her phone and took a few snaps. Then she spotted Perry walking towards her. 'Okay, that's enough. I'll await the forensics from it now. Nice to meet you, Christian.'

'Likewise.'

Perry drew level with her, his cold cheeks red against the dullness of the day. 'Got anything?'

'No useful intel yet. Fiona Abbott is living with Billy Whitmore, though.'

'What, just her, or the girls too?'

'All three of them.'

Perry sighed in despair. 'Thought you might like to know the word is out who he is.'

Allie groaned: the negatives of social media. People and the press spreading things before the police had time to confirm and release them to the public. They often didn't realise how damaging it could be to relatives and friends, whether they knew what had happened or not. Even though

Fisher Grove wouldn't take long to drive to, it was imperative they reached Billy's mother soon.

Once she could see everything was in hand, that details would come through to her as and when they were actioned, she searched out Frankie. He was coming out of the garden of number fifty-two.

'Anything interesting?' she asked.

'No. I've been trying to find out online whose crew Billy belonged to lately, but no one's talking.'

'Maybe he worked alone because he'd become unreliable.'

Frankie considered this for a moment. 'Perhaps that's his problem.'

'*Was* his problem.' Allie shook her head. 'It seems a little neat to me. There don't seem to be any signs of a scuffle. Although to be fair, if someone pushes a knife in you, there wouldn't be much time to fight back.'

'He had defensive stab wounds on his hands and arms, though?' Frankie questioned.

'If he was drugged up, that might be why.' Allie pointed at the disused pub again. 'Or someone lured him to the back of there to give themselves time, and a quiet spot, to kill him.'

'I can't believe this has happened around here,' a woman said from the house which they were standing outside. 'You lot should have moved the druggies on a long time ago.'

The woman was in her early twenties, with bright blue hair, a child on her hip and one racing around the front garden pretending to be a superhero.

'We did when the pub closed. It's been quiet for ages,' Allie replied, making a mental note of the number of the property. Forty-six.

'*Some* people still cause a nuisance.'

'And do you know any names of these troublemakers?'

'No. But you should. You're always quick to get round

here when something bad happens, but what about the rest of the time?'

'That's what the phone is for,' Allie snapped. 'Funnily enough, we've never been able to be in two places at once. And we're here now.'

'I'm just saying.'

'I bet you are.' Allie rolled her eyes at Frankie as they set off for the car. 'Pop back and see her this afternoon too. She seems keen to talk.'

CHAPTER EIGHT

Riley Abbott's call to Carlton was answered after two rings. It was unusual for them to speak on the phone. Typically they sent messages via WhatsApp or text, umpteen each day.

'Hey. What's up?' he asked.

'We've had the police here,' she cried. 'Billy's dead.'

'But I saw him yesterday. What happened?'

'He didn't come home last night. Mum was furious. She thought he was sleeping something off, but the police called round and told us. He was stabbed, behind the old Red Lion pub.'

'Fuck. Do they know who did it?'

'No, they're looking into it now. But Mum has something she needs to get out of the house before they come back. She has Billy's notebook full of names, and there's some money inside it. She wants you to keep it safe.'

There was a pause on the line. 'Can you get out without anyone seeing you?'

'I think so. There's no police here yet, but they'll be back any minute.'

'Okay. Meet me on the main road. I'll be in the Co-op car park in fifteen.'

Riley disconnected the call and turned to her mum. 'He's coming to get it.'

'Thank God for that.' Fiona held Riley's coat out to her. 'Get this on and go out the back way.'

Riley slid her arms into the sleeves, pushed the plastic carrier bag her mum gave her inside it, and fastened the zip.

'Thanks, love.' Fiona pulled her in close for a hug. 'Everything will be fine. Wait and see.'

Riley's nerves got the better of her. It wasn't her mum who was going to be in trouble if she was caught sneaking something out of the house.

'I really don't think I should be doing this.'

'You have to, please!' Fiona squeezed her tight. 'It'll be done and dusted soon.'

Riley was all of a shake, but seeing the worry etched on her mum's face when they drew apart, she relented.

Outside, she ran along the path and into the cobblestoned alleyway behind. Her trainers ensured she was silent as she jogged towards the end which would take her on to the next street and then to the main road, away from prying eyes.

She held in sobs, still unable to believe that Billy was dead. She'd been having a laugh with him yesterday morning about the state of his hair cocking up everywhere. Now, she'd never get that chance again. Who would do such a thing to him?

The police hadn't given them all the details yet and, even though she didn't want to hear how he'd died, she needed to know. Because it might narrow down who had attacked Billy or, at the very least, if he knew his killer.

Having said that, Riley reckoned most of the men on the estate carried a knife, some of the women as well. It wasn't too rough during the day, but at night it was a different matter. Carlton was always telling her to be careful when he collected her at the main road. He wouldn't come to her house often; said he didn't want the feds to catch him there.

At the end of the alleyway, Riley peered around the wall. There were no police nearby; she supposed they'd be working Redmond Street for a while yet. She hurried across to the main road and on to the supermarket.

Carlton wasn't there when she arrived, her shoulders dropping in panic mode, wanting to get rid of the parcel tucked inside her coat. What if *she* got stopped with it?

It was a few minutes until his car came along. Despite the circumstances, Riley's heart beat a merry tune. Carlton was a heartthrob on the Limekiln Estate, and she couldn't believe her luck in him wanting to be with her. Sometimes he scared her with his intensity and moodiness, but deep down, she knew she was fortunate to see the sweeter side to him.

He was boy band material, chiselled jaw, strong Roman nose, and perfect teeth. He always wore the best clothes, today sporting designer jeans and a jumper. God, how she wished it was the night before when she was curled up with him on the settee, both their clothes in a pile on the carpet.

He pulled into a parking space and, almost breathless with anxiety, she ran over to the car. Then she climbed in the passenger seat and flew into his arms.

His brown eyes shone, wide and curious. 'What the hell's been going on?'

'All I know is Billy's dead.' Riley tried to hold in a sob, but it escaped. 'The police didn't tell us anything more than that. But he's dead!'

She cried for a few seconds, and they broke apart. As he glanced at her, she had to ask.

'You didn't have anything to do with it, did you?'

'Me?' Carlton seemed astonished. 'No, I liked Billy.'

'Well, perhaps someone thought he was dealing and got stroppy when he had nothing on him.'

'*I* hadn't given him anything.' Carlton paused, his eyes narrowing. 'Are you saying he was working with another dealer?'

'No.' Riley shrugged. 'I'm trying to think what he was doing behind the pub and who would have known. What about Kenny Webb? Do you think he would do this?'

'He might do. He was pretty pissed that Billy was getting more and more wasted. Milo told me Kenny called him a liability.'

Riley flinched. Being called that meant no one had your back because you'd screwed up too many times.

Carlton held out his hand. 'Where's the notebook?'

She took the bag out of her coat and gave it to him.

He looked inside. 'How much money is there?'

'A couple of hundred, Mum says.'

'Are you sure this is all he had?'

'That's Mum's. Billy was due a load from you, so he went out with nothing. He told Mum he was collecting, not dealing.'

Carlton ran a hand through his hair. 'Fuck!'

'What's up?'

'Oh, nothing. Just... upset, that's all. I liked Billy.'

'Me too.'

Carlton shoved the bag into the glove compartment. 'You'd better be getting back.'

'I'd rather stay with you.'

'You know there's nothing I'd like more, but they might miss you. You'd be comforting your mum, wouldn't you, if you weren't getting rid of the book?'

'Yeah, I suppose.' Riley didn't really want to leave, feeling better with him. But of course, he was right. It would seem suspicious if she wasn't there when the police came back. She kissed him before getting out of the car.

'Call me if you find out anything?' he shouted through the open window.

'Yeah, you too.'

She waited as he pulled away, watching until he was out of sight. Then she ran.

Hopefully that would be the end of the matter.

CHAPTER NINE

Allie parked in Fisher Grove and pointed to a bungalow. 'That's the one. Have you met his mother before?'

'I don't think so,' Frankie replied.

'She's a sweet old thing but she has a demon mouth on her.'

Gladys Whitmore took a while to get to the door.

'Wait a minute,' she shouted to them.

Allie smirked as she heard her trying to locate a key, cursing loudly. Finally the door opened.

Gladys seemed to have shrunk into herself since the last time Allie had seen her, her eyes almost hidden within hooded lids. Her clothes hung from her. But her silver-grey hair was set, and her face bright with rouge on her cheeks.

The sneer on her thin lips was an obvious distaste for her visitors.

'Oh, it's you lot.' She shuffled to one side to let them in. 'I'm surprised you found me. Did he tell you he made me leave Forest Avenue? What has he been doing now?'

They followed her inside.

Allie pointed at a seat. 'May we?'

'It's that serious?'

'It is. Please come and sit next to me.'

'He's dead, isn't he?'

Allie waited for her to settle. 'Yes, we found him this morning. I'm so sorry for your loss.' She reached for Gladys's hand.

Gladys pulled it away, and it shot to her mouth. Her initial guard dropped.

'Oh, no. Please no.'

Seeing the woman shrink even more into herself wasn't pleasant but inevitable as the news was tough to hear. Allie gave her a few moments for it to sink in.

'Are you okay to continue?' she asked then.

'Yes. I've been expecting this for quite some time now. I knew it wouldn't be easy to deal with.' Gladys fished a tissue from her sleeve and wiped at her eyes. 'I bet the silly fool only had himself to blame. How did it happen?'

'He was attacked behind the old Red Lion, on Redmond Street.'

'Around the corner from his home? Was he dealing?'

'We don't know for certain. The scene is being worked on as we speak, so we'll know more soon, and we'll be sure to keep you informed. I'm so sorry.' She paused, realising what she was about to say would upset her even more. 'Gladys, we need someone to identify the body. Do you think Sheryl would do that?'

Gladys recoiled and then, just as quickly, sat upright. 'I can do it.' She nodded fervently.

'If you're certain? There's no need if you don't feel up to it, we'd understand.'

'Sheryl can come with me.' Gladys turned to them both. 'I want to do it.'

'Okay. If I can make it, I'll come along too but I'll arrange for an officer to collect you all the same. Would this evening be all right for you?'

'Yes.' Gladys let out a sob. 'It will help, won't it? With your enquiries. Once you can tell everyone his name, you can find out which bastard killed my boy.' Almost as suddenly as she'd started crying, she stopped. 'I must be mad to cry for him, after what he did, but I can't help it.'

'He's your flesh and blood,' Allie soothed.

'Only this morning, I was cursing him. He threw me out of Forest Avenue, my home for over fifty years.' Gladys shook her head. 'He made me sign the tenancy over to him so he could put me in this box while he moved whatever woman he's with now in with him.'

'And I bet you couldn't protest,' Allie replied meaningfully.

Gladys huffed. 'You knew Billy. He didn't give me a choice. And to be fair, life has been a lot quieter since I came.' She wiped her eyes. 'But I miss my old neighbours. They're not as friendly around here. Some days, I barely see a soul.'

Allie decided to ask a few more questions. 'When did you last see Billy?'

Gladys paused as she cast her mind back. 'A few weeks ago, I think. He came when he was after money. I told him I had none, and yet he was still in my purse when my back was turned. He took a twenty-pound note, the bloody thief.'

'Sorry to hear that.' Allie gave her a sympathetic smile. 'So there's nothing you know that might help us to find out who did this to him?'

Gladys huffed. 'I bet half of the estate will be happy he's gone.'

'I'm sure that won't be true.'

'It will. He was quite the nuisance.' Glady's face screwed up and she burst into sobs.

'Why don't I ring Sheryl for you?' Allie said, eventually. She was struggling with her own emotions, seeing the distress it was causing the woman she had known for years. Sensing the pain that was yet to come for her.

But Gladys came back in her usual fighting spirit. 'No, I want to do it.'

Gladys contacted her daughter, handing over the phone to Allie when it came to breaking the news. Afterwards, Allie mouthed to Frankie, asking if he was okay and he nodded.

They stayed for a few minutes longer. Allie didn't want to see the woman sitting alone, but Gladys assured them she would be fine until Sheryl arrived.

'We'll be in touch later this afternoon.' Allie handed Gladys a card with her contact details printed on it. 'If you or Sheryl need to speak to me before then, please call.'

'Did you know he threw me out of Forest Avenue? Fifty years I'd lived there.' Gladys's voice tailed off as she bit her bottom lip and gazed out of the window.

Allie paused, waiting for her to look back, but she didn't. It worried her that Gladys had mentioned the same thing three times during their short conversation. Was she confused because of the shock, or did it run deeper than that? She wished she didn't have to leave her alone until her daughter arrived. But she needed to get back to the station sometime today. Thank goodness she had Sam there to co-ordinate everything coming in. Her head was full of far too many questions right now.

And so much sorrow for the victim's mother.

CHAPTER TEN

Once out of sight from Riley, Carlton turned into the next street and parked up to gather his wits. Traffic was heavy on the main road, but down here, it was quieter. Unless there was some old bag nosing through any of the windows in the row of terraced houses, he could sit here while he caught his breath.

Questions were flying through his mind as he thought about what had happened to Billy. More to the point, he hoped it hadn't landed him in trouble.

He and Billy had got a good thing going on. Billy had collected money owed that Carlton was supposed to, and in return, Carlton paid him in drugs. Of course, Billy had never known that Carlton made a tidy profit that way.

But all that would stop now, and Kenny Webb trusted him to deliver *and* to collect. He groaned, knowing how much he hated it. The people who owed it were hard work to get it from, and he didn't enjoy hurting them if they hadn't got the required amount each week.

Billy hadn't minded that, maybe because he was older and

from a different generation. As mean as Carlton was, he didn't like preying on the weak unless absolutely necessary.

He wondered if he knew the officers who had found Billy at the back of the pub. It was probably a dead cert. Carlton had been in trouble for one thing or another since he was about ten years old. Now twenty-two, he'd already been in juvenile detention twice, and then prison for a six-month stretch once he was nineteen.

He'd started off as a runner for Billy, but when it became clear he did a better job of things, Kenny had made them swap positions, and he was over the team now. There were seven kids, boys and girls, and they did as he said for the most part. If they didn't, they knew what they'd get. He had a good reputation on the Limekiln Estate, and he wouldn't let anything, or anyone spoil that.

It was a good life. Everyone younger than him respected Carlton the way he'd looked up to others on the estate in his earlier years. He was going places, building his empire quietly, until it was big enough to take people out with a bang. Trust Billy to mess things up for him.

Either Fiona or Riley would have to start collecting the money now that Billy was gone. Fiona was savvier than Billy, that was certain after she'd given him the book and money to keep safe. He knew she'd be fine with what he was going to supply her with from now on. Maybe he could persuade Kelsey to work for him too.

He cast his mind back over the past few weeks, unable to recall if Billy had upset anyone. There didn't seem to have been a problem, not that he'd heard about anyway.

He banged his fist on the steering wheel. Had someone been talking – Billy, perhaps – and said too much? He didn't know all the details of the murder yet, but he would get them later from Fiona. In fact, he'd probably have them before anyone else because of Riley, so there was that.

Reaching into the glove compartment, he peered inside the bag that Riley had given to him. He counted the money: two hundred and twenty notes. Shit: he needed treble that to give to Kenny. Billy could even have some of it on him. He'd never get that back now.

Would Fiona dare to have taken any? He wouldn't put it past her to have grabbed some of it before passing it to Riley. He'd check in with her, sound her out later. Because if she had, she'd definitely be working for him to pay off the debt.

The money was nowhere near enough, but he'd take it anyway. He reckoned he could make a couple more hundred pounds by the end of the day. Perhaps that would be okay until he could get the rest.

He took out his phone and sent a few messages. He needed to find out the talk about Billy, who knew what.

A few minutes later, he started the engine and drove off quickly before he was spotted.

When he was away from the estate and in his flat, he relaxed. The messages back weren't telling him anything he didn't know. Before he went to work, he would go through the rest of his contacts too. Someone had to know what had happened to Billy.

More importantly, someone had to know why.

After the detectives had left, Gladys sat for a while, trying to take in what had happened. Could it be true, Billy was gone? A tear dripped down her cheek, and she wiped it away. She never got to say goodbye.

She pushed herself to her feet and shuffled over to a wall unit at the back of the room. From there, she pulled out a photo album. There were so many pictures of Billy and his brother and sister as children.

She flicked through the pages: Billy as a baby, Billy and his siblings dressed for Christmas, Billy in his school uniform, and Billy and his friends as teenagers.

There was a group photo of family and friends. Gladys wept as she gazed at her husband. When he was eleven, Billy's father had died of a heart attack, and she was sure this had been the catalyst for all his troubles. He and Billy had been so close, and he'd been devastated at his death.

It was when he'd moved into high school that things changed. Billy got in with a crowd on the estate, a gang of kids that everyone was frightened of, that terrorised the streets. It toughened him up, too much, in fact, because when the ringleader ended up inside for life on a murder charge, Billy took his place.

Things went from bad to worse. Billy even joined him in prison for two years. When he came out, you'd have thought he'd have wanted to have a new start. But no, he went back to his earlier ways. Ever since he was a teenager, the drugs he was experimenting with had brought out the worst in him.

Gladys had hidden herself away from him on many occasions; called the police too. It had seemed like a betrayal, but sometimes it had been more than necessary, when she knew she'd get hurt if she didn't.

Next was a wedding photo, when Billy had married his first wife, Dawn. Even though it had been a volatile relationship, the best thing had been the grandchildren. At least they still visited her, despite having their own lives now.

The image of Billy at his wedding was nothing like he'd been when he'd died. Back then he was fit, healthy, quite stocky. The last time Gladys had seen him, she'd told him off for not taking care of himself. He'd become so thin, dark circles under his eyes, yellowing teeth, and needed a good wash.

What on earth changed him into the selfish idiot he

became? Often, she'd told him he would wind up dead because of it. She hated herself for that now.

She ran a finger down his image, more tears forming. Her arms longed to hold Billy one more time, her lips to kiss his cheek to say goodbye. She wanted to ruffle what hair he had left, tell him how much she loved him. No matter what he'd put her through, she had brought him into this world and, although she'd never expected him to turn out like he had, he was still her son.

There was a knock on the door and a voice. 'It's me, Mum!'

Sheryl appeared in the room before Gladys had time to stand properly. They fell into each other's arms and wept for the man they had lost, perhaps forever now, but a long time ago regardless.

CHAPTER ELEVEN

At the crime scene, Allie was eating a sandwich on the go as she approached Perry who was in front of the pub. Being so close to everything in her role as a police officer, she couldn't imagine what it must be like to have a murder investigation on your doorstep. It was often the first thing residents said to her. "Nothing like this ever happens around here." As if murder was restricted to certain areas and people. Murder happened most days, and it happened anywhere and everywhere. No road, house, area was immune, no matter how close the community or how tidy the street was kept.

'Have you eaten?' she asked Perry.

He nodded. 'Someone did a lunch run. How was Gladys?'

'She took it quite well, to be honest. Sure she was upset, but not entirely surprised.'

'Sounds about right with Billy's past.'

'I suppose.' Allie agreed, although sad about it all the same. 'Anyone see anything from the flats across the road?'

'Two people were in – saw and heard nothing. The other two were left contact cards.'

'Ah, right. Because I've only been here a couple of

minutes, and there's someone in the upstairs flat peeping around the curtains.'

Perry glanced up. 'Neighbours have said there are some comings and goings in that one.'

'I'll have a nosy before we go.'

She finished her lunch and then, leaving Perry talking to one of the uniformed officers, made her way across the road.

There were four flats in the block, two on each floor with side entrances. Mostly they were for one or two occupants as they were so small inside, with shared gardens that weren't really suitable for pets or toddlers. However, there were lots of single parent families living in them across the estate, usually with an abundance of kids sharing a bedroom.

Even before she'd reached the steps to the path, Allie clocked a man in the top right window moving out of sight when he spotted her.

While she was there, she tried the downstairs flat again. A man in a blue uniform came to the door. His name badge said Daniel, and he seemed to be early twenties. Dyed-blond hair spiked with gel, black kohl around his eyes, and well-defined eyebrows.

He smiled. 'Can I help you?'

'Yes, are you the tenant?' Allie held up her warrant card.

'No, that'll be Mr Barratt. Henry. I'm his carer.'

'Ah, I was hoping to talk to him.'

'About the murder across the road?' Daniel held the door open. 'Can you say who it is yet? I've been hearing the commotion all morning and I missed someone calling earlier so I was going to chat to you once I finish my shift in half an hour.'

'We're still making enquiries at the moment.' Allie couldn't help but grin at the warmth intermingled with his curiosity. 'Is Henry available for me to talk to?'

'Yes, but he's often out of it due to the medication for his pain. He's also in the back bedroom, so I doubt he heard anything.' Daniel lowered his voice. 'He's got a matter of weeks. Cancer.'

'Oh, sorry to hear that.' Allie noted the boxes of medical equipment piled in front of them and realised there was no point in going in herself.

'Is he always in the rear of the flat?'

'Yes. He's been bedridden for two months now.'

'Ah, okay. My apologies for disturbing you.'

'Not at all. I hope you catch whoever did it as soon as you can.'

The next door was to the upstairs flat, where Allie had seen the figure earlier. She knocked and while she waited for it to be answered, she glanced to her left. An officer was bringing out a dog. Allie watched as the spaniel jumped around, eager to get going. His handler locked the car and walked to the back of the pub.

Finally, the door was opened.

'Hi. I'm Detective Inspector Shenton.' She flashed her warrant card. 'And you are?'

'Andrew Dale.'

He was tall to Allie's five foot six, with dirty-brown hair cut short. His jumper had stains of an earlier meal down the front of it. A watch on his wrist looked to have cost a packet unless it was a knock-off.

She smiled. 'Would you mind if I come in for a moment?'

She followed him upstairs to the flat, pleasantly surprised to see a spotless living area, a kitchen coming off it. A three-piece suite huddled around a coffee table, and a huge TV hung above the fireplace. Games consoles were piled in a plastic box in an alcove.

'You like computer games?' she asked, hoping to build a rapport. When he nodded, she realised that although he seemed to be in his late twenties, his mind was a bit behind his years. He continually messed with his nails rather than meeting her eye.

She sat down and patted the seat at the end of the settee.

Andrew perched on it.

'Have you heard what's happened across the road, Andrew?' she started.

'Yes.'

'It's a terrible shame that someone has died. I wondered, as you're so close, if you could have seen something? Or heard anything that might be of help to us?'

Andrew shook his head, still not connecting with her.

'Do you have any friends who visit? Or a girlfriend?'

There was a glimmer of a smile at this but then another shake of the head.

'How long have you lived here?'

'Two years.'

His tone sounded juvenile; she'd been right with her assumptions, so she chose her questions carefully, asking basic things to put him more at ease.

'Do your family live nearby?'

'Mum lives in Tunstall. Dad died two years ago.'

'Sorry to hear that.' She paused. 'I wanted to ask who visits you, to keep you company.'

'No one.'

'What about the boys who hang around outside? Are they your friends or do they cause a nuisance?'

'They're okay.' He shuffled on the seat, moving away from her an inch or two.

'You have a very tidy home. Do they come in here and play games with you?' Allie raised a hand at the look of fear that crossed his face. 'It's okay if they do, as long as you invite them in.'

'No, they don't come in here.'

'You would tell me if they misbehaved?'

He shrugged.

She got out a contact card and gave it to him. 'If you can think of anything that might help with the incident across the road, can you let me know? I promise no one else will find out.'

He glanced at her briefly then. 'Someone told me it was Billy Whitmore. Is that true?'

'We believe so. Did you know him?'

A shake of his head, this time vehemently.

'He never visited your flat?'

Andrew gulped before shaking his head again.

It was the proof she needed that something was going on here, something she didn't like. Whether it would stop with the death of Billy would become clearer in time.

'Did it hurt?' he asked.

'Yes, but we think it was quick.'

Allie hoped that would put his mind at rest. She decided to leave things for now, perhaps have a word with Grace to get her to visit in a few days on the premise of finding out what had happened to Billy Whitmore. Sam could then find out if Andrew had a social or a care worker too. Allie was worried about him.

CHAPTER TWELVE

Bethesda Police Station was situated in the lower part of Hanley. It shared the street with the City Central Library and the Potteries Museum and Art Gallery, the *Stoke News* offices, the crown court, and a large multi-storey car park on the other side. To the left was a fenced area where Perry parked the force car and signed it back into the logbook. It was six p.m. Allie was glad to be getting back after almost a day on site.

They went in through the rear entrance. As she passed the main reception area, she greeted the duty sergeant at the desk.

'Hey, Stu – how's that bonny baby of yours doing?' Allie knew he'd become a father three weeks ago.

'He's grand, ta.' Stu beamed and pointed to his face. 'Can't you see the matchsticks holding open my eyes?'

'Oh, it gets much worse than that.' Perry laughed. 'It's when you feel like the walking dead that you realise how many years you have of it coming to you.'

'Yeah,' Frankie joined in. 'They still wake you up at ridiculous o'clock but by then they've learned the art of creeping and jumping on you while you're still asleep.'

Allie giggled at Stu's bewilderment intermingled with a smirk before heading upstairs.

The first floor was a hive of activity. In the briefing room at the far end, through half glass-panelled walls, Sam was busy adding things to the large whiteboard on the wall. Frankie went to make a brew.

'Briefing in five minutes, guys,' she spoke to everyone in the room.

'Want a cuppa, boss?' Frankie shouted across to her.

'I thought you'd never ask.'

After gathering her thoughts, Allie checked the small line of Post-it note messages on her desk to see if any were urgent and then went to join everyone.

Whether it was huddled around the digital screen watching CCTV footage or viewing forensic slides on the projector, they spent a lot of time in the briefing room. A row of filing cabinets lined one of the longer walls, windows at desk height along the other overlooking the car park and the D road.

The large oval conference table seated twenty people comfortably around it, every chair taken, a few officers trailing in left with standing room only.

Allie marched to the front of the room and turned to face them all.

'Okay, everyone. We have a new case; everything will go under Operation Moorcroft. Billy Whitmore, forty-five, IC1, received multiple stab wounds resulting in his death. It happened sometime yesterday evening – to be confirmed with the post-mortem – but we believe to be between eight p.m. and midnight. Scenes of crime officers are combing the area, and uniform are out conducting house-to-house as we speak.'

She pointed to the screen where Sam had located a portrait image of the victim.

'Billy was a career criminal. He'd been in and out of prison most of his life and was heavily involved with Kenny Webb, although Webb will deny that, I'm sure.'

'It's a wonder Billy doesn't have a plaque with his name on it over a prison cell,' Frankie joked.

There were a few snorts and mild laughter.

Allie rolled her eyes, but she was smiling. Despite the fact that someone had been murdered, she let it go because it was banter.

'Does everyone know the Kennedy brothers?' She addressed the room again. 'One of several crime families in the city and a rival of Terry Ryder. The eldest, Steve, has recently come out of prison after a stretch for murder. As soon as he was back in Stoke, he reclaimed his patches.

'Billy is a known dealer working for him. We think further down the chain, Kenny Webb is in between. But we could never get to Steve through Billy, sadly. Billy would take the rap before grassing anyone up. I'm not sure if that was through fear or loyalty, though. Thoughts, anyone?'

'From the people I spoke to,' Perry said, 'it seems the car park is a regular hangout for troublemakers. There and in the flats across from the pub.'

Allie's ears pricked at the mention. 'Anyone say anything about flat seven?'

'Yes, I caught someone this afternoon.' Frankie flicked back through his notebook. 'Mrs Faraday from number twenty-three says there are often groups of teenagers hanging around, causing a nuisance. But when Billy comes along, they scarper. She says she's seen him going in and out of the flat too.'

'That's interesting.' Allie updated them on her chat with

Andrew Dale. 'Frankie, can you visit him tomorrow, please? And check if there've been any cameras seen? I know the area isn't covered by CCTV, but maybe someone has their own installed, or one of those doorbell systems that are all the rage nowadays.'

'Yes, boss,' he replied.

'Billy's phone records are in,' Sam told her. 'I've already started checking through them, and once the tech team have looked at the phone, I'll get on to collating the digital footprint.'

'I took photos of the pages in the notebook – did you get my email?'

'Yes, boss. I'm already on it.'

'Great. Anyone else want to add anything while we wait for forensics?' Allie glanced around the room. When nothing was forthcoming, she designated the rest of the tasks and then brought the meeting to a close.

'The first press release is due to go out within the hour, confirming Billy is our victim. Make sure you grab something to eat before we start staring at screens and answering phones all evening. Good luck, everyone. Let's get this in the bag as soon as we can.'

CHAPTER THIRTEEN

From behind the curtains, Andrew peered through the window at what was going on in the street below. It was dark, and some big lights had been brought in to illuminate the street and make it look like it was daytime.

Earlier, he'd watched a police dog and his handler. The little spaniel had been so excited, barking like crazy and twirling around in circles. He wondered if it would find anything, sniff out the evidence. Dogs were much better than humans for that. He'd read up about it online.

There were other police officers too. Andrew had never seen so many, except on the TV. He loved watching reality shows. *Police Interceptors* was his favourite. It was like being on the job with the bobbies. He enjoyed fictional detective series like *Vera* and *Line of Duty* as well. *Midsomer Murders* was another one, but his favourite was *Endeavour*. Young Morse was a great character.

He wished he could watch more TV, but it was usually being used to play games on. When Milo and his friends didn't come round, he watched it all evening.

He was glad it had been his day off today so he could see

what was going on. Billy had been taken away in a black van, but there was still a lot of activity across the road.

A police vehicle, like a caravan, was on the car park at the front. Andrew had seen people coming in and out of it all day. It was good to have something happening outside that he could watch, but he didn't want to get involved. He'd be in trouble if he said anything out of place.

The lady police detective who'd come to see him had been very nice. She reminded him of his supervisor at work. Kate was always kind to him, even when he made a mistake with the counting. Andrew often had errors.

But he always kept his mouth shut about what went on in his flat. That was a slip-up he definitely didn't want to make.

An officer came from behind the building and Andrew watched until he disappeared into a van. Andrew would like to be a police officer one day. It would be so much fun to arrest people and lock them in the cells. He knew of lots of people he would like to do that to. But he wouldn't dare, because they would come and wreck his flat, like they did last month.

Andrew hadn't been able to sleep for a few nights, recalling the memories of what the boys had done. He'd been in bed when they'd banged on the door. At first, he hadn't wanted to let them in. But they kept shouting through the letterbox. They were *so* loud, and Mr Barratt had just come out of hospital. So he'd let them in.

There had been five of them, Milo the noisiest. They were all drunk and had brought more drink with them. As soon as they'd got upstairs, he'd been shoved into the corner of the room while they sat playing games on his TV. Said it belonged to them so they could use it whenever.

It didn't belong to them. It had been a gift and it was his.

But he hadn't said anything. There were too many of them for him to feel comfortable, so he'd kept his mouth shut. Even when one of them peed in the corner of the room.

That had been the start of it. They'd laughed and then all took turns peeing. Some on his settee, some on his cushions. Two on the carpet and one over all the games consoles, which he'd thought was a bit stupid. He'd got a clout around the ear from Milo for saying so.

They'd left shortly afterwards. It had taken him ages to clean the mess, and even now he could often smell a whiff of urine. It was rude of them. Luckily, they hadn't asked for his key, so they couldn't get in when he was at work. That wouldn't have been very nice. He'd have worried about what they were getting up to without him.

Milo was the worst one. Andrew didn't like Milo. He remembered a couple of weeks back when he'd visited on his own and demanded a drink. When he said he hadn't got anything but orange juice, Milo had punched him in the side of the head and pushed him down onto the settee. It had hurt where he'd hit him, but he'd tried not to show it.

Then, Milo had taken off his smelly trainers, put his feet on the coffee table, and demanded that Andrew made him some toast. Milo had taken his last three slices of bread, so Andrew had to have cereal the next day. It hadn't been a cereal day, and it upset his routine.

'What the fuck are you looking at out there?' a voice came from behind him. 'You know the feds can see you because it's dark outside and the light is on in here.'

Andrew jumped back from the window. Milo, who had been there for half an hour now, was using his phone to ring round people he knew.

Milo held up a mug. 'Make me some more tea.'

Andrew said nothing as he went into the kitchen. Sometimes he wished he had proper friends, so he didn't have to do whatever *they* chose to do. They were never nice to him,

and he wasn't sure how nasty they would be if he said
anything wrong. Which reminded him: he'd better tell Milo
in case they thought he was a grass. That's what they called it
on the TV, wasn't it?

'She came to visit me today,' he said, when he placed a
mug of tea in front of Milo.

'Who did?'

'The lady detective.'

Milo narrowed his eyes. 'She came in here?'

'Yes.'

'And what did you say to her?'

'I said I didn't know Billy Whitmore.'

'Good man.' Milo got back to his phone. 'Keep it that
way. Because if I find out different, I'll break every bone in
your body. You got that?'

Andrew nodded and moved out of his way sharpish.
Carlton had rung him earlier and said he would do the same
thing if he told tales. He didn't like Carlton either.

And he didn't want them to figure out that he *had* seen
something. He'd watched the man approach Billy, then go to
the back of the pub. Billy had followed him. There had been
nothing for a while, and he'd got bored, but as he was about
to draw the curtains across and settle for the night, he saw
the man appear again.

But Billy hadn't.

Andrew could have gone across to see why, but he had
been scared. Now, learning about Billy's murder, he wasn't
sure if he felt good about it or not.

CHAPTER FOURTEEN

Perry closed the front door quietly and popped his keys on the hook inside the cloakroom, away from preying thieves who might try to steal them through the letterbox. It was ten to eleven. He couldn't wait to chill out with a beer after his long day.

'Hey, you.' Lisa was in the kitchen.

Now there was a sight for sore eyes, he mused. His wife in her pyjamas and still as gorgeous as the day they'd met. Her blonde hair was loose, long now, and her face devoid of makeup, but in some ways, stripped back, she was even better. Age had been kind to her. To him too, except for losing his hair a few years ago. Now he thought he sported the look of Jason Statham.

Lisa popped the top from a bottle and passed it to him, giving him a kiss. 'I have a pizza in the oven. It'll only be a few minutes longer.'

'You're a star.' The smell of her perfume, vanilla and spices, enticed his senses, even though the scent of her familiarity alone was more than enough. 'How's work been today?'

'Not bad, actually.' Lisa had been a foster care support worker for two years now.

'Thanks for staying up. You must be tired.'

'Hardly. I've just woken up after an hour on the settee.' She grinned. 'You seem done in, though. It's been on the news.'

Perry had called her earlier to say he was going to be late, but that was all she knew so far.

'It was a shock to see someone I know lying there, that was for sure.'

He thought back to seeing the body of Billy Whitmore, the one he would dream about during the night. He always dreamed about murder victims on the day they were found. It was harder when you knew the victim too, whether you liked them or not.

'How's Alfie?' he asked as they moved through to the living room.

'Fine. There's been no trouble today.'

'That's good to hear. I hope he settles soon.'

Alfie had been doing well at school until a new boy had arrived. Freddie Benson had taken an instant dislike to their popular lad and started a vendetta against him. After being tormented for a month, which had involved Lisa visiting his teacher twice, Alfie had stuck up for himself when Freddie punched him in the back while Miss Brown hadn't been watching. He'd pushed Freddie, and they'd started to fight.

Alfie had given as good as he got, ending with Freddie coming off worse. Of course, Alfie had then got into trouble for it, despite saying he wasn't the instigator.

'You wouldn't believe they were both six.' Lisa tutted and they dropped onto the sofa. 'I hope they get along soon or it's going to be war for years.'

'Knowing how Alfie wins everyone over, him and Freddie will be the best of buddies because they'll see it's in their best interests. I like that he's popular, but I also like how he's been challenged by Freddie coming in and changing the dynamics.'

'Like young Frankie, you mean.' She giggled.

'Yes, exactly. But he's a dickhead, and I don't want to be his best buddy,' he joked. 'Ever.'

'You love it, really.' Lisa laughed. 'I'll check the pizza. Can I have a slice of it?'

Perry rolled his eyes but then winked at her. 'Course you can.'

'Good answer, Mr Wright.'

He sniggered, watching her leave the room. He and Lisa had been together for nineteen years, and even though they only had Alfie, they were a complete family of three. Although Alfie was going on and on about getting a dog. To the point that he was wearing them down to say yes pretty soon. They'd discussed it and decided to wait until the summer months and see what they could find. Alfie wanted a big dog: he'd have to compromise on a small terrier. Perry knew any puppy would win him over.

His thoughts returned to Billy Whitmore. Billy was four years younger than him, and yet their lives couldn't have been more different. Here he was in a home he owned because the mortgage had been paid off, with a wife and a son he loved dearly, and a job that although testing, was all he lived for.

In sharp contrast, Billy had been divorced and had two children he barely saw. He'd been in a string of failed relationships, had a criminal record as long as his arm, not a true friend to his name, and was now lying in the mortuary until they found out who had murdered him.

Growing up in Stoke-on-Trent, with its population of just over a quarter of a million, Perry knew a lot of the residents of the city, whether that be from the wrong side of the law or the right. It amazed him how most people got on with their lives, tried to make as much of it as they could, and yet others would take, take, take until they either killed themselves or someone else did.

Although Billy Whitmore was a known addict and dealer, Perry would love to think that there was one less scrote on the streets of the Limekiln Estate. But he knew Billy would be replaced soon, if not already.

Before going through to Lisa in the kitchen, he went upstairs to Alfie. He probably wouldn't see much of him over the next week or so. Perhaps the odd few minutes in the mornings if his lad was up early enough.

The hall light was on, his bedroom door ajar. He pushed it open slightly, trying not to make a noise. Alfie, for once, was asleep under his Spider-Man duvet. His son was obsessed with the superhero, something Perry was delighted about, having loved all the Marvel characters himself when he'd been Alfie's age. Still did if truth be known.

He leaned over him, just about able to see his face, content in sleep. His mousy hair was short and was always a mess every morning, spiking up everywhere. When he came into him and Lisa, jumping on the bed in his pyjamas, he often reminded him of Macaulay Culkin in the film *Home Alone*.

He was a sweet kid, and Perry hoped he'd stay that way. He'd see to it that he respected others, but there would also be times when his son would have to learn by his own mistakes. He vowed to keep him on the straight and narrow if he could.

Creeping downstairs again rather than risk going in and waking him, he joined Lisa in the kitchen as she was putting his plate on the table. At times like this, when his emotions were on high alert, he loved her so much he could burst. Ten years his junior, so always making him feel younger too.

Most of the time she was understanding about his job. Being in the Major Crimes Team rather than on a beat with shifts meant he got to spend more time with her and Alfie now. And that, he hoped, would never change.

He pulled her into his arms and held her tightly, smelling the scent of her shampoo.

'What was that for?' she asked.

'Do I need a reason?'

He could tell she was smiling. It was a standing joke between them.

He hoped they'd never stop feeling comfortable with each other.

CHAPTER FIFTEEN

Allie finally arrived home shortly before midnight. There was only the outside light on to greet her. She sighed: obviously Mark was annoyed she'd be so late. But he knew the score by now, and quite frankly, after they'd fallen out that morning, she was glad he'd gone to bed.

She made herself tea and toast, enjoying the silence as she sat at the kitchen table. The day had been long – no one ever clocked off early when a murder came in – and yet they didn't seem to be far along with anything.

Cases went like this. Sometimes crimes were solved within the first day or two. More often than not it was weeks, months even, before things diligently fell into place. There had been occasions when they'd worked solidly, when one clue led to another and another, until boom. Job done.

Their roles were satisfying for the most part, getting killers off the street and justice for the families of the victims. But in other ways, it was often frustrating, annoying, and tedious when there wasn't enough evidence to back up crimes that had been committed. With the courts and prisons full, getting a case to stick was proving harder. But electronic footprints were the best way of catching criminals and ensuring convictions.

Allie scrolled through her phone while she ate, checking any posts about the murder. There was a lot of local chatter, and she knew the team would be monitoring it, but she wanted to see if anything came up once or twice.

There was nothing except RIP messages, which she found equally comforting and distasteful because most people thought Billy Whitmore was a scrote.

Afterwards, she went through to the lounge and relaxed into the settee. The house was quiet, not a creak or a groan to be heard. She thought back to meeting Christian earlier, recalling the scent of his aftershave as it wafted upwind at her. Far more impressive than most of the aromas she'd encountered that day. She definitely liked what she'd seen of him. He had a friendly manner, approachability, and she hoped they'd get on well.

Yet the easy feel to their conversation had emphasised how much trouble Allie's marriage was in. She and Mark had barely had a civil conversation for weeks.

Things had been steadily getting worse for them since her sister died in 2015. Karen had been the victim of a vicious attack when she was twenty-five. It had left her physically and mentally incapacitated. There was no way she could live independently anymore, and her parents had taken her home so they could give her the care she required.

Their father had died two years afterwards of a heart attack, and when their mother had passed too, Allie made the agonising decision to place Karen somewhere she would receive the care that she couldn't provide. She and Mark had been married for seven years then; they were young and unable to do what was necessary. Even happy to concentrate on their careers and put children off until later, they weren't able to be there for Karen around the clock.

The decision to admit her sister to Riverdale Residential Home had haunted Allie for months, but it had been the right thing to do. Until her death, Karen had been well looked after, and the staff always welcomed her and Mark.

Finally catching her attacker just before Karen died had put an end to the constant wondering, the anger that he was still out there. The frustration that he might do what he'd done to her to another woman.

He'd come after Allie in the end, wanting his piece of her too. Afterwards, she'd sat with Mark, safe in the knowledge that it was all over. But it was then that their troubles had begun.

Mark had often talked about starting a family. Being a police officer and having a sister to visit didn't give Allie enough time to concentrate on what was important to them as a couple. It was mostly her fault – she had to take the blame for it – because her work became her shut-away from it all.

The anger at her sister's attacker being out there had consumed her. And even when he was caught, she wondered if Mark had ever questioned if it would be enough to patch them up again, the way she often did.

Without Karen in their lives, Allie had spare time, but she'd found herself working more and more. When Mark raised the subject of adoption, she'd pushed it to one side. She knew she'd hurt him, but she felt unable to look after anyone again. She understood she might not be able to keep a child safe. The worry it would bring might outweigh the benefits. She couldn't do it.

Over time, it had soured their relationship. Mark was nearing fifty, and Allie had passed her best years a while ago. Even though it might be possible for her to become pregnant, she hadn't wanted to put her body, or herself, through it. Nor had she wanted them to be older parents with a baby.

Their marriage had become a union of confusion, she thought.

She glanced at a photo on a shelf in the built-in unit beside the fire. It was of her and Mark, laughing as they shared a drink on a summer holiday. She wished she could transport them back to that moment. Holidays were for relaxing, chilling out, and getting together again.

Like most couples in long-term relationships, there were times when the sex became infrequent. They used their beach holidays to get together again, often at it like rabbits. It was something they looked forward to even, the more times the better. Like second honeymoons really, and enough then to get them through the dry spells when they returned to normal life. Busy days and tired evenings. Weekends spent catching up, visiting friends or decorating to fit everything in.

They needed to rekindle their relationship soon or else.

Sometimes she loved Mark with all her heart. She would know they'd get through this; they were meant to be together.

Other times, it was like living with a stranger, who she neither loved nor despised. She just felt... *indifferent*.

She ran a finger over her tattoo on the inner side of her wrist. One word: *Believe*. Should she have faith in their relationship still or had it gone past the point of no return? She gave a dramatic sigh, unsure what to think right now.

So it was at times like these, when she had a head full of her latest case to solve that she relished. They took her out of a world that she no longer fitted in, to inhabiting one that she loved.

And it made her forget a marriage she wasn't sure she wanted to be a part of anymore.

CHAPTER SIXTEEN

Debbie Mayhew reached for her glass of wine, trying not to roll off the settee in the process. The TV was on too loud, but she couldn't be bothered to find the remote to turn it down. Instead, she had to put up with some woman on a farm with her kids, cute but not her thing at all.

Living at home with her mum hadn't been on her life plan, nor any part of her teenage dreams. Still, the bungalow she was sharing with her was much better than some of the squats and shitholes she'd lived in over the years.

She pulled up her head long enough to take a sip of her drink and then flopped back again. Everything was too much effort. She hadn't even had a shower today.

Once Mum had left that morning to stay overnight with her aunty Janice, Debbie had planned to spend the day lounging around. But hearing about Billy's death had sent her completely in turmoil. She'd gone to the pub at lunchtime, mainly because she'd needed someone to talk to about it. Everyone knew Billy, and she and him went back at least twenty years.

A huge crowd had gathered in The White Horse, mostly

in shock, some in disbelief. But there was respect for the main part. They'd raised toast after toast in his honour.

She still couldn't believe he'd been murdered. *Stabbed*, even. Rumours were rife about what might have happened, who it could have been. No one really wanted to say what they were thinking. Was it one of his crew who had done it for revenge? He'd certainly been a character in his time, that was for sure.

Afterwards, a couple of her mates had come back with her but, luckily, she'd managed to get rid of them while she'd slept off her hangover.

Now the place was a tip, and her mum would go ballistic if she didn't tidy it before she came home tomorrow afternoon. Still, there was plenty of time for that, and as this was the first night she'd spent on her own in safety for what seemed like forever, she was going to enjoy every minute of it.

She'd eaten well, for once. She'd cooked chips and a burger. Well, she'd shoved it all in the oven, but it had been wonderful to sit in the kitchen and eat it without her mum fussing over her.

Then again, she wished she was here now. Mum would make her a mug of tea. Mum wouldn't have let her get drunk, nor take a quick fix. Not even after what Debbie had done the week before.

Embarrassment flooded through her. When Nathan had thrown her out for not paying her rent, Debbie had come here and asked if she could stay. She promised it would only be for a couple of nights – the bungalow was too small for two people really.

At first, Mum had been reluctant, but Debbie had pleaded, finally winning her over. That had been five weeks ago, and she had no intentions of going anywhere anytime soon.

When she'd come in leathered at three a.m. last weekend,

Mum had read the riot act to her. Of course, Debbie being Debbie hadn't taken kindly to it and had screamed in her face before slapping her. She'd been mortified the next morning. Both assumed those days had been far behind them. Because it had been a regular occurrence twenty years ago.

Debbie was forty-two and ever since her teens had been in trouble of some sort. She'd gone off the rails as soon as she'd left school, getting in with a crowd who'd introduced her to drugs. Her parents had tried to keep her on the straight and narrow, but to no avail. Her dad had died a couple of years ago now, and she didn't think she'd ever made him proud to have a daughter, something she'd tried to put out of her mind on many occasions. She'd been an embarrassment to him, she was sure.

Moving in with Mickey Elkin had been her worst mistake. At nineteen, he'd got her addicted to heroin. She'd got pregnant twice, miscarrying one baby and carrying the other to full term, only to give it up for adoption. At that stage in her life, it seemed as if the whole world was against her.

She often wondered what her daughter was like. She would be twenty-one this year... or was it twenty? Perhaps twenty-two? She cursed loudly, annoyed that she couldn't remember.

Nothing she did ever worked out. She'd get a job but then be sacked for either not turning up or thieving from the till if she needed a fix.

She'd had friends who'd stood by her at first but then had slowly drifted away when she became even more addicted.

And then she'd got hooked on monkey dust. It had worn her down, tore away any dignity she'd had left. Although she'd still managed to come grovelling back to her mum, it was because she didn't want to sleep rough again. At her age, it was too much.

The news came on the TV, and she was surprised to see it

was ten p.m. Where had that evening gone? She hauled herself from the settee and trundled off to the loo. The room was spinning but at least she hadn't thrown up. Yet.

Staggering back, she dropped into the settee and wrapped the duvet around her. She might as well settle on here for the night, as long as she'd taken enough to knock her out. If not, she would nip around to Harrison House to see Milo for another fix.

An hour later, she jumped as something woke her up. She relaxed, thinking it had come from the TV.

Then the doorbell chimed. Who could it be at that time of night?

She dragged herself up once more. By the time she got to the hall, the bell had gone again.

'Okay, okay, keep your hair on. I'm coming.' She opened the door. 'Oh, it's you.'

As Debbie turned and went back to the living room, her visitor closed the door to the night.

CHAPTER SEVENTEEN

TUESDAY

Before the morning briefing with her team, Allie went upstairs to the DCI's office. All higher-ranking officers shared the top floor of the station, and she smiled fondly at Verity, their secretary, receptionist, and personal assistant.

DCI Jenny Brindley had been in her role for several years now. Allie had trusted her previous DI, Nick Carter, impeccably until she'd found out he'd double-crossed everyone by being in the pocket of The Steeles, a notorious crime family. Nick had hidden his deceit well, she and him having worked together until he'd retired. It had been the ultimate betrayal.

Jenny, though, looked after Allie. Since Allie had run a few successful investigations, Jenny had given her more control, often not sitting in team briefings, trusting Allie to tell her what she needed to know whenever necessary.

Allie realised the woman had her back, and that meant so much in a world that could become corrupt within seconds.

One line crossed, one mistake capitalised on, and you could be in someone's pocket for the rest of your career. Allie knew that with Jenny she had found an ally, as long as she delivered the goods.

She knocked on the door and waited for the command to go in.

'Morning, Allie.' Jenny removed her glasses and beckoned for her to sit. 'How's Operation Moorcroft going?'

'All in hand at the moment, Ma'am,' Allie replied. 'A few potential leads and lots more to follow on. The post-mortem results are due in this morning, possibly some forensics.'

'Likely cause of death?'

'Stab wound to the heart.'

Jenny sighed, running a hand through her short brown hair. 'When will these people ever learn? Billy Whitmore's been quite the man in his time. Do you feel it's drug-related?'

'I expect so. We've found a notebook with names and a wad of cash inside it.'

'Hmm. And there was a silk floral scarf found too? That's a bit strange.'

'It is. I'm hoping we'll get some forensics from it, but I'd also like to show it to his partner and then his mother. He could have stolen it for either of them as a gift.'

'Or taken it from one of them. Who's his partner?'

'Fiona Abbott.'

'Did the woman not have enough with Trevor Ryan?' Jenny raised her eyebrows, then let out a huge sigh. 'I'll get a further press release out this morning, appeal for witnesses et cetera. All family have been notified?'

Allie nodded. 'People will be chattering about him now. We're keeping a watch on social media.'

'Very well. Let me know as you need to.'

'Yes, Ma'am.'

Jenny popped her glasses on and was back looking at the

screen again. Allie left, feeling quietly confident. It was great that Jenny put so much trust in her, but knowing she was good at her job and finding a killer was another thing. Still, she'd done it before. And no doubt she would do it again.

Downstairs, she said good morning to her team as she walked through to her office. Then she checked her emails. There was one from Christian. Quickly, she scanned through it and stretched her arms to the ceiling to relieve some tension in her neck. It was time to update everyone of their findings.

In the briefing room, Allie perched on the table and spoke to the team gathered.

'The preliminary path report has come in,' she said. 'I'm shocked it's so early, but I'll take it.'

'Perhaps the new boy was out to impress,' Frankie joked.

Allie smirked. 'Luckily for us, it's his first week on shift, so he's not got much work backed up yet. Give him another month and we'll have to wait in line as usual.' Allie pointed to Billy's photograph on the screen. 'As we know, Whitmore died from a stab wound to his heart. There were nine entry wounds altogether, including several lacerations on his hands where we assume he tried to defend himself. Not many forensics to go by yet.

'There are numerous footprints in a pile of mud, but most were damaged by the rain. A large size, though, probably belonging to a male. Where are we with sightings from Redmond Street, Sam?'

'I've got the camera from Hamil Road, nothing closer,' Sam replied, checking through her notes. 'I'm watching a few cars, and there are several people I can see. A few couples, a gang of teens, and three lone males and one female. Nothing stands out, and no one is running or rushing around. But you know as well as I do that the Limekiln Estate is a maze of rat runs. Our killer could have had a car parked off any of the side streets and slipped by without being seen.'

Allie ran a hand through her hair. 'Well, let's keep searching.'

'I've also been thinking, boss, about the names in the notebook found on his person,' Sam added. 'If it isn't drugs, it could be a record of something else. It might be money people owe.'

'Let me see.' Allie took the image from her. 'I never had him down for a debt collector, though.'

'They're paying him for something. I've checked them all out – none of them are known to us.'

Allie frowned. 'That surprises me.'

'Yes, me too. I've emailed Becky White to see if they are any of her tenants. If I get no joy from her, I'll start on the housing associations.' Becky was a housing officer for the local authority and one of their first ports of call when they needed information on the estate.

'Thanks, Sam.' Allie addressed the group. 'So, our new pathologist, Christian, says we're looking for a small knife, easy to conceal until needed. All the surrounding areas are still undergoing a thorough search as we speak.

'Time of death has been narrowed down to between eight and ten p.m. Most people would have been inside their houses shut away from the dark and the cold. Frankie, did you liaise with the FLO at Billy's home, to see if Fiona Abbott had anything else to add?'

'Yes, boss, but she's said nothing so far. And just a thought, *The First Hour* was on TV from nine p.m. From a quick scan on social media, every man and his dog seemed to be watching it. That might explain why we didn't get many calls when the appeal went out last night.'

'I can't wait to catch up with it... not.' Perry rolled his

eyes. 'Like a busman's holiday while I shout at the screen at all the discrepancies.'

There were a few snorts of laughter and a muttered general agreement. Allie held a hand up to silence them.

'There's also the mystery of the scarf found in his pocket.' Allie showed them the other image she'd printed off from the email Christian had sent to her. 'We'll get a photo and take it to Fiona and Billy's mother to see if they can shed any light on it.'

'I can do that, boss,' Frankie offered.

'Great, thanks. As well as the money Billy had on him, he was left with his watch and phone too, so we might be able to rule out a robbery gone wrong. Obviously, let's keep an open mind about this as it could be a decoy for someone stealing something we don't know about, and then leaving everything else behind purposely to throw us off the scent.'

Officers put their heads down, taking notes. She waited for everyone to finish and look up.

'Anyone got anything else to add?' When there was nothing, she got to her feet. 'Okay, you know what to do, so let's get cracking. I expect it's going to be another long day, but we have it covered.'

CHAPTER EIGHTEEN

'Where shall we start?' Perry asked Allie as they left the police station by the side door. He stopped when he realised she wasn't heading towards the car park.

'Thought we might have a wander into town,' she explained. 'See if we can spot any of Billy's mates.'

They went onto Bethesda Street and up Piccadilly, recapping everything that had gone on over the past twenty-four hours.

Alongside the Regent Theatre, there were all sorts of shops on the pedestrianised walkway. Eateries, clothes, beauty, and hairdressers. Insurance companies, estate agents, and charities. During the day, it could be quite drab and depressing, wanting to be so much more. The summer evenings, however, gave the place a European vibe.

As they were almost at Stafford Street, the top of Piccadilly opened into a larger area. Allie grimaced at the smell of urine when they reached the blocks of concrete seating.

The area had been paved and was somewhere local workers might stop to eat their lunch on a nice day. In reality, it seemed to be a no-go zone due to the down-and-outs who congregated there. For the most part, they were harmless, but it was their sense of menace that had people rushing past them, women clutching on to their handbags.

Now, there were two men and two women sitting in a line on one seat. From the look of them, their habits dictated whether they slept in a cell for the night or huddled in a shop doorway, perhaps the odd stay in a hostel.

As they were spotted, a groan went out from one of them, and the rest turned to see why.

'What do you want?' the man nearest to them asked. 'We haven't done anything wrong.'

'Yet,' smirked the woman sitting next to him.

Marian and Pete Kennington were a couple in their fifties. Both were hooked on heroin, and boy, could you tell. Pete's teeth had gone, his skin pale and wrinkled, his eyes almost dead. Marian's long blonde-grey hair had seen far better days, her face covered in spots. Cracked lips smiled as she eyed Perry, her tongue snaking across the top one.

Allie groaned inwardly. They were both clearly high at the moment.

'We have some bad news,' she started. 'Unless you already know.'

'About Billy Whitmore?' a voice from the far end said.

Allie looked to see a man in his twenties, thin and scraggly in dirty clothes that seemed ready to walk off of their own accord. He wasn't known to her; neither was the woman, who she suspected was his partner.

'We found out about an hour ago,' he added.

'You, being...?' she questioned.

'I'm Tony.' He pointed to the woman he was with. 'Sandra.'

'Haven't seen you around here before.'

'We've just relocated, from Stafford.'

'To?'

'No fixed abode.' He smirked.

'No fixed abode.' Sandra giggled.

'We loved Billy,' Marian said.

'You love everyone, you dirty cow.' Sandra nudged Marian to indicate she was joking.

'Show some respect,' Pete snapped. 'The man is dead. He was a good friend.'

They all murmured in agreement. Some heads turned when a bus went past, revving after slowing at the pedestrian crossings.

'When was the last time any of you saw him?' Allie asked, once the noise had died down.

'Last week, I think,' Tony said, eyeing Sandra for confirmation. When she nodded, he went on. 'Yeah, last Friday.'

'And how was he?'

'His usual self.' Tony seemed unwilling to say anything else.

'How about you, Pete?' Perry asked.

Pete shrugged. 'I saw him Friday too. He seemed fine to me.'

'He never mentioned having a run-in with anyone?'

'Nope.'

'Do any of you know who might have wanted to harm him?' Allie glanced at them all in turn. 'He used to sit here with you a lot.'

'Only when he had gear to sell.' Marian put a hand over her mouth as if she'd spoken out of turn.

'Shut up!' Pete warned.

Allie said nothing too, leaving Perry to take her lead. Sure enough, the silence was filled.

'We loved Billy,' Marian repeated. 'But he could be quite nasty if he didn't get his own way.'

Pete glared at her, but she continued.

'He had a right go at me the other week. Pete had to drag him off. He was going to thump me, like this!' She raised her fist in the air. 'I didn't even know what I'd done wrong.'

'He had been getting a bit more wired lately,' Pete admitted with a shake of his head. 'He was starting fights all the time, swearing at passers-by, that kind of thing. It wasn't on, but we couldn't say anything. We try to keep a low profile, as you know.'

Allie laughed inwardly. If none of them got locked up, they'd no doubt call it a successful day. Their custody suite was home to a lot of the regular down and outs. However, some would often get arrested purely to have a bed for the night. The system was broken when it came to some.

They chatted for a few more minutes, but when it became clear the group could be of no help, they walked back to the station. There wasn't any point in knocking if no one was home. By the look on Marian's face, it would surprise Allie if she ever remembered her own name.

'How on earth do people get like that?' Perry said, shaking his head as they fell in step.

'Easy access to it, and once you're there, you're hooked,' Allie replied, although it sounded patronising because it was a rhetorical question.

'I wish we could stamp it out. The city centre is becoming so drab with the number of shops that are closing as well. It's becoming a ghost town.'

'Yeah, Hanley was buzzing at the weekends back in the day.' She grinned. 'And who'd have thought then we'd be working together in the Major Crimes Team?'

CHAPTER NINETEEN

Twenty minutes later, they were in a pool car and on their way to the Limekiln Estate. Before they got to Redmond Street, Allie parked in front of the shops. Like Hanley, several were boarded up now but there was a Co-op, a chippie, The Caff and an off-licence that all did roaring trades. It was still early, so there weren't many people around. But the two she'd spotted straightaway were the ones they wanted to talk to.

Gary and Malcolm Parker were twins in their thirties. Shifty and Shortie, they were known to the police, the only way they became distinguishable. Gary could never keep still; Malcolm the slightly shorter one of the two.

They were sitting on the floor outside the entrance to the Co-op. No doubt they'd be moved on a few times today and return once the manager was out of sight.

Allie wanted to get them a coffee and a bite to eat but knew she'd be encouraging them to stay so she refrained. Besides, she couldn't offer a drink and a sandwich to everyone she thought was in need.

'Ner ner. Ner ner. Ner ner,' Malcolm said, laughing as they drew level with him.

They were wrapped in a dirty blanket, woolly hats covering what hair they had, a red nose apiece and the wind trying to blow through them.

'Ayup, lads.' Allie ignored their chants when Gary joined in too.

Malcolm shuffled his feet. 'We don't know anything about Billy Whitmore.'

'That surprises me. I thought you two knew everything before we did,' Perry humoured. 'You're honorary detectives in my eyes.'

That had them laughing again.

It wasn't hard to join in. Both Allie and Perry had known the men since they were in their teens. They weren't troublemakers, simply a couple of kids who'd been dealt a crap hand in life: parents who hadn't cared about them as much as their alcohol addictions, a father who'd died when they were in their twenties; a mum who'd had a heart attack soon after.

Since then, they'd shared a flat across the road from the shops, but they chose to spend their day hanging around outside, no matter the weather.

'We heard he had a hand cut off.' Malcolm looked at them for a moment.

'No, that was a lie.' Allie sighed. 'Is that all you've heard around the estate?'

They nodded.

'That's a shame. I always had you down as good cops.'

Their laughter filled the air again. Allie was tired of playing games, though. She'd thought these two might give them something to go on. Perhaps whisper a name or an address they could check out. They were the eyes and ears on this block, despite being known for not telling anyone anything. Everyone seemed to like them, which was lucky for them as they were ripe for being taken advantage of.

She tried one more time to engage with them. 'Had you seen Billy lately?'

'He was in the car park on Friday,' Gary said.

'This car park?'

'Yeah, he was with K...' He stopped when his brother nudged him sharply in the ribs. 'Ow, what was that for?' He groaned and held his side.

'He was with...?' Perry asked.

Silence.

Allie sighed inwardly. They were getting nowhere. A young woman coming towards them with a pushchair chatted away on her phone, oblivious to the shoe that her toddler had thrown out on the pavement. Allie pointed at it, the woman's anger at being interrupted clear to see once she stormed back to pick it up. No thanks were forthcoming when she continued past. Charming, she thought.

Perry was still trying to get information from the twins. She decided she would treat them to something before leaving after all. Perhaps they'd talk when she was inside the shop. Sometimes the general public found two police officers together, especially detectives, intimidating.

As she waited for the coffee to come out of the machine, someone prodded her shoulder. She turned to see Mallory Whittaker, one of the kids she knew from the estate. Mallory was fourteen and the middle girl of seven children, all still living at home. Some kids ruled the estate; others wanted to keep the peace. Their mother tried her best to make them stay in line, but it was never any danger guessing as to who was winning.

'Hey, Mallory, how are you?' Allie added sugar to the two cups now full of liquid. 'No school today?'

'Free period.' The girl trotted the words off as if it were second nature.

'Fair enough. What're you up to now, then?'

Mallory shrugged. 'Just getting some bread and stuff.' She showed Allie a five-pound note. 'I'm paying before you get the wrong idea.'

Allie smirked. Mallory had been forever in trouble for shoplifting until the food bank had opened. She wasn't your typical child who stole makeup or fancy pens. She lifted food to help her family survive.

Allie sensed she'd come to talk. 'Any gossip you want to tell me?'

'I heard about Billy Whitmore.' Mallory leaned on the wall with her hands behind her back. 'Shame, I liked him.'

'A lot of people did.'

Mallory glanced around to see if the coast was clear before moving closer. 'You should talk to Carlton Stewart. He's been hanging around Redmond Street.'

'Has he now?' Allie wondered what the relevance of that would be. 'When did you see him there?'

'I was with him a few times.'

Allie locked eyes with her. 'You're not messing around with him and his crew?'

'No!' Mallory looked at the floor.

The way she spoke gave her away, the blush rising on her cheeks even more.

Allie pushed lids onto the drinks. 'You be careful. He's far too old for you.'

'I'm fifteen soon!'

'So grown up!' Allie widened her eyes in mock surprise.

Mallory giggled and went on her way.

When Allie came outside again, Perry was nodding profusely at the brothers. She handed everything over, and they left them to it.

'What was all that about?' she asked as soon as they were out of hearing range. 'Got anything useful?'

'Apparently, Billy was hanging around in a flat opposite

the old Red Lion. Tenant is Andrew Dale. Wasn't that the bloke you spoke to yesterday?'

'It was indeed, you charmer, you.'

Perry smirked. 'I got them talking about *The First Hour*. It's a great icebreaker, I'll give it that.'

Allie raised her eyebrows. 'Well, *I've* been told that Carlton Stewart has been seen in Redmond Street – in the flat opposite the pub.'

'Really? Something is definitely going on there then.'

'Yes, I'm going to have Grace look into it.'

They walked in silence to the car, each deep in thought.

'Do you think this will be linked to Kenny Webb?' Perry said when they reached it.

'One way to find out.' Allie unlocked the door and pulled it open. 'I'll call on him this afternoon. You can visit his second-in-command.'

CHAPTER TWENTY

In Redmond Street, Allie caught up with everything. Officers were still going house-to-house and, although the scene was less frantic now, she doubted the residents liked the intrusion. Nevertheless, she braced herself for any forthcoming snide comments but was pleased not to receive any.

She called to see Andrew Dale, but there was no one in. Instead of leaving a card for him to contact her, she called Grace as she walked back to the pavement.

'Bit of a shock about Billy Whitmore,' Grace remarked after they'd said hello. 'How's it going?'

'So-so. Nothing concrete yet, you know.'

'Is it drug-related?'

'Possibly. I wondered if you could do some work around Redmond Street for me, please, in particular around the block of flats across from the crime scene?'

'Sure. I have two residents who complain about a group of teens coming and going but I can never catch them there. I can check in on them again, if you like?'

'I was thinking more of you seeing what you could find while you're out and about round there? You know they'll talk to someone they trust a little more. I'm particularly interested in flat number seven. Tenant's name is Andrew Dale. He seems vulnerable, and my spidey-senses were alert when I spoke to him. Since then, I've been given his name a couple of times.'

'Gotcha. I'll see what I can do. I'll also have a word with Becky, the housing officer who covers that patch too.'

'Cheers me dears.'

A message came in on her phone, so she finished the call. She looked to see it was from Simon.

Are you at the crime scene? If so, fancy oatcakes for lunch – my treat?

Allie beamed. Always the way to a Stokie's heart. Her mouth almost watered at the thought as she messaged back.

Excellent idea. Where are you?

Coming up to High Lane Oatcakes.

Go on then. Bacon and cheese, please. The same for Frankie and Perry – I'll pay.

Be with you in ten.

True to his word, a few minutes later his car pulled into Redmond Street. She got in the passenger seat, and he passed her a brown paper bag.

'Ooh, thanks!' She delved into it, unwrapping the silver foil parcel. 'I've just been speaking to your better half.'

'About what? Not the W word?'

'We don't *always* talk about the wedding. I wanted to ask her something work related.'

'Ah. She's made for that job, Allie.' Simon undid his parcel too. 'She never stops talking about it. The things she can say, obviously.'

Allie smiled. They all trod a fine line between telling their partners as much as they could but often a little more when they needed to offload, or to have another opinion on things.

Grace and Simon worked exceptionally well together,

their roles as police and press quite hard to juggle. She could imagine how easy it might be to have slipped up, and something then used by a partner for their own means. It happened a lot more than anyone was privy to.

But they were a team, Grace and Simon, loyal to each other, and it worked well. They were getting married at the end of the month. Allie was looking forward to the wedding. If nothing was going on, it would be a chance for the team to have another get-together as they'd all been invited.

She swallowed her food. 'Right then, Simon. I need your help.'

'Great! Is there something you can give me about the ongoing murder first?'

'Straight to the point as usual,' she teased. 'Did you get any sachets of brown sauce?'

'*Really?*'

'What?' She turned to catch him screwing up his face.

'Oatcakes should be eaten naked.'

Allie almost choked as she laughed. 'I can't wait to have them for breakfast this weekend, in that case!'

'I mean, without any condiments. A Staffordshire oatcake is a delicacy. It's meant to be eaten without it.'

'Says who?'

'Says Simon.'

Allie sniggered. 'Simon Says,' she teased, referring to the children's game they'd played when they were young. It had been called simple Simon Says, but she felt it wouldn't be right to use that term now. 'I suppose it will have to do in its naked form.' She bit into it, her shoulders dropping. 'So good.'

'Anyway, you were saying?' Simon said between bites.

'Perry and I went to talk to some of the druggies in town this morning. I have a feeling they knew more than they were letting on. So I'd like to reach out to the people who knew

Billy Whitmore, the ones who won't come to the police with info but might talk to you?'

'Sure. I can even interview some of them, if you like. Under the guise of doing an article about the drugs in the city.'

'That was exactly what I was after.'

Their conversation came to a halt, and they continued with their food.

A minute later, Allie's phone rang. Wiping her hands, she whipped it from her pocket. 'Frankie.' She listened to what he had to say. 'Give me five minutes.'

'Duty calls?' Simon queried.

'Yes, I'll have to catch you later.' She wrapped one oatcake in a napkin to take with her and finished the other. 'Stoke never stays still for long, but I'm not leaving my oatcakes behind. Thanks for these. And Simon?' She retrieved the parcels for Frankie and Perry and handed him a tenner. 'This conversation stays between me and you?'

'Of course.' He waved the money away.

'You trying to bribe me, Cole?' she chided.

'Of course,' he repeated with a laugh.

Allie found Frankie and gave him his oatcakes, which he took with enormous gratitude.

'I've come from Gladys Whitmore's home,' he said before tucking in. 'The scarf is hers.'

Allie frowned. 'I didn't have Billy clocked as someone flamboyant enough to want a pale-pink scarf with red roses emblazoned all over it.'

'She was shocked when she saw it. She had no idea it was missing.'

'When we spoke to her yesterday, she told us she last saw Billy a few weeks ago. I wonder if he stole it then.'

'To give to a woman, Fiona perhaps?'

Allie shook her head. 'I don't buy that. Either Billy lifted it or someone else did. We'll have to see whose prints come back on it. In the meantime, once I've given him his lunch, Perry's going to talk to Martin Smith, and then we can nip over to see Kenny Webb. Perhaps between the two of them they might be able to shed some light on things.'

CHAPTER TWENTY-ONE

As evidence was being gathered around Billy Whitmore's death, there wasn't much Allie could work on until the actions came in, alongside further forensics. The murder weapon still hadn't been recovered yet: she was on standby to be told as soon as. So it was a good time to visit Kenny Webb in Longton.

There were six branches of Car Wash City, one in every suburb. It was a lot to watch, and Allie was certain they had missed things over the years, but one day it would all come together. And she would be waiting to arrest her old foe, Terry Ryder, for something else, hopefully before he set foot out of the walls of his cell. Now, wouldn't that be nice.

The south of the city was known to be Steve Kennedy's patch now. Word had it that Kenny was looking after it for Ryder while he was in prison, so Steve seemed to be staying clear. A garage services depot was adjoined to this one, also known to be a front.

There had been many face-offs between Allie and Kenny over the years. She knew there was more going on at the car washes. He knew the drugs team and the fraud squad were watching the buildings. So Allie wasn't expecting a welcoming party, but a lead was a lead, no matter how tenuous the link right now.

Before they got out of the vehicle, she took some discreet photos of the front of the building. She had no interest in the cars that were being washed. She wanted images of the ones that belonged to the employees, parked to the right.

'You know what to do while I'm inside?' she asked Frankie.

'Act like everyone's best friend.' He grinned.

They strode across the forecourt of the business. Several young lads were washing cars, not batting an eye at either of them. They were good workers, she'd give them that. On the many times they'd had to visit these premises, there was always a queue of cars waiting to be cleaned.

However, Allie was more concerned with what went on behind the scenes. She knew whatever they'd shut down in the past would likely have been started up again. Perhaps with a new team of men. They all seemed to be dispensable.

Every month, the force worked on gathering more evidence to keep Ryder inside. Despite being locked up, he was still running all his businesses. There would always be minions such as Kenny Webb to help him out.

Above the sign, it still showed Terry Ryder was the proprietor. Allie groaned inwardly at the name. Serving a life sentence for the murder of Philip Kennedy, Ryder was due out soon. She rued the day, expecting him to come after her.

Even now, she could recall the anger and disbelief on his face when he thought he'd got away with murdering his wife. Still, he was locked up for now, where he belonged. Where she hoped he would stay.

She knocked on the office door and was shouted in. Kenny's face dropped when he saw her.

Kenny was forty-seven, with a shaved head, tanned skin

all year round, piercing dark eyes, and a scar down the side of his cheek where he'd been slashed in his teens. Usually she'd find him in casual gear, today being no exception as he was in a grey designer tracksuit and expensive trainers.

He was the epitome of someone who lived in the gym. Allie assumed it was because he now owned Steele's Gym, where most of his crowd trained. Until recently, it had belonged to the Steele family, but since the police had closed an arm of their illegal business, Eddie Steele had sold up and moved out of Stoke.

Allie was always impressed with anyone who took the time to work on their physique unless it was steroid enhanced. In her line of work, she'd seen some of the men turn nasty, dangerous even. It was a heady mixture of testosterone and strength.

To look at Kenny, she wasn't sure if he took steroids or not. She'd always known him to be affable, if a little standoffish.

'To what do I owe this displeasure?' he said.

'I need a quiet word.'

'*Word* has it that Billy Whitmore has copped it?' Kenny replied, not inviting her to sit. He chuckled at his joke. '*Copped* it. Geddit?'

Allie ignored him and moved to the window, seeing a yard, cars and paraphernalia everywhere. A mechanic was struggling to get a wheel off an old Range Rover, a youth pulling at it with him. Another group of young men were laughing at something on one of their phones. It seemed like any other work day out there.

She turned back, leaned on the sill, and folded her arms. 'Care to elaborate?'

Kenny pursed his lips and raised his eyes to the ceiling, as if deep in thought.

He was mocking her, the bastard.

'Can't say I know anything about it, no.'

Allie posed another question. 'Did Billy still work for you?'

'I don't know where you heard that.'

'Eyes and ears everywhere. You know what we do.'

'Yeah, and you know what *I* do too. And I don't kill people.'

'That's right.' Allie nodded slowly. 'You'd get someone else to do it for you.'

Kenny glared at her before sitting back in his chair and lacing his hands together behind his neck.

'Terry would love to see you again,' he said.

Allie rolled her eyes. If he was trying to rattle her, he'd have to do better than that. Ryder might not be in her nightmares anymore, but she knew he'd be waiting and watching. She wasn't going to give either of them the satisfaction.

'So you don't know anything about Whitmore's demise?' she went on.

'I had no idea he was dead until an hour ago.' He jerked a thumb at the window that overlooked the forecourt. 'I found out from Nicko. He showed me on his phone. It's all over Twitter. I don't know how you figure out the truth from the lies.' He glanced at her. 'I doubt his hand was cut off?'

Allie neither confirmed nor denied, then thought better of it. 'He was stabbed, multiple times.'

'The exaggerating tossers.' Kenny sniggered. 'There's a bit of difference between the two.'

'You don't seem too bothered. Is that all you've heard?' she pressed him.

He was quiet for a moment, contemplating what to say next, no doubt. How much to give, to get them off his back.

'All I know is that it's nothing to do with us.'

'Us being you and Car Wash City, or us being you and whatever you get up to when we're not around?'

'You're quite determined to pin something on me, aren't you?' He laughed. 'I'm telling you all I know. Whatever happened to Billy Whitmore had nothing to do with me, nor any of the lads that work for me.'

'For *Ryder*. They work for him.'

'Are you listening? That's not my style. I gave Billy the heave-ho a few years ago. He became a liability, taking more drugs than he was selling.'

'So who was he working with before he died?'

He shrugged. 'That's your job to find out.'

His reply was disappointing. Allie kept her sigh to herself. For some reason she thought he was telling the truth. But she had to stay open-minded to work the case. She wouldn't rule anyone out.

But she would flush them out. If they had anything to hide, Kenny and his men would be finding out intel of their own. It would get back to them one way or another.

She left, fully satisfied she had rattled his cage if nothing else. It was always good to show up every now and then. To keep Kenny on his toes. He'd tell Martin Smith they'd been, so she'd see if Perry had managed to get anything from his chat.

She re-joined Frankie who was scrolling on his phone.

'Find out anything?' she asked.

'Not a dicky bird, boss. No one wanted to talk.' Frankie shook his head. 'That Milo bloke is a dick, isn't he?'

'You have an excellent deduction of character.' Allie laughed. 'And if nothing else, we will have got Kenny thinking about why we came to see him.'

CHAPTER TWENTY-TWO

Car Wash City's Hanley branch was set up legitimately to keep the police from the scent of the other five. Situated on Leek Road near to the Staffordshire University campus, it was a couple of minutes from Hanley or Stoke in either direction.

With the click of a fob, Perry locked his car and jogged through the traffic that was at a standstill due to a red light.

The forecourt was awash with action, a radio blasting out the sounds of R'n'B. Three drivers sat in their vehicles, waiting in a queue for them to be cleaned. Several young lads climbed over a fourth as they gave it a spit and polish. If it wasn't an establishment they were keeping an eye on, he'd have let them do his motor too. They had a good reputation for doing a thorough job.

One in particular gave him the eye the nearer he got. He turned to another and nodded his head in Perry's direction. They sneered at him, clearly knowing he was police. He didn't recognise them and continued past. Neither stopped him.

The office was at the rear of the public area. He walked around to the back. Inside the building, he stepped into a small vestibule and knocked on a door to his right.

A voice shouted. 'Come in!'

Martin Smith was the same age as Perry. They'd matured well, each refusing to give in to the beer belly look a lot of men in their generation sported. Both had a penchant for designer labels but, whereas Perry was always suited and booted for work, Martin wore black jeans, a checked shirt, and Timberland boots.

They'd gone to school together, so went back a while, and knew a lot about each other. Occasionally, they met on the celebrations circuit – big birthdays, the odd wedding, and a fair few funerals recently.

Perry had really liked the man until he'd started working with Kenny Webb. After all the trouble with the Ryder family, and the Kennedy brothers while Terry was in prison, he couldn't understand why Martin would get in with their crowd, especially turncoat Kenny Webb whose only loyalty to a big boss was what was in it for him. Martin wasn't a player so there had to be an ulterior motive he'd yet to find out. Still, he'd keep a civil tongue in his mouth to get what he wanted. It mostly paid off.

'Leftie!' Martin greeted Perry with his schoolboy nickname. With his surname, it had been bound to happen.

'Martin.' Perry shook the hand he offered.

'How's the wife and that bonny son of yours?'

'Good, thanks. He's six going on sixty now.'

Martin roared with laughter, ran a hand through a floppy greying fringe, and pointed to a seat. 'Come, sit. I suppose this is business and not pleasure. Can I get you a drink?'

'No. I'm good, thanks.'

'Okay, what can I do for you?' He leaned forwards on the desk, clasping his hands together.

Perry came straight to the point. 'I expect you've heard about Billy Whitmore?'

'Yes, terrible news.' Martin smirked. 'I never could stand

the fella. He was an idiot getting hooked on drugs for so many years. I'm glad he didn't go to our school. He'd have been eaten alive.'

Perry chuckled. 'Any idea who he was working with?'

'No. He'd been a loner since his last stretch inside. More to do with him being unreliable. Where did it happen again?'

'Redmond Street,' Perry replied.

'Ah, yes. Was he still with that dippy Fiona?'

'That's not very nice, but yes.'

'He recently shacked up with her, so I heard. Threw his mother out to move her and her kids in. Nice of him.' Martin shook his head. 'I bet you have a list of suspects a mile long.'

'Yeah, Kenny being at the top of it.'

Martin sat back. 'You think this is connected to him?'

'That's what we're trying to find out.'

'I doubt it'll be his thing. Have you checked with the local druggies?'

'Not yet.' Perry wasn't going to give him unnecessary information. Of course they both knew he was lying.

Martin paused. 'So why come to me?'

'Sources, you know.'

'I'm not sure why someone gave you Kenny's name.'

'They didn't. I assumed.'

'I doubt he's been near the Limekiln Estate for a good while.'

Martin's mobile phone rang. He picked it up, glanced at the caller and muted the sound. Then he moved the mouse to wake his computer, turning to the screen.

Perry knew he was about to be dismissed, but he wanted more. Martin had always been good for intel, always his first call, and he wasn't sure why he wasn't getting anything from him today.

'Like I said, Billy's time was up,' Martin added. 'He was too old for that game anyway.'

'Still not a good way to go. I expected him to overdose rather than be killed.'

'Yeah, me too.'

'If you do hear of anything, you'll be sure to give me a bell?'

Martin nodded profusely. 'Of course. You know I'm always happy to help.'

They stared at each other, holding it long enough for them both to know the meaning behind his statement.

Perry left, annoyed he hadn't got what he'd come for. But as he passed the window outside, Martin was on his phone. No doubt he'd be letting Kenny know what they'd discussed.

He grinned. Martin was one of the best informants he'd ever had but, like Allie had said, it never hurt to rattle a few cages.

CHAPTER TWENTY-THREE

It was past four p.m. when Allie's phone rang. It surprised her to see Kelsey Abbott's name showing on the home screen. Even though she had given her a contact card, she very rarely used it.

'Hi, Kelsey, how are you doing?' She kept her tone light.

'I'm okay.'

'I'm so sorry about what's happened to Billy.' Allie covered her ear to drown out the sounds of the traffic in the background.

'Thanks.'

A pause down the line and she wondered if they'd been cut off. But then Kelsey spoke again.

'Could – could I see you?'

'I'm a bit busy, as you can imagine.'

'Please? Just for a few minutes.'

Concerned by the anxiety in Kelsey's voice, Allie checked her watch. 'Where are you?'

'Hamil Road, coming onto the estate.'

'I can spare you half an hour. Fancy hot chocolate at The Caff?'

Her destination only a couple of minutes' drive from where she was now, Allie scanned her emails, made two quick calls, and then was on her way.

Curiosity was killing the cat as she parked and then went inside the café. Allie had known Kelsey since she was ten. Now fourteen, she was growing into a beautiful young woman, one she prayed wouldn't be taken advantage of like her mother.

Kelsey's blonde hair was tied away from her face, showing bright-blue eyes and a bit too much makeup for Allie's liking. Her eyebrows were thick and black, eyeliner to match. Red lipstick, and she seemed way older than her years.

In school uniform, she was even more prime prey. Luckily, Kelsey seemed to be able to look after herself. Whether that was to do with what she'd seen her mum going through, she didn't know.

But Allie did know, more because of her work, what could happen to vulnerable young girls, regardless of how streetwise they assumed they were.

The Caff was run by two women from the estate who had set it up as a not-for-profit organisation in memory of their sons. Stella Phillips and Rebecca Nightingale's teenagers had been killed when a fight between two groups of lads had got out of hand. In the fracas, they'd both been stabbed. Matthew Phillips had died at the scene, David Nightingale the next day.

It had been a tragic event, yet during the outpouring of grief, it had worked to pull the community together. The kids had nothing to do, nowhere to go and meet friends where they felt safe, so the café had been run with them in mind.

At first, opening hours had been limited to a couple of hours after school and during the holidays but it had proved to be so popular for everyone on the Limekiln Estate, it was now manned by volunteers and open all day, most days.

Allie sat down once she had their order. Kelsey had gone
for hot chocolate and a blueberry muffin. Allie had her usual
breakfast tea and an oat cookie.

She removed everything from the tray, balanced it at the
side of the table, and waited for Kelsey to begin. It often took
a few minutes to start a good conversation with her, so she
decided to begin with small talk.

'How are you really doing?' she enquired.

'Not so bad.'

'And school? Any better now?'

Kelsey had been bullied before Trevor had gone to prison.
Back then, they didn't have much money, and what they did,
Trevor had used for drink. Kelsey became known as one of
the scruffy kids at school. Always clean and tidy but with
worn and hand-me-down clothes. She'd never fitted in with
the girls in her year because of it, had resorted to fighting and
getting into trouble on several occasions.

Although meeting her through Fiona, Allie had got to
know Kelsey well when she'd arrived at one of Grace's work-
shops on the estate at the beginning of last year. In her own
time, Grace had set up some things for the girls to do,
teaching them above all useful bits of self-defence they could
use to ward off anyone they didn't want near them, or they
felt afraid of.

'School is school.' Kelsey took a sip of her drink. 'It's
better, though. And I didn't want to stay at home.'

Allie took a bite of her cookie as Kelsey ate her muffin. It
was peaceful sitting here after the hustle and bustle of the
day. Even though there was music playing, mixed with the
sounds of the coffee machine, the clatter of cutlery, and the
noise of the other customers, it was all in the background. It
was quite soothing, giving her mind time to have a break
from all that she was carrying inside it. Cramming into it,
actually.

Kelsey started to speak without a prompt.

'My mum loved Billy, you know.'

Allie was surprised to hear that, but she didn't say, nor did she give it away with her expression. She was good at keeping a poker face after all the years of practice. Instead, she waited to see what Kelsey would say next.

'I liked him too.' Kelsey stirred her drink purposely to avoid looking at Allie. 'He was kind, funny, and quite gentle when he wasn't high.'

'And when he was high?'

'He was too wasted to do anything but lie around.' Kelsey's baby blues glistened. 'I miss him.'

'I'm sorry, duck. Do you know anything that might help us catch his killer?'

Kelsey's eyes went down, then she turned to stare out of the window. 'I don't like Carlton.'

'You mean Carlton Stewart?'

'Yeah. Riley has been seeing him for a few weeks.' She looked back. 'She's *obsessed* with him. I'm worried about her.'

It broke Allie's heart to think how much this kid had been through in her short life, and yet here she was, concerned for her sister. She'd always thought Kelsey was the stronger of the three women. Even when she was ten, she'd been feisty, but clever with it. Kelsey had a knack of getting under Allie's skin too.

'Did Billy get on well with Carlton?' she asked next.

'He was at our house a lot.'

'And that wasn't to see Riley?'

'Sometimes it was. He... like I said, I don't like him.'

Allie paused, then reached across to touch Kelsey's forearm. 'What aren't you telling me? Don't be afraid. I won't say anything to anyone.'

Kelsey sat back and Allie cursed inwardly. Had she lost her?

But then Kelsey sat forward again and whispered, 'I think he had something to do with Billy's death.'

'Okay, why don't you tell me what you know?'

Kelsey gnawed on her bottom lip before finally speaking. 'I heard him and Riley talking in the kitchen, about what job they were going to do next. Carlton said he wanted another bungalow. Riley said she wanted to stop.'

'Stop what?' Allie probed. 'Did you hear what the job was going to be?

'No. And then I went to school, and Mum called me out because Billy was dead.' Kelsey wiped a tear from her cheek.

Their conversation slowed to a halt. When she offered to buy more drinks, Kelsey declined.

'I hope Riley won't get in trouble,' she said softly.

'I won't use the information unless –'

'Not with the police. I don't want Carlton to ruin her the way Trevor damaged Mum.'

Allie nodded her understanding. She wished she could help the young girl more, but she had to draw a line somewhere. She wasn't her family. She couldn't meddle, despite wanting to.

'Would you like a lift home?' She needed to get back to work, even though she was technically finding out information. 'I'm in a marked car but I can drop you off discreetly.'

Kelsey shook her head. 'I'm going to my friend, Leah's, for tea.'

'Okay. Have a good time.' She stood, leaving Kelsey to finish her drink. 'Take care of yourself, missy.'

As she walked to her car, she looked across the car park, spotting Fiona popping into the Co-op. Excellent timing – if Riley was home, she might get a few minutes with her before Fiona got back.

That niggle of a gut feeling was getting to her now. Riley

could be involved in something, and she needed to find out what.

She started the car, reversed out of the space, and shot off towards Forest Avenue.

CHAPTER TWENTY-FOUR

As a lot of the press coverage was concentrated on Redmond Street, it was fairly quiet in Forest Avenue. A uniformed officer was stationed outside Billy Whitmore's home, no doubt taking care when arranging the ever-growing array of flowers that were collecting on the pavement, leaning against the boundary wall. At the moment, he was standing alone.

Allie greeted him quickly before moving indoors. She'd rung ahead to let Rachel know she was coming but asked her not to alert Riley.

'Hi, Rachel.' She smiled at her as she opened the front door. 'How're things?'

'Okay. Riley is in the kitchen.'

She stepped inside and followed her through the house. Riley was sitting at the table nursing a mug of coffee. She glanced at Allie and then quickly away again.

'Hi, Riley.' Allie greeted her with a warm smile. 'How are you today?'

'Fine, thanks.' Riley didn't smile back.

Allie pulled out a chair and sat across from her.

'I was passing, and I thought I'd have a quick chat with you.'

'What about?'

'Nothing in particular, but I know how worrying this must be for you after what happened with Trevor. I wanted to reassure you that we will catch whoever did this to Billy as quickly as possible.'

'You mean you know who it was?' Riley's eyes widened.

'Not yet, but we have a lot of leads.' Allie saw no harm in bending the truth to her own advantage. 'I'm confident we'll catch his killer soon. I was wondering if you'd thought of anything else since we spoke, that might help us with our enquiries?'

'Such as?'

'Have there been any regular visitors to the house lately? Billy must have had friends who came to see him?'

Riley looked into her mug but gave a small shrug. 'Can't think of any.'

'That's good then. I'd hate for you and Kelsey to be worrying unnecessarily.'

'What do you mean?'

'Well, Billy often mixed with a bad bunch, and I wouldn't want you to be troubled because of it.'

The door opened, and Fiona bustled in, stopping in her tracks when she spotted Allie.

'Ah, Fiona.' She smiled. 'How are you today?'

'I'm okay.' Fiona held up a carrier bag. 'I needed a few essentials.'

'Rachel can help with that if you feel unable to go out at any time.'

'I wanted a bit of fresh air. I didn't think I needed to tell you everything.'

'You don't.'

'Good.' Fiona paused. 'Was there something you came to see us about?'

'Oh, yes. I was wondering if you'd recognised the scarf we found on Billy.'

'Rachel showed it to us, didn't you?'

Rachel nodded.

'Oh.' Allie pretended to be flustered. 'I'm sorry. As you can imagine, I have so much on my mind, I must have forgotten.' She smiled. 'My mistake. So you don't know whose it might have been?'

Fiona shook her head. 'Neither did Riley.'

Allie glanced at Riley who, after a moment, did the same as her mother.

'Okay, not to worry.' Allie stood up. 'I'll leave you with Rachel now. If you need anything, let her know.'

Rachel showed her to the door, and Allie rolled her eyes.

'That didn't quite go to plan,' she whispered.

'A hunch?' Rachel spoke quietly too.

'Yes. Can you keep an eye on them for the next half hour, see if you can catch anything they're talking about? Perhaps get them to chat about Billy again? I'm trying to find out if anyone has been calling lately. In particular, I want to know if Riley has a boyfriend, without asking her outright.'

'Yes, Ma'am.'

Allie left then. She didn't want either woman to think something was afoot. Nor did she want anything coming back to Kelsey if she mentioned their chat.

Not until she'd found out exactly what was going on.

Allie and her team had worked flat out that day, evidence slowly coming in. Forensics had found two sets of fingerprints from the scarf, one of them belonging to Gladys Whitmore. The others didn't match any they had on record. There was still no sign of the murder weapon. Uniform were going back to as many house-to-house calls as possible when people hadn't been at home yesterday.

Allie had not long been back at the station and was catching up with a few emails, reading some and asking for details from others, when her desk phone rang. It was the control room.

'We've had a call from a paramedic,' an officer informed her. 'There's been another fatal stabbing.'

Allie grabbed a pen and wrote down the details. Within a minute, she was out of her room and on the main floor.

'We have another murder, people. A female in her forties has been found stabbed in her home. You'll never guess who it is.' She paused, quite unable to believe it herself. 'She's been identified by her mother as Debbie Mayhew.'

'*Debbie Mayhew?*' Sam repeated.

'No way!' Perry said a fraction of a second later.

'Isn't she one of the monkey dust crowd?' Frankie piped up. 'I used to arrest her regularly when I was in uniform.'

'Yes, which links her to Billy Whitmore,' Perry added as he pulled on his coat.

'And also means we could have an attack on Kenny Webb going on, someone taking down his minions,' Allie went on. 'Sam, can you get me as much intel on Debbie's recent dealings with us and ring it through? Perry, Frankie, you're with me.'

CHAPTER TWENTY-FIVE

The suspicious death was in Smallthorne, a mile from the Limekiln Estate. Perry had grabbed keys for a pool car and was driving them to the scene on blue lights.

'Two in one week, boss?' he asked as he negotiated the traffic.

'Yes, that can't be a coincidence. The call to emergency services was a bit garbled by all accounts. The paramedic who attended said Debbie was found unresponsive by her mum. It wasn't until he removed the duvet and saw all the blood. Three stab wounds, one probable fatal.'

There was barely room to park their vehicle, so they left it on the main road and walked into Rose Avenue, a cul-de-sac of privately owned semi-detached bungalows. Even in the dusk, Allie could see that each homeowner took pride in their property, despite being next to Harrison House, a L-shaped, three-storey block of flats that were known for housing some of the roughest families in the city.

There didn't seem to be too much of a commotion yet, although several doorways were open with residents shadowed inside them. The ambulance was ahead, lights slicing through the dusk.

'Too close for comfort, boss?' Perry jerked his head in the direction of the flats.

Allie wasn't sure if he was referring to the residents being likely suspects of the suspicious death or the murders that had happened there over the past seven years.

'We'll see. Ask Sam to get names of anyone known to us in there at the moment. Any run-ins uniform have attended too.'

While Perry was on his phone, they continued towards number fourteen. Several clusters of neighbours stood at the bottom of driveways, all curious and wondering what was going on.

'Sam's checking on Harrison House, boss,' Perry said once he'd disconnected the call. 'The last collar Debbie had was shoplifting in Tesco a few months back.'

'She's caused nothing but strife since she moved in,' a man shouted at them when they went past.

'Be quiet, George,' the woman beside him urged. 'She hasn't been that bad.'

'They need to know,' he went on. 'She's a disgrace, her and the friends she hangs around with. This has always been a respectable avenue. We had to call the police out a couple of weeks ago due to the noise. What's she been up to now?'

'We'll make sure and come back to you when we can tell you more, sir,' Allie continued past. Although she was always interested in what neighbours had to say, right now she wanted to see what had gone on at the crime scene. 'Frankie, be sure to visit them. Find out what you can about the friends he mentioned.'

'Will do, boss.'

A small hatchback was parked on the driveway. They

squeezed past and along the side of the bungalow where a door was open. Allie glanced around to see if anything was out of place, but it looked pretty clear. There were no windows broken on this side of the building, everything seemed neat, nothing to suggest foul play. The door itself hadn't been forced.

Before going inside, Allie wrapped her hair in a band and then pulled on latex gloves and shoe covers. It would have to do for now. Although mindful of the crime scene, it didn't seem appropriate to dress in a white suit to speak to the victim's mother who had been asked to stay in the kitchen until they arrived.

They stepped into a long hallway decorated in cream and pale-blue striped wallpaper. Laminate flooring was under their feet, a grey rug covering the length of most of it. Two doors either side were closed, but ahead, the living room and kitchen doors were open.

In the kitchen was a woman sitting at a table, her back towards them. A young female paramedic sat across from her. Allie spotted another and went into the living room on her left.

'DI Shenton,' she said, as the man got to his feet. 'Did you call it in?'

'Yes, Andy Salisbury. Patient's name was Debbie Mayhew. She was forty-two. ID'd by her mother.'

'Thanks.'

'It's a nasty one. I reckon she died last night.'

Allie moved past him and came face to face with their victim. Debbie lay on her side, dressed in skinny jeans, a black T-shirt, and red socks. A single duvet soaked in blood had been moved to the floor. From first sight, there were no immediate signs of sexual assault.

Debbie had been wrecked by her drug addiction. Allie could vaguely remember a better phase in her life when she'd been a beautiful looking woman with wavy brown hair, a gym-bunny figure, and took a real pride in herself. After mixing with the wrong people for a few years, she'd managed to clean herself up and get away from them. Sadly, it didn't last. As with most addicts, the draw was too much to walk away from permanently.

Now, her nails were bitten to nothing, and her hair was a mane of tangles and grease. Spots ravished the skin around her mouth, both arms covered in track marks and self-harming scars.

What happened to you, Debbie Mayhew?

It was vital they worked out Debbie's last known movements as soon as possible, especially after what happened to Billy Whitmore.

'I'll go and speak to Mum. Is her GP on the way?'

'Yes,' Andy nodded.

'Why don't you cancel that call? I'll get the pathologist out. This is a murder enquiry.'

CHAPTER TWENTY-SIX

Once in the kitchen, Allie acknowledged both women and turned to their victim's mother.

'I'm Detective Inspector Shenton,' she said, feeling no need to show her warrant card. 'Please call me Allie. Could I sit down?'

The woman nodded.

'Debbie was your daughter?' She spoke gently, seeing she was in shock.

The woman nodded again.

'And your name is?'

'Irene Mayhew.'

'Thanks, Irene. I know it's hard, but can you talk me through your day, until you got here, please?'

'I-I'd been to visit my sister, Janice, overnight. We don't see each other that often but we always keep in touch by phone. When we spoke last week, she suggested I come and stay over. I had a lovely time.' She let out a sob. 'If I'd have known what had happened, I would have been home earlier.'

'None of this is your fault, Mrs Mayhew,' Allie soothed. 'So you arrived back today at...?'

'Half past five. I shouted Debbie's name but got no reply, so I took my things into my bedroom and left them on the bed. Both doors to the living room and kitchen were closed, so I went into the kitchen. The place was in a right mess.' Her laughter was high-pitched. 'Debbie wasn't the tidiest of people. So I cleaned her mess and made a mug of tea.'

Allie knew she might have got rid of vital evidence, but she kept that out of the conversation.

'Was it then you went into the living room?' She sensed Irene didn't want to relive what she'd seen, but equally knew its importance.

'I-I was expecting it to be empty and there... there she was. I dropped my mug and I screamed. I could tell right away that she was... I said her name and nudged her all the same. But there was no response.' She stared at Allie through watery eyes. 'That's when I rang for an ambulance. I didn't know who to call.'

'You did the right thing,' Allie mollified. 'And there are no signs of forced entry anywhere?'

'I don't think so.' Irene went to stand, but Allie rested a hand on her arm.

'We can do that.' She glanced at Perry who went to investigate.

'When the paramedic pulled back the duvet, there was so much blood.' Irene shuddered. 'I'll never forget that look in her eyes for as long as I live.'

'I'm so sorry.'

'Someone came into my home. You have to find out who it was.'

'We're already working on it. Does anyone else have a key besides you and Debbie?'

'My neighbour, Mary. Mary Westbourne. She lives at number two. We have each other's, for emergencies.' A sob escaped her. 'But knowing Debbie, she could have given hers to anyone.'

'Irene, we know Debbie,' she explained. 'You don't need to tell us everything.'

Allie almost cried at the relief that crossed Irene's face. It must be so hard for parents of drug-addicted children to talk about things, especially in difficult situations such as this.

'We'll need to have a word with Mary.' Allie raised a hand when Irene was about to protest. 'It's procedure.'

'We've been friends since before Debbie was born. Debbie was hard work towards the end, but Mary wouldn't hurt her. She loved her, as did I. On her good days, she was lovely. She could be funny and generous and kind.' Irene looked at Allie with so much pain. 'You need to find who did this to her. She was an innocent victim.'

Allie nodded, unsure of that last sentence for now. 'We will do all we can, Irene, I promise you that.'

'Thank you.'

'Can I ask if Debbie had any visitors lately? People who you've had a bad feeling about, perhaps?'

'I haven't let her, although I'm not sure who was here when I wasn't. I did have a few neighbours saying there had been loud music on occasions, and shouting, but Debbie always denied it. Said they were wanting to cause trouble to get her out. What could I do?'

'I understand. It must have been so hard for you.'

'The man she was with was worse than her.'

'She had a boyfriend?'

'Sort of. She was living with him, but he kicked her out.'

'Do you have his name?'

'Nathan, I don't know his surname. I couldn't see her on the streets, so I had to have her here. It's such a small place, and she was a feisty soul, so it wasn't easy. But, no, I can't think of anyone else.'

'Could I ask you to make a list anyway in case something jogs your memory? Your visitors too so we can have a quick chat with them. Someone might have information that we would find useful. It's all evidence-collecting for now.'

Irene burst into tears.

Allie needed to get her out of here. She didn't want Irene to be in the thick of it, nor should she be present at the scene.

'Do you have any family you could stay with? You mentioned a sister?'

'She lives in Stone – it's too far. I want to stay nearby.' Stone was fourteen miles away.

'Shall we call Mary?'

'Yes, please.' Irene pointed to a drawer. 'My phone book is in there.'

'I can do that.' Perry came in behind them. 'Everything's fine on the property, boss. No sign of forced entry.'

So Debbie knew her killer, Allie mused.

'Thanks, Perry. Can you nip down to Mary instead, please? She lives at number two. I'd prefer her to find out in person. Then we can take Irene to her property.'

'Yes, boss.' Perry disappeared again.

Allie stayed seated with Irene and the paramedics. But it was time to establish if Irene's clothes needed bagging up for evidence.

'I know this is a difficult thing to answer,' she said, 'but can you tell me if and where you touched Debbie when you found her?'

'I didn't do anything.' A tear dripped down Irene's cheek. 'When I saw she was dead, I panicked and left her there. I rang for help, though.'

'Oh, no, that's fine. I just needed to see if you should change out of your clothes straight away.'

'For evidence you mean?'

Allie nodded. 'I would prefer it, although there's no saying
_'

'I'll do it.'

'Thank you.'

Allie stayed in the hallway while Irene changed. She came
out in fresh clothes, the ones she'd been wearing folded up,
her shoes sitting on top. She passed them to Allie.

'Thank you,' she acknowledged.

A few minutes later, there was a knock on the front door.
She turned to see Perry outside with a woman.

'Mary is here,' she told Irene. 'I'd like to move outside
rather than bring her indoors.'

Allie helped Irene out of the bungalow, along the pretty
hallway, and into the cold where Mary Westbourne was
waiting for them. She was the same age as Irene, dressed in a
pair of dark jeans tucked into fake Ugg slippers, and a blue
jumper. Grey hair was styled into a bob.

'I came as soon as I could,' Mary said, tears visible in her
eyes.

Irene rushed into her arms, crying.

Allie introduced herself as Mary comforted Irene.

'Can I see her again before I go?' Irene asked.

'Not at the moment,' Allie said. 'We'll make sure she is
her best for you at the mortuary, and you'll get a chance to say
goodbye later too.'

The colour fell from Irene's face. 'Someone did that to
her. I want to know who it was.'

Allie needed to get them both out of here.

'Mary, do you think Irene could stay with you overnight,
while we carry out our investigations? '

'Yes, of course.'

'With your permission, Irene, we need to have a look
through Debbie's belongings too. I promise we'll be
respectful.'

'I want to stay,' Irene interjected.

'I know and I respect you for that. But this is a crime scene, and we must preserve evidence as well as search for it. Why don't you go with Mary, and when we have to contact you again, we'll come there to you? In the meantime, I'll arrange for a family liaison officer to be a point of call for you.' Allie pondered. 'Is there a back way you can go?'

Both women shook their heads.

'Come on, ladies,' Perry said. 'I'll escort you both.'

Once they were out of her vision, Allie breathed a sigh of relief. Dealing with grieving relatives was the worst part of the job and often made her think about Karen. After joining the police, she now knew from experience how terrible it would have been for the police officers breaking the news to her parents, that one of their daughters had been assaulted and left for dead.

Which was why she would always see to it that families got justice.

CHAPTER TWENTY-SEVEN

It was seven p.m. Rose Avenue was now flooded with emergency services, and everywhere was cordoned off as necessary.

Unfortunately, no one could stop the residents in the higher floors of Harrison House overlooking from the walkway in front of their homes. Luckily, they couldn't see that much, and only at the rear.

Christian Willhorn was present, and Dave Barnett with his team of forensic officers. Uniform were going house-to-house. As both victims had been stabbed, it was now imperative they found a connection or, at the very least, ruled out its similarity. A search of the property and surrounding area was underway.

'On first feedback, residents in the bungalows haven't seen anything suspicious today, boss.' Frankie brought her up to speed, checking his notebook while he talked. 'A few have said there have been disturbances at the property since Debbie moved in, but nothing too bad.'

'Okay, thanks, Frankie.'

As he went over to join a group of officers, Allie mentally

ran through a list of things she had to do. First and foremost, she needed to update DCI Brindley with news of today's further developments.

Christian came out to speak to her.

'Hi,' she said. 'Not exactly a great welcome to Stoke. It isn't usually this bad, I promise.'

'It's certainly keeping me on my toes,' Christian acknowledged. 'I thought you might like to know that the victim seems to have been drugged before she was attacked.'

'Yes, she's a known user.'

'This is different. My bet is Rohypnol. Whether that was because the murderer anticipated a struggle, I don't know.'

Christian's accent suggested he was from Northumberland. A little teasing was allowed on second meeting.

'I dunna know, either. Ast herd ight else?'

'Come again.'

'Ast herd ight?'

'Sorry, I don't understand –'

Allie smirked. 'It's Potteries slang. It means have you heard anything else?'

'Oh! I thought my hearing had gone funny.' He laughed quietly. 'I'm not actually listening for it, but there's been no chat, if that's what you mean.'

'Well, that's interesting about the sedative, and different from Billy Whitmore.'

'He's an addict too? There's obviously signs in and on his body but I'm ever the optimist that someone can clean themselves up.'

'Yes, there're too many around here, sadly. Bloody monkey dust is the worst thing ever. Was it rife where you've come from?'

'Isn't everything?' His smile was faint this time.

Once he'd gone back inside, Allie checked her watch.

Already she knew it was going to be another late night. She got out her phone and called Mark.

'Hey, good day?' she asked, keeping her voice light.

'So-so. You're not coming home early this evening, are you?'

'No. There's been another murder.'

'What, so soon? Are they linked?'

'Possibly. It only came in at six and there's a-'

'So I won't wait up then?' He sighed down the line.

Allie pinched the bridge of her nose. 'No, Mark. It's best that you don't. I might be really late and -'

'You know, sooner rather than later, we'll have to talk.'

She stayed silent, as if she wasn't aware there was a problem, rather than admit there was.

'And throwing yourself into work all the time isn't going to change things,' he continued.

'You say that as if I plan these murders to keep me here.'

His tone was a tad less sharp when he came back to her. 'I'm merely saying, that's all.'

'I know and we will talk, if that's what you want. But I can't think about anything else right now.'

'Yeah, as ever, your work comes first.'

'That's not what I meant! Mark, I... Mark?'

The line was dead. She let out a low growl. Her job had never been a big issue over the years. Sure, they rowed about her long hours every now and then. But Mark also made it clear how proud he was of her, how he knew she was meant to do the job.

Yet lately, they'd been like passing ships in the night. She was staying late: he would be asleep. She might catch him for a few minutes in the morning, which would be terse because he was angry, and then it would be back to work.

So hearing him wanting to talk filled her with apprehension. She was glad her days, and evenings, were full at the moment. Because she was dreading the outcome of sitting down with him, for fear of what was to come.

Allie stayed at the crime scene for a couple more hours before thinking of leaving for the station. Spotting Simon trying to get her attention, she walked over to him, about to speak when he beat her to it.

'Two in one week, Al – doesn't look good.' Simon glanced around to see if they were out of hearing range. 'Do you have any ideas yet?'

'Yes.' She snorted. 'Not that I'm telling you any of them.'

'Which means you have no clues.'

'Give us time, you sarky git.'

His smile gave away his sentiment. 'I thought you might like to know that I didn't find anything out when I went to talk to the crowd.'

'That was quick!' Allie had known she could rely on him to get the job done, but that was a speedy response regardless.

'No flies on me. I worked on it this afternoon. There were quite a crowd of them, luckily. I managed to speak to twelve.' He handed her a slip of paper. 'Here are the names. Most were either shocked or tight-lipped. I couldn't get any of them to be in my feature, though, which was a bit of a bummer.'

'Sorry about that.' Her apology was sincere. 'Do you think they're hiding anything?'

Simon shrugged. 'One or two of them were genuinely upset that he'd been killed. Mind you, Mickey Elkin was annoyed that Billy owed him money because he wasn't going to get it back.' He rolled his eyes. 'The grand sum of seven pounds and fifty pence.'

Allie sniggered. 'Well, thanks for trying. I'll let you know once I have anything I can share about today.'

'Not even a name?' He stuck out his bottom lip like a child.

She paused. 'It's Debbie Mayhew.'

Simon frowned. 'But she and Billy are-'

'Which is why we won't be officially releasing the name until the morning.'

'Gotcha. I'll start digging in the meantime.'

She went back to Perry who was scrolling on his phone.

'It's awash on social media, but only with what we've given them so far,' he told her.

Her shoulders drooped. 'I expect Debbie is fairly unknown in Rose Avenue.' She pointed to Harrison House. 'I bet someone in there knows something. We need to figure out her last movements. Take me laddo here and go and grab a drink at The White Horse. See if anyone offers you any information.'

CHAPTER TWENTY-EIGHT

When a neighbour was taken in such a brutal way, Perry often had people approach him. But a lot of the time, they were uncomfortable to be seen with the police in public.

Inside the pub, it was busy, yet clear within minutes that no one was willing to be seen with them, so they went back to the car.

They waited for a further quarter of an hour, on the off chance someone would come looking for them. But no one did.

'Well, that didn't work.' Perry started the engine. 'Maybe the estate gossip has let us down this time.'

'I suppose it is a bit early.' Frankie fastened his seatbelt. 'Perhaps people haven't heard yet.'

'Are you kidding? Things get out around here in minutes, not hours. I think people are avoiding us for some reason. Debbie's mum mentioned she had a fella called Nathan. I'll take a guess on that being Nathan Spiers. He wasn't in the pub, and it's his regular haunt. I reckon we should pay him a visit before we go back to the station.'

Nathan Spiers lived in Addison Street, a few minutes'

drive from Rose Avenue. The block of flats were council-owned, eight to a floor and three storeys high with an outside walkway leading to each door. They jogged up to the second floor, to flat 207.

Perry knocked but there was no reply. He knew someone was in, so he banged on the window, shouting his name.

A few seconds later, Nathan opened the door, holding on to it to steady himself. He was thin, partially toothless, with a chequered cap covering his hair. The glazed look in his eyes told Perry all he needed to know.

'What the... oh, it's you.'

'Can we have a word inside?' Perry stepped in before he had time to object.

Nathan sighed. 'Close the door behind you then.'

They went into the living room. Lounging on the settee were two further men. Perry recognised them both straight-away. Tom was Nathan's son, twenty-two, and a younger image of his father, sadly. Carlton Stewart was sitting next to him.

Nathan burped loudly as he sat down, and the three of them laughed.

Perry glanced at Frankie and rolled his eyes. They were all pissed, the room stinking of alcohol. He glanced around, unearthing no drugs paraphernalia, although he would search a lot harder if he felt the need to bring any of them in. For now, he wanted facts on Debbie Mayhew and to break the news to Nathan.

Nathan pointed to the cans on the table. 'Help yourself to drinks.' He smirked.

'Funnily enough, we're not in the entertaining mood.' Perry glared at them all in turn. 'We're wondering if you've heard about the murder in Rose Avenue?'

'You mean about Debs being stabbed to death?' Nathan asked.

'That hasn't been confirmed yet,' Perry replied.

'It's true though?' When Perry said nothing, he went on. 'Yeah, sad that is. Especially as Billy is dead too.' He frowned. 'You've not come here to say they're linked? Are they after me next?'

Typical Nathan Spiers, Perry thought. Not interested in anyone but himself.

'We're making enquiries now.'

'Yeah, right.' Carlton sneered. 'You probably think it's one of us who killed them.' He looked at the others. 'Because we didn't have anything to do with it, did we, lads?'

'Have anything to do with what?' Tom asked.

Perry thought he was being sarcastic until he realised Tom probably didn't know what they were talking about. He hated druggies when they were spouting shit.

'So where were you all last night, from around ten p.m.?' Frankie asked, getting out his notebook.

Perry was thankful for it. Hopefully that would move things along.

'We were here,' Nathan said, as quick as a flash.

'Yeah, we were here,' Carlton concurred. 'All of us, all evening.'

'What were you doing?'

'Pretty much what we're doing now.' Nathan pointed at Tom. 'Of course, there's no point in asking him. He'll never remember.'

The laughter that followed had Perry sighing inwardly. It wasn't the answer he was looking for. Normally, someone would say they were watching TV, the easiest option. He'd then ask what programmes they'd viewed, and it often flummoxed the liars to think on the spot. He changed tack, glancing at Nathan.

'I gather you and Debbie were an item?'

'Not for a long time now.' Nathan shook his head. 'She used to go out with Billy too. What happened to her again?'

'Details will be available in the morning. Maybe you can tell us when you last saw her?' Frankie asked.

'It would have been Monday, when we'd all heard about Billy. She was in the pub. The one you've just been in.'

They ignored the remark. Obviously, someone had contacted Nathan once they'd left The White Horse.

'How was she?' Perry continued.

'Like her usual self but upset about Billy. We ended up reminiscing about the olden days. Then she left.'

'Around what time?'

'About four?' He reached for his beer bottle and took a swig. 'We stayed until six, I think.'

'Is there anything else you can tell us that would help with our enquiries?' Perry urged. 'Did she get on with her mum? Had she been in trouble lately?'

'Her mum is great,' Nathan said, and the other two men nodded in agreement.

'What about any friends?'

Carlton shrugged. 'I wouldn't say she was the type to get close to many people. She could be quite clingy. Needy even.'

'Yep,' Tom agreed, surprising them all as it was the first word he'd spoken in a while.

Beside Perry, Nathan was falling asleep. The visit was useless. He doubted any of them would even remember they'd been in the morning. But then Carlton spoke out.

'This is another gang, isn't it?' His eyes narrowed. 'Moving into our territory.'

Nathan's eyes opened, and he sat up abruptly. 'In that case, you'd be best talking to Kenny. He might tell you if he's heard anything on the grapevine. He knows *everything*.'

Carlton kicked him, and Nathan yelped. He was about to

give Carlton a verbal assault when he saw the snarl on his face and shut his mouth.

Perry saw it too, deciding to stay quiet also. It was time to leave. They were getting nowhere.

'What a waste of space,' Frankie said once they were out on the walkway again. He shuddered as if he wanted to rid himself of the atmosphere. 'It smells rancid in there.'

'Yeah, they're dirty scrotes, bloody useless too.' Perry rubbed his hands together. 'Won't put me off food. Fancy grabbing a dirty burger on the way back?'

'Absolutely.' Frankie grinned.

They got in the car again and Perry thought back over the conversation with the three men. Nathan Spiers might not be involved in Debbie's murder, but he was good for information, possibly about Kenny Webb. So too was Carlton Stewart.

It could be worth leaning on them over the next few days.

Carlton went to the window, watching the detectives drive away. When they were out of sight, he turned to lay into Nathan, only to find him out of it completely. He grabbed the neck of his jumper and pulled him closer, but Nathan pushed him away and flopped back down.

At least the police had thought he was in the same state. Carlton was as sober as a judge, playing them into thinking he was drunk.

What the hell had the pigs come round here for anyway, getting in his way of things? He should have realised Nathan would be one of their first suspects after Debbie had been shanked.

But he had been able to vouch for him, and vice versa. If he needed an alibi, he had one. Because he couldn't let anyone find out that he went to visit Debbie last night.

She'd called him to say she needed a fix. But when he'd got to Rose Avenue, she was so spaced out that she hadn't known what she was doing. He'd given her something for tomorrow and left her to it. He'd known she'd be out of it for the rest of the evening.

Yet he'd left her very much alive. If she'd died of an overdose, he might think everything was fine. But someone had murdered her too.

First Billy, and now Debbie, and both could be linked to him. Was someone trying to set him up?

And then his blood ran cold. He would have left fingerprints in Rose Avenue.

CHAPTER TWENTY-NINE

Over in Longton, Kenny had been nursing a whisky while he contemplated whether to call it a day. He still couldn't get his head around Billy Whitmore's murder, the fact it had happened to someone he knew so well. He'd put one of the lads onto sourcing out more information but so far, he'd drawn a blank. Either no one was talking, or they didn't know anything.

There was a knock on the door, and Martin appeared. He seemed mithered about something, his face ashen.

'What's up?' he asked.

'I thought I'd come over and see if you were still here. Have you heard?'

'About what?' Kenny lifted his glass. 'Want one?'

'No, thanks.' Martin pulled out a chair and sat down. 'Debbie Mayhew is dead. Word is out she's been stabbed.'

'What the... tell me what you know.'

Martin enlightened him, Kenny's mood darkening by the second.

He took a sip of his drink. 'I bet that prick Carlton is

behind this. It could have been him that finished Billy Whitmore off too.'

'What makes you say that?'

'A hunch. The lad is a cocky shit. I need to talk to him about some money he hasn't paid me. He's been keeping an eye on the workers.'

'Ah.' Martin pulled back his head. 'Does he know too much?'

'Either that or he's playing me. I gave the job to Carlton, and yet when I've checked into things since Billy copped it, it seems *he* was collecting my money for him.'

Martin's brow furrowed. 'Why would he do that?'

Kenny shrugged. 'I can't work it out. I'll arrange to see Carlton tomorrow. Figure out what's going on.'

'Did he know both Billy and Debbie?'

'Yeah, they move in the same circles, I suppose, even though they're older than him. All idiots together.'

'Do you think anyone else could be involved?'

'I'm certain they are. Carlton isn't capable of murder and getting away with it, especially twice. Nor would he risk setting me up.' He shook his head. 'Someone is messing with us.'

'Another crew?'

'I think so, don't you?'

Martin whistled through his teeth. 'It's possible, but who would dare?'

'That depends. Someone could be trying to wipe out my dealers. Or perhaps making me think that there's a bigger ulterior motive.'

There was a moment's silence.

'What about Steve Kennedy?' Martin asked. 'Do you think it might be him getting his own back?'

'More than likely.' Steve had never forgiven Kenny for

going to work for Ryder, but money was always his motivator. He'd do anything for the right price.

'Want me to put feelers out?'

'Yeah. Get a message to Terry too. He needs to know.'

'Will do.' Martin paused before continuing. 'Perry came to see me.'

A nerve in Kenny's eye flickered. 'And what did he want?'

'He mentioned you in connection with Redmond Street.'

'Did he now? So they're already thinking it's me when I've got nothing to do with it?'

'It's probably because Billy got killed there. But Debbie being murdered too, well, it kinda puts more emphasis on you, in a roundabout way.'

Kenny's brow furrowed. This was turning out to be worse than he'd imagined. Someone *was* trying to get at him.

His focus fell on a photo on the wall. It had been taken at his fortieth birthday party a few years ago. Both Billy and Debbie were on it, Carlton too. He cast a glance around everyone else. Was there a mole in his camp, or an idiot trying to muscle in?

He gnawed on his bottom lip. 'Either way, we need to put someone else in there now that Billy isn't around, once everything has died down.'

Martin nodded. 'Is Carlton out of the picture now?'

'Not necessarily, but I don't trust him. He's getting too clever.'

'What about Milo? He's keen and up-and-coming?'

Kenny thought for a moment. 'Perhaps. In the meantime, you find out what you can?'

'Of course.' Martin smiled. 'I'd be happy to.'

Once he'd heard Martin's car pull away, Kenny picked up his phone and rang Carlton. The call went unanswered, and he cursed loudly, resisting the temptation to hurl it across the room in temper. Where the fuck was he?

Nothing would express his anger more than a fist in Carlton's face. If he was here in his office, he'd have floored him, perhaps not stopping until he'd done some serious damage. Hell, he might even do that when he saw him tomorrow. Regardless, somehow the lad must have landed him in it. Who else was he working for?

Kenny was a fool to have given him a chance after he'd found him on the take last month. It had only been a small sum of money he'd caught him stealing, and Carlton had paid him back, but to think he was doing it again was taking the piss.

He glanced at the clock: it was too late to do anything about it now. He'd sit tight, see if Carlton came to work in the morning, and if not, he'd go over and see him.

It took a few minutes before Martin's heart beat its normal rhythm. He hated going to Kenny's office. It brought back how powerful he was; how things could change from good to bad in seconds.

He'd seen it so many times. Men younger than him unable to walk for weeks after he'd bashed their legs. Older men unable to breathe after he'd smashed a few ribs. Kenny didn't care whether he was right or wrong. Whatever he heard that he didn't like, he acted on. Which was why he was looking after the business for Terry now, staying loyal to him rather than Steve Kennedy.

Luckily, Terry liked Martin much more than he did Kenny.

Being an informant from all sides was a dangerous game he played, and it was always best to be one step ahead. And he much preferred keeping Perry sweet rather than Kenny.

Especially as he was being paid well on the side by Ryder.

CHAPTER THIRTY

Allie and the team had gone through everything they could for the day, and while they waited on the post-mortem and first forensics to come through for Debbie Mayhew, they could at least get a good few hours' rest until the morning.

As she entered her home, it was near midnight again, but there was a light on downstairs this time.

In the hall, she shrugged off her coat, the kettle reaching boiling point the first thing she heard.

Mark appeared in the kitchen doorway. 'Tea or something stronger?'

'Tea would be lovely, thanks.' She smiled faintly at him.

'You look exhausted. Go sit down and I'll bring it to you.'

A few minutes later, he came into the room with two mugs and a packet of biscuits. Seeing him in his pyjamas, tears brimmed in her eyes when Allie realised why he might have waited up for her. It wasn't because he missed her, or wanted to see her, or was checking in to see if she was okay after her hard day. It was because he wanted to get things over with, no matter how late it was.

Their chatter was small talk, and it was tinged with a "we

both know what's coming after this" vibe. They couldn't put things off any longer. Nor could she face what he was going to say.

Despite such a harrowing day, she'd been trying to close her mind to what would happen once she was home. How she would react; how Mark would respond. How everything she valued would be gone.

She fought back tears and looked everywhere but at him.

'You know I wanted us to talk,' he began at last.

'Hmm-mmm,' was all she managed to reply.

'I took it really bad when you said you didn't want to look into adopting a child.' He held up his hand as she was about to speak. 'I shouldn't have reacted the way I did. I withdrew from you, and that wasn't fair. But I couldn't deal with the thought of not doing it.'

'I'm so sorry.' Allie truly was. 'It's not that I don't want to do it for you, but it wasn't enough. It would *only* be for you. There was no way of compromising. I even said I'd try fostering, but you were adamant you wanted to adopt.'

Mark gnawed his bottom lip. 'Like I say, I was so entrenched in my own needs and wants, that I hadn't thought how it would affect us. I thought you'd say yes, and it hurt when you couldn't. Our marriage has always been built on compromise.'

'I know. You gave up so much when Karen was alive, and I —'

'That's nothing to do with it. Karen was your sister, and what happened to her was tragic. You cared for her as best you could until she died.'

'But it changed the course of everything we'd dreamed of, hoped for.'

There was silence, and she held her breath until he spoke again. This was it, the moment where everything ended. She jumped in first, not wanting to hear what he had to say.

'Mark, I –'

'I should have been willing to meet you halfway from the beginning,' he cut her off. '*I'm* sorry about that. So what I was going to say was, shall we see about fostering?'

Allie's mouth dropped open for a moment.

Mark went to the drawer and pulled out a handful of leaflets. 'If we're accepted, we could foster older children, teenagers. Apparently, the council is crying out for people to help with that age group. They're obviously challenging but also, they're the most independent too. Not so demanding time wise. We could try it, have a child or two stay with us. What do you think?'

Allie said nothing while she gathered her thoughts. Mark stared at her until she continued, tears welling in her eyes.

'I thought you wanted to talk about getting divorced.'

His eyes widened in surprise.

'Oh, Allie.' He reached across for her hand, giving it a squeeze and holding on to it. 'I don't want that at all. But I must ask why you'd think I would. And more to the point, do you still want to be with me?'

'Of course I do!' She squeezed his hand back. 'I know we haven't been getting on lately. Even when I've not been working a case, you've been going out for a drink with John before coming home. I've been catching up on paperwork to avoid meeting your eye when I walked through the door. I thought...' She took a deep breath as emotion flooded through her. 'I thought you'd had enough.'

'I have, of what we've become. But we're a team. For better, for worse. We've always had our ups and downs, like many couples who've been together as long as we have. But that doesn't mean I want it to end. I just...' He ran a hand through his hair, sitting back. 'I need to do something.'

She stared at him, the man she had loved for over twenty

years. He had been there for her through so much, and yet she hadn't been able to do this one thing for him.

She couldn't blame him for being angry when she'd refused to see into adoption. Having a small child would have meant too many changes for them. It could have been the beginning of the end. And so permanent. Allie knew she'd been selfish, but still, it had to suit them both.

Mark had been devastated. He'd closed himself off from her, but now he was telling her why. And he was giving her an option that she'd wanted to take in the first instance.

Would fostering work for them? She thought of her chat with Kelsey, how she wanted to help her more than she was able to. How Kelsey had been dragged up and how that might affect her for the rest of her days. Could they make a difference in a child's life, someone like Kelsey?

'You know teenagers can be the worst?' she said, quietly, interlinking his fingers with her own.

'I remember how awful I was to Mum and Dad.' He sniggered. 'But this way, we wouldn't have to be around all the time. They'd be at school for one thing. You could still do your job, with no worries as I'll be there when you're not. I'm at home more often now. I think we could wing it to see if it might work.'

'What about the things I may have to cancel on short notice if a job comes in?'

'We can switch roles and I'll go.'

'I'm not sure you'll fit into my clothes, especially my dresses.'

Mark laughed. 'I'll play my version of mum and dad combined.'

Allie reached for one of the brochures. There was a photo of a couple in their late forties with a girl of about ten on the front. They were all smiles, as if they knew it would work out, no matter what.

There was a hole in their life, room for it to be filled.

She almost laughed at the thoughts she'd been fighting with earlier in the day. They'd have to sell the house, split all their possessions. Start again, move out and get on with life without each other. She hadn't been able to contemplate it at all. Now she didn't have to.

'At least think about it?' Mark pleaded.

How could she refuse that look, the one he'd won her over with so often over the years?

She smiled. 'I will. Just give me some time?'

Mark moved to sit next to her, turning his face to hers. It was the closest they'd been in a long while, and they kissed, their eyes locked together afterwards.

It was all she could promise for now. But it seemed it was enough.

CHAPTER THIRTY-ONE

WEDNESDAY

Allie awoke the next morning with a huge grin on her face. She'd thought she'd be too tired for some good loving, but after their conversation the night before finished in a much better way than she'd anticipated, when Mark had kissed her goodnight, one thing had led to another. It had meant her mind had switched off and she'd had the best sleep in a good while.

'Morning,' Mark said, reaching across to pull her near.

'Morning. I slept like a baby. It was bliss!' She snuggled into him.

'You worry too much.'

'I had every reason to.' She thumped his thigh playfully. 'I'm glad things are good between us again.'

'Me too. It's been really shit these past few months.'

'Don't hold back, Mr Shenton.'

He chortled. 'I won't.'

'But yeah, you're right.'

They lay together in silence until the alarm went off. Allie sighed. 'Time to face the day.'

'Have a good one.'

Allie wished she could stay in bed for an extra hour, and then work from home for the day. It would be nice to hang around, do a few conference calls online, make some phone calls while sitting in the conservatory. Although she was doing Mark a disservice as his job involved far more than that. But all the same, it seemed a comfortable option to the day ahead she'd no doubt be having.

'I don't suppose you'll wait up for me this evening and we can have a repeat performance of last night?' she queried.

'What, the chat?'

'No!'

'No chance.'

'You charmer, you.'

Mark's laughter rang in her ears as she drove to work. She was glad they'd sorted things and was quite excited about the future for the first time in ages. Fostering might be something they tried and found it didn't suit them but equally, it could be a huge opportunity for them to grow further as a couple by giving a child somewhere safe to stay.

Traffic was heavy but now at the station, she checked in on what had come in overnight before briefing the team. Jenny would be joining them as the case had evolved. She was glad of it. Two murders were better to crack when there were more heads than hers at the helm to do the thinking and the problem-solving needed. There was so much to remember too.

They were waiting in the briefing room when Jenny came in.

'Morning, everyone,' she greeted.

'Cup of tea, Ma'am?' Frankie offered, getting to his feet.

Jenny raised her eyebrows, and Allie watched a blush

spread upwards from Frankie's neck, settling on his face within seconds as he wondered if he'd overstepped the mark. But it wasn't unheard of to ask a superior officer if they wanted a brew. In fact, it was a smart move.

Jenny smiled her appreciation. 'That would be great, thanks. I haven't had time to grab one yet. One sugar and a spot of milk, please.'

'We have him well trained,' Allie remarked. 'He makes the best tea.'

She brought Jenny up to speed with everything that had happened the day before and what they had been planning to do before the call about Debbie Mayhew had come in. It was a lengthy meeting as there was much to discuss. This time yesterday there had been the one murder, which was much easier to keep abreast of, but two, and so close together, meant there was a lot to get through.

'Where are we with any video evidence?' Allie's gaze fell on Sam.

'Nothing else found on the city CCTV, nor at all in Redmond Street. There was only one security camera fitted on the houses at the rear of the pub. It doesn't cover the crime scene, but I checked it anyway and drew a blank. It's the same with Billy's phone too, although a couple of the names in the notebook found in his pocket match numbers stored in it.'

'Let's look into those. Can you action that, thanks?'

'Do we need to visit or ring them?'

'Visit. I doubt they'd say anything over the phone, and I don't want to spook anyone. Get on to the providers for addresses.'

Sam nodded. 'Yes, boss.'

Allie watched her typing on her laptop at double the speed she thought was possible. Again, thankful for her analytical mind, she recognised the job was in capable hands.

Jenny had sat back for a while, but Allie knew she was paying attention to what she was doing. Luckily, she didn't seem annoyed that she'd missed anything. In fact, it seemed quite the opposite.

'You've obviously been extremely busy,' Jenny told them. 'Thanks, everyone. Allie, there'll be a press release going out this morning. We should think about doing a Q and A session in the station too now we have two deceased.'

'I need to speak to Debbie Mayhew's mum this morning,' Allie told her. 'Would you like me to ask her anything?'

'See if she's had any more thoughts, obviously, and if she's up for it, I might do an appeal between both families. Can you make sure she's okay with that? It could be too soon after her daughter's death to do them both together, but parents like to help so you never know.'

'Yes, Ma'am.'

The briefing ended, and Allie collared Frankie before he left the room with everyone else.

'Smart move re the tea,' she teased.

Frankie blushed. 'I was mortified it came out.'

'We're all part of the same team.'

'I know but –'

'That's not why I stopped you, you eejit. I want you to call on Andrew Dale while we're out, on the quiet. I haven't heard anything from him and, I know we're busy, but I had it in mind for Grace to visit him in a couple of days. I don't want him to fall through the net.'

'I'll go this morning.'

'Thanks.' She held up her mug. 'Just got time for another cuppa before I leave.'

CHAPTER THIRTY-TWO

Allie was fond of working with the elderly population, a throwback from her role as a social worker. In some ways, that job had been very satisfactory, but the red tape and lack of funding that stopped her from helping her clients became soul-destroying.

It was when her sister was attacked, and Allie had been involved with a lot of the local police, that she'd decided to join the force. At least now she could get some resolutions, although in some ways things were the same. The constant cutbacks and longer hours took their toll.

Yet she knew she could never leave. She enjoyed her role as a DI immensely. While serving as a detective sergeant, the role was hands-on, with two or three staff to monitor, and she'd been apprehensive at first about overseeing a larger operation. But her stint in the Community Intelligence Team had given her confidence to manage a larger team.

When she wasn't needed as a senior investigating officer, her role was much more involved with budgets, meetings, and general rules and regulations. But it all stopped until cases like Operation Moorcroft were either closed, passed to the CPS or, sadly, sometimes, when the trail went cold.

It was drizzling when she and Frankie got to Rose Avenue. After having a catch up with everyone who was still at the crime scene, they walked to number two.

Mary Westbourne answered the door, and they followed her along a narrow hallway and into the living room, the same layout as Irene Mayhew's property.

"Irene is lying down. I'll check to see if she is awake.' Mary turned to leave but then stopped. 'Would you like a cup of tea? I'm sure you need warming up.'

Allie smiled. 'We're fine, thank you.'

While she was gone, Allie took the opportunity to have a scan around the room, a hint of vanilla mixed with musk wafting around her. A settee and an armchair were pushed against the back walls to make room to squeeze in a small bookcase and a TV on top of a unit. The gas fire was on high, the heat warming her up.

The back wall was covered in family portraits. Allie spotted several with Mary and a gentleman, some with a red-haired little girl through to her teenage years. Several were of the girl as a grown-up with what seemed to be her own family. It was a lovely collection.

Mary came back into the room. 'I'm afraid she's still asleep.' She closed the door quietly and sat down.

'Not to worry. You have a lovely home. Have you lived here long?' Allie asked, prepared to make small talk before they left.

'Four years, since my husband died.' She pointed to the man in the photos. 'That's my Harry. We were married for forty-three years.'

'Wow, that's true love for you. And is that your daughter?'

'Adopted one, yes, Sharon. Harry and I couldn't have our own, but we were blessed with her. Do you have children?'

'I don't,' she replied, not feeling the guilt that she usually did after her conversation with Mark last night. 'But Frankie has a young son.'

'Yes, Ben. He's four.' Frankie smiled.

Allie made to stand, but Mary began to talk.

'I'm glad Irene is asleep actually,' she said. 'Because it will give me time to have a word with you. It's...'

'What is it?' Allie sat forwards, sensing whatever Mary said was going to be a revelation, but uncomfortable for her to discuss.

'I've known Debbie from the day she was born.' Mary's eyes lit up. 'She was a bonny baby, and we used to look after her a lot until our Sharon came along. Harry and I adored her. But we had no idea what was going on back then either.' She paused to clear her throat. 'Debbie's uncle sexually abused her when she was a teenager. He raped her continually, the poor girl.'

Allie's heart sank. No wonder Debbie had lived a chaotic life. It was despicable to think of what she must have gone through. Although the authorities, as well as the force, tried to keep on top of sexual exploitation nowadays, it was hard to hear it from years gone by. Children had been more at risk because there was no one to confide in, or they didn't dare because they were warned of the dangers if they said anything to anyone. To a certain extent it was still like that now, but sometimes photographs, pornography and online forums made the evidence they needed accessible rather than putting up a child against an adult in court.

'She confided in me a few years ago,' Mary went on.

'Did Irene know?' Allie questioned. 'And her father?'

'That's the thing, I'm not sure. Irene never told me, and I could never ask. But by then it was too late for Debbie. She'd turned to drugs to wipe out the memories.'

'I'm sorry to say this as it sounds disrespectful, but did you believe Debbie was telling the truth?'

'Yes.' Mary's hand went to her neck as if she was trying not to transport herself back to that harrowing time. 'She was tormented and cried like a baby after telling me. I let her stay for the night. Before she left the next day, she thanked me for listening and asked me to promise not to tell Irene. Well, I was torn but I agreed. She brought me some flowers in the afternoon.'

'Did she visit you much?'

'Once or twice a month. It depended on what she was up to or how she was feeling.'

'You mean how dependent on drugs she was?'

'Yes, sadly. Oh, I have something for you.' Mary passed a slip of lined paper to Allie. 'Irene made a list of people, like you asked.'

'Thank you.'

They drank their tea, and when Irene still hadn't stirred, Allie decided they would come back later. At the front door on her way out, she handed Mary her contact card.

'If you can let us know when Irene is ready to talk, one of us will come and see her. In the meantime, if you can think of anything else, no matter how small, that might help with our enquiries, please don't hesitate to come forward. You can call me anytime at the station. If I'm not there, an officer will get a message to me.'

Mary nodded.

'Thank you for letting us know,' she said quietly. 'I'm glad Irene has you for a friend.'

CHAPTER THIRTY-THREE

In the bedroom, Irene was awake. She was waiting for the detectives to go; didn't want to face them. She knew what they must think of Debbie, and yet Irene had tried so hard to make things right.

She had broken her promise as a mother. She'd said she would look after her daughter, but she hadn't known what was going on with Debbie and her uncle until it was too late.

What kind of a mother did that make her? Of course she'd tried to make up for it, even though he'd never been charged with what he'd done. Now it was too late as he'd died last year.

Her body wouldn't stop shaking, she supposed it must be due to the shock. And relief perhaps, because it meant Debbie might be at peace now.

Her daughter had been a huge part of her life, but for the most, Debbie had been disruptive and emotionally damaged by what had happened to her when she was fifteen. It had taken her until she was in her thirties to tell her what had happened.

Irene had never told a soul, not even Mary. More out of

shame really. Because Ralph had taken advantage of her too, soon after her husband, Stan, had died.

Stan hadn't got on with his brother, and they'd lost touch over the years. It was at Stan's funeral that she'd reconnected with him again. At first, Ralph had been friendly and, when he'd started to visit her unannounced, it had been nice. He'd be attentive to her needs, bringing her flowers and chocolates.

It hadn't been long before she'd realised his motive. Ralph wanted to sell his bungalow, pocket the money and move in with her. And that wasn't on.

When he'd said he loved her, Irene had been surprised. She hadn't wanted to hurt his pride because she didn't feel the same. But she had to be sure he understood. She liked her own space and had no intentions at her time in life of starting again. Memories of Stan were all she needed. She had a good social life, seeing friends most days and some evenings.

But Ralph had been hurt by the rejection. He hadn't visited for a fortnight, and then out of the blue, one evening, he'd knocked on the door. It had been ten p.m., and Irene hadn't wanted to see him. He'd been drinking too.

Eventually, he'd talked his way in. Irene had been worried about upsetting the neighbours with the noise he was making.

It was the worst thing she could have done. She was in the kitchen, making a cup of tea when he'd come behind her, wrapped his hands around her waist, and kissed her neck. She'd squirmed, told him to stop and tried to push him away. But he'd turned nasty. She would never forget the look on his face.

She closed her eyes, trying to block out the image of what he'd done next.

At her age, it had hurt very much. All he'd done afterwards was gone to sleep. She hadn't dared move as she lay next to him all night.

And then the following morning, he'd woken with a smirk on his face, not recalling what had happened. Or he'd fooled her, making her think it was all consensual.

After that, he'd appear late in the evening a couple of times a week. She hadn't anyone to talk to about it – there was no way she could mention it to Mary. Each time he arrived drunk, and each time he left sober.

She'd tried to stop him on the first few occasions, but he'd got so rough with her that she'd had to concede. And besides, it was always quick, if he finished at all before falling asleep.

Was she certain he didn't think they were in a relationship? She wasn't sure. But he never took her anywhere. Never saw her outside of her home.

And then Debbie had turned up one morning while Ralph had been there from the night before.

Debbie had gone wild, thrashing out at him, calling him every swear word Irene had ever heard. Ralph had tried to stop her, but after she'd scratched his face and punched him several times, she'd marched him to the front door and threw him out, telling him never to come there again.

Debbie had sat with her then and told her everything. Irene had confessed to what he'd been doing to her, and for a time they'd understood each other. It was *his* fault, not theirs.

But her daughter had been ruined by that man. Barely a woman, on the cusp of living a life she could be proud of, happy to be a part of, Ralph had taken that from her.

Had Irene known at the time, she might have been able to do something about it. And although there was no excuse for Debbie's behaviour recently, at least she'd understood why.

He'd stayed away but she'd lived in fear. So when she'd heard of Ralph's death, relief had flooded through her. There would be no more jumping at a knock on the door. At last now she would be able to relax in her own home. It was terrible what could go on behind closed doors.

She hadn't gone to his funeral. Whether anyone thought ill of her, she didn't care. She never wanted anything else to do with that vile, despicable man.

She wondered now if she should tell the police. Would it help them to find Debbie's killer? She wasn't sure how it could, but it may help them understand Debbie better.

Deep down she knew that she *had* to tell them. It was a matter of when she could get the words out. Not today, tomorrow maybe.

A knock came at the door, and Mary walked into the room with a mug of tea and a sandwich.

'I thought you might try and eat something, duck,' she said, placing them on the bedside cabinet. Then she sat on the bed. 'How are you?'

'A bit numb.'

'That's understandable.' Mary patted Irene's arm. 'It was all so sudden and... such a tragedy.'

'I-I don't want to talk about it yet.'

Mary stood promptly. 'Of course. I'll leave you alone. But if you need anything, I'm a shout away.'

Irene said her name just as Mary got to the door. She couldn't let her go without saying something.

'I don't know what I'd do without you.'

'That's what friends are for.' Mary gave a faint smile. 'You should be able to go home soon but you're welcome to stay with me for as long as you need.'

'Thank you.'

As Mary left, Irene buried her face in her hands and cried again. How was she going to live without her daughter?

CHAPTER THIRTY-FOUR

Once at the car, Allie turned to Frankie.

'Ugh, that wasn't pleasant to hear. Are you okay?'

'Yeah, I'm good. It turns my stomach, though.'

'Mine too. I love this job, but equally it's depressing at times.' She held up the list that she'd been handed. 'Still, we have a consolation prize. There's a person of interest on here who's also visited Gladys Whitmore. I think we'll pay her a visit.'

While Allie drove, she couldn't get Debbie Mayhew from her mind. What a shame she was unable to tell her mum for so long because of the humiliation she'd felt.

Allie hated how people preyed on the vulnerable, particularly their own family members. A lot went on in private, far too much for them to police even if all the public came forward to ask for their assistance.

And yet the people who didn't need their help, who rang for emergency services over the slightest thing, were always the ones to waste their time and think nothing of it.

They arrived outside Billy Whitmore's home. The door was answered by PC Joy.

'Hi, Rachel, how's it going?' Allie smiled.

'Everything is calm, but Fiona isn't talking much.'

'Is she on her own?'

'No, Riley is with her.'

'Good.' She stepped inside, followed by Frankie. 'Because that's who I've come to see.'

They went into the living room to find Fiona sitting in the armchair and Riley on the settee.

The two women glanced at each other quickly.

'How are you doing, Fiona?' Allie asked first.

'It's not sinking in yet.' Fiona's face screwed up a little.

Allie wasn't sure how to take her. It didn't seem as if she was heartbroken, but grief often stayed hidden away when relatives of the deceased took care of everything that needed to be completed in a robotic state. Fiona had changed her clothes, and her hair was freshly washed, so she was coping, but who knew what she was like once she was alone.

Did she cry herself to sleep, or did she say a silent prayer that Billy was no longer here? It was all so different for every individual, and private unless necessary for their investigation for them to know more. Allie feared she was about to make things worse as well.

'How's Kelsey taking the news?' She still didn't mention that they'd already spoken, unsure whether Kelsey would have told her family, and she didn't want to lose her trust if not.

'She's okay but upset,' Fiona answered. 'She liked Billy, got on with him really well. She's gone to school, though.'

Allie pointed to a seat. 'May we sit?'

'Be my guests.'

Riley's cheeks reddened and Allie frowned. It didn't make sense, especially as she was here to talk to her about a trivial matter. Unless there was more to it.

When Frankie was settled beside her, she decided to jump

right in, rather than mention Debbie Mayhew. She assumed Rachel would have told them by now anyway.

'Riley, you work for a company called HomeHelp Stoke, is that correct?'

'Yes.' Riley looked on in confusion.

'Let me start by saying you're not under caution at this moment in time, but I do need to ask you a few questions. As you know, we're investigating Billy's murder, and I requested a list of people who had visited recently from his mum.'

'Why?' Fiona butted in.

'It's routine procedure.' Allie kept her eyes on Riley. 'When it came back, we noticed that you'd been to her home.'

'I see a lot of people.' Riley's voice rose to panic mode. 'I can't remember them all.'

'Do you know which client is Billy's mum?'

'Yes, she lives in Fisher Grove. She's nice. Always makes me a cup of tea.'

'When was the last time you visited her?'

'I think it was Friday.' She paused. 'Yes, last Friday. I did her two hours of cleaning. She can do most things herself, but I do some of the heavier lifting and carrying type of things. She's very fussy – likes things just so.'

Allie smiled, because what Riley had said tallied with Gladys's version too. 'You also visited Irene Mayhew, in Rose Avenue?'

'That's Debbie's mum.' Riley sat forwards. 'Debbie was murdered yesterday too.'

'Yes, did you know her well?'

'She was drunk whenever I saw her.'

'Oh, *her*,' Fiona muttered.

'What do you mean by that?' Allie turned to her.

'I told Mum about Debbie,' Riley said. 'I stopped going to Rose Avenue a couple of weeks ago because she wouldn't let me in. She hurt my arm when she grabbed me and told me to get lost. It's not even her property, but Mrs Mayhew wasn't there. So I complained to my supervisor at work, and I never went back.'

Frankie took out his notebook and jotted down the details.

'So can I reconfirm where you were between seven p.m. and ten p.m. on Sunday evening, Riley?' she continued.

'You've already asked me that. I was here with you, Mum, wasn't I?'

'That's right.' Fiona folded her arms. 'I told you that the last time you visited too.'

Allie ignored Fiona. She looked at Riley again.

'I was here.' A blush appeared on her cheeks the moment the words were out.

'And yesterday?'

'I was at work – ten until six. You can check, if you like.'

Allie nodded. Until they'd seen the client rota, she wouldn't rule Riley out, and even then, Riley could have slipped in after work to have a go at Debbie, to get her own back. And there was Carlton Stewart to think about too. Had they gone together, and something went wrong?

'Riley wouldn't do anything to hurt her, if that's what you're suggesting,' Fiona said.

'No!' Riley insisted, sitting forward to protest. 'I couldn't, not even to someone like her.'

'Okay.' Satisfied for now, Allie stood up, Frankie doing the same. 'Riley, if you can think of anything unusual during your last few visits to see Billy's mum, I'd be grateful if you could let us know. You can tell PC Joy, Rachel, if you prefer.'

'How did she die?' Riley asked when they were almost at the door, her voice carrying a slight tremor.

'She was stabbed.' Allie would give her that, but nothing

else for now. They still weren't sure what Debbie had been sedated with, nor for how long.

'Like Billy,' Riley said quietly.

Allie could see things beginning to sink in. Although she couldn't rule Riley out of the investigation, she was sure she wasn't telling her everything. At the least, their conversation seemed peppered with things she didn't quite understand yet.

All she could assume was there may be a link between Riley and their murder victims. Obviously, there was no evidence to say she had attacked and murdered either one or both, but something wasn't right.

Although Allie could have mentioned it, she didn't want to ask about Riley seeing Carlton. She'd save that nugget of information for now.

'We'll be in touch if I need to speak to either of you again,' she finished before leaving.

While Allie was outside with Rachel and Frankie, Fiona rounded on Riley. She kept her voice low, conscious they might be listening.

'What the hell was all that about?'

'I don't know.' Riley shook her head. 'I saw her through work, that's all. I didn't bloody kill her.'

'I know that, but they're fishing for something. It was the same the other day when she was talking about that scarf.'

Riley folded her arms. 'I'm telling you the truth. Don't you believe me?'

'Of course I do, but I wouldn't put it past Carlton to be involved.'

'I don't know what you mean.' Riley blushed.

'You know something.' Fiona pointed at her. 'You'd better make sure it doesn't come back to us. I can't get into trouble because of Carlton. You have to speak to him.'

'I have to go to work soon!'

'Call in sick. They can give you another day off. Say you're still upset about Billy.'

'It's only four hours. And quite frankly, Mum, I'd rather be away from the house for a while. I'm beginning to feel smothered.'

'Don't be so dramatic.'

'Me? I'm not the one who's in continuous panic mode.'

'Just ring him!' Fiona cried in exasperation.

'No! I'll call and see him this afternoon.'

CHAPTER THIRTY-FIVE

As soon as her shift finished that afternoon, Riley was straight round to Carlton's flat. It had been a good idea to be at work. As well as needing the money, it was a chance for her to switch off for a while. A pounding headache hadn't eased at all. The constant pressure not to slip up in front of the police was stressing her out, especially when they turned up unannounced like they had this morning.

Carlton answered the door, a frown on his face. 'What's up with you?'

'The police have been around to see me.' Riley flew past him.

'*You?* What for?'

'About Debbie Mayhew!' She paced the tiny living room, being careful not to trip over the mess on the floor. 'They came because Billy's mum and Debbie's mum are clients I clean for, and I've visited them both recently. I've had to provide alibis for when Billy *and* Debbie died now!'

'Relax,' Carlton urged. 'It wasn't you.'

'The police don't know that. And now I'm worried that

they'll link me to things, and everything will come out and I'll be sent to prison, and I won't be able to see you and –'

'Slow down!' Carlton interrupted. 'You're overthinking. No one is going to link you to anything.'

'How do you know?' Tears welled in her eyes.

'Because you've done nothing wrong.'

'It was me who –'

'No one knows that except you and me.' He put a finger to her lips. 'I'm not telling the feds anything, and it looks as if you haven't either.'

She shook her head.

'Then we're home and dry. They'll be too focussed on the murders to think about anything else.'

'So we're going to stop?'

Carlton paused. 'For now, yes. Then we can start again once it's all sorted.'

Riley saw this as her chance to air her thoughts. 'I don't want to do it anymore. It's not right, really and it's put the creeps up me having the police coming round with their questions.'

'But you told them nothing, right?'

'I-I said I was with my mum when Billy died.'

'Why?'

'I *panicked* because they thought I had something to do with it. Besides, I was covering for Mum. She was on her own.'

'Are you sure she didn't have anything to do with it?'

Riley folded her arms. 'It wasn't her.'

Carlton paused. 'And what about Debbie?'

'What about Debbie?'

'Did your mum –'

'No, she did not!'

'So why did the police question you?'

'Because I might have been at work when she died. They don't know the exact time she was murdered yet.'

'That means I need to figure out *my* alibi for when Billy died. Why didn't you tell the truth? You've landed me right in it.' Carlton narrowed his eyes. 'You'll have to come clean and say you lied.'

'I can't do that. Besides, you don't need an alibi, do you?'

'You know what the cops are like with me.'

She hesitated, confused by his reply. 'Were you involved with Billy's murder?'

His tone became calmer, and he gave her a quick hug. 'Of course not, babe.'

'You weren't with me all evening. You went out for an hour.'

'I was with Kenny, but I don't want to drop him in it, if I can help it, so let's stick to your story. You were at home, and I was here both times. Do you want a drink?'

She nodded, thinking back over his words with a frown.

He came back with two bottles of lager, passing one to her as he sat down.

'What were you doing with Kenny on Monday?' she pressed.

'Collecting some stuff for him.'

'What stuff?'

'Just... things.'

They sat in silence for a few seconds. But she couldn't stop thinking there was more to it than he was telling her.

'I don't like this,' she said. 'You're hiding something from me.'

'No, I'm not.' Carlton flicked on the TV, the conversation seemingly over. 'If you're staying, we could watch something.'

She snatched the remote from him and threw it onto the settee. 'Carlton, *listen* to me. If I'm going to get in trouble, then at least have the decency to let me know what for.'

'For fuck's sake, Riley. Quit with the nagging.'

Riley stopped. She didn't want to upset him again. Last time she had, he didn't contact her for two days, and in the end, it was her who'd had to grovel. Was she overthinking?

'I'm sorry,' she relented. 'It was the police wanting to talk to me. And I'm scared something might happen to you. I-I don't want to lose you. Not after what happened to Billy and Debbie.'

'I'm nothing like them.' Carlton sneered.

'Aren't you scared, though?'

'About what?'

'Someone coming after you next?'

'They'd have to be quick to catch me.'

Riley groaned. Why couldn't he get it into his thick skull that she was trying to protect him? It wasn't as if she wanted to know where he'd been, unless he was with another woman.

'Were you seeing –'

Carlton's eyes snapped her way, his mood darkening. 'Riley, go if you're going to continually question me. What I do in my spare time is up to me.'

'But –'

He waved at her sarcastically. 'Close the door on the way.'

He didn't even look at her. Exasperated, she flounced out, making sure she banged the front door as loud as she could.

That man! He could be so infuriating at times. Was it too hard for him to admit where he was when she was covering for him? For all she knew, he could have killed Billy and now be using her to cover his tracks. He could even have done it with Kenny Webb. They might both have something to do with Billy's death.

Then a thought struck her, burying itself deep into her brain, and she stopped to catch her breath. Would Carlton have made a quick visit to Debbie Mayhew after he'd dropped her off at home at ten last night? And if so, was it because he was seeing her on the side or supplying her with drugs?

Or even worse, had Carlton killed Debbie on Kenny Webb's instructions?

She glanced at the flat, wondering whether to go back and have it out with him. Then she decided she'd be better keeping away from him until she found out what had been going on.

CHAPTER THIRTY-SIX

Carlton cursed as Riley stormed out. He needed to keep on her good side so he could stay close to Fiona and hear what was going on. But he wasn't going to go after her. He couldn't stand her whining all the time. She was such a stupid girl. He'd had her down as being far more mature than she'd proved to be.

But she had got him thinking.

Of course he never mentioned the police at Nathan's last night. And at least now he had time to think what to do next because he seemed to be in deep shit from all directions. First with Kenny Webb because of Billy and now with the police because of Debbie Mayhew.

Unbeknown to Riley, Carlton had been hiding out in his flat for most of the day. Already, his phone had six missed calls from Kenny, and he knew he'd be in for it once he caught up with him. Four hundred quid he'd have to find, or work for, once Kenny found out what had been going on. There was no way he'd get away with it.

But he needed to keep Fiona sweet too. He'd have to make up with Riley as an excuse to visit, go when that family liaison officer wasn't around. He hadn't been able to ask Fiona anything as she'd been there all the time, and he didn't want to ring or text because of the paper trail, so to speak.

Carlton wished there was a way he could find out who'd paid for what before Billy was murdered. His book obviously must have been on the older man, along with the money, because it wasn't in the bag Fiona had given to him. That was a dealing book. Hopefully Billy had stashed it somewhere because Carlton was in for it if not. It could lead back to Kenny, and that would be his fault.

He thought he'd been safe.

He'd been a bloody fool.

He couldn't even get in touch with any of the people in the book because he didn't have their numbers. He purposely didn't contact them on his mobile and he always made a conscious effort to delete anything that might get him into strife later. There was no way he wanted that racket coming back to him as well.

Then he thought of Andrew, in Redmond Street. He always paid on time. Perhaps he'd have more money by now, or access to savings. He'd call there later.

And he did know some of the addresses of the people in the notebook, so a few surprise visits might do the trick.

It was nearing six when there was a knock on the door, a banging of a fist straight afterwards. Carlton rushed to the window to see Kenny's car parked outside. He held his head in his hands for a moment. Fuck, there was no running from this now.

With trepidation, he opened the door. 'Hey, I was about to –'

The door was shoved into his chest as Kenny burst in.

'Where the hell have you been?' He pushed his finger into Carlton's face.

'With Fiona, like you told me to, keeping an eye on things. Since Billy died, she's been upset and –'

'I don't give a flying fuck.' Kenny glared at him, his eyes dark beads of nastiness. 'You're late paying my money.'

'I have most of it and I'll get the rest to you as soon as I can.'

'You should have it all by now.'

Despite thinking earlier that it was a good idea to come clean, he knew already it might not be the right move. But he didn't have another one. Which was freaking him out because he'd been there when Kenny had done over Danny Burton the other week. It was never easy to watch, and yet he hadn't taken any notice, sure he wouldn't do that to him. Now he was thinking, he'd better brace himself for something similar.

Why had he thought he could get one over on him? You didn't cross Kenny without knowing there was a good chance you'd get hurt. Kenny was a scary bastard at the best of times, but when he was like this? There was no other word but dangerous.

'Well?' Kenny yelled at him.

'I think Billy had the money on him when he was shanked,' he admitted. 'The police must have it.'

Kenny punched him in the stomach. 'You expect me to believe that someone killed him but didn't rob him?'

Carlton groaned. 'It's true! The feds told Fiona there was a wad of notes. They didn't say how much but –'

'Why had he got my money?'

'I... he was collecting it for me.'

Another punch to the stomach. A further groan as he doubled over.

'Finally you admit it.' Kenny sneered. 'I gave you the job of getting it, you idle bastard.'

'No, wait!' Carlton put up his hands. 'You know Billy was using more than he was selling? Well, I used my initiative and did a deal with him. I'd supply enough for his own use if he collected the money for me.'

'Yeah, right. I wasn't born yesterday. What was in it for you?'

'Nothing.' He gulped.

'Don't take me for a fool. You'd be quids in because you'd be able to sell more drugs.' Kenny stopped, his face screwing up in anger. 'Did he have anything else on him?'

Carlton didn't dare speak for fear of saying the wrong things. But his silence infuriated Kenny more.

He screamed into his face. 'Did he have the fucking book I gave you, with names and phone numbers?'

'I don't know, okay!' he lied.

Kenny's eyes bore into his again. His lips turned into a snarl and he looked like a rhino ready to charge. A moment later, his forehead crashed down on Carlton's nose.

Carlton's head flew back as fists came at him. Even if he wasn't against the wall, there was no way he could have defended himself. It was an insult to push the big man away.

Kenny was a street fighter, every punch hitting its target. It took seconds for Carlton to drop to the floor. When the kicking started, he curled into a ball, praying it would be over soon.

Eventually, Kenny was spent. He stood over him while he caught his breath.

'Clean yourself up and get back to work. I want the rest of my money by the end of the week. And for your sake, the cops better not have my book.'

Carlton coughed. His eyes were barely focusing, but through the open door, he watched Kenny retreat. Then he passed out.

CHAPTER THIRTY-SEVEN

THURSDAY

Allie was at the station by seven a.m. All her team were in and, after grabbing half an hour reading through evidence reports that had been sent for Billy Whitmore and Debbie Mayhew, she'd just delivered them a batch of toast from the canteen.

She was perched on the edge of Perry's desk as they tucked into it.

'It's so sad about Debbie being a victim of sexual abuse.' She wiped her fingers after her latest bite.

'I suppose in some ways, it explains why she went the way she did,' Perry remarked. 'Maybe she wanted to get rid of the pain, or her shame, when it was nothing to do with her. Merely a sick bastard who should have known better.'

Frankie, with a mouthful of toast, nodded in agreement.

'It makes my blood boil.' Allie grimaced. 'No child should have to put up with that. Not once, not ever.'

'Even though she's no longer with us, I'm glad it's over for her,' Sam added.

'And luckily for him, he's already passed, or else I'd haul him in and nail his balls to the wall,' Allie finished.

'Any more forensics back on her?' Perry asked, reaching for his drink.

'She was given Rohypnol, by the looks of things. We also know it's likely to be the same murder weapon. Christian says the size of the wound fits, which freaks me out because our killer might be planning to use it again.'

Frankie had finished his toast. 'So we have a link to two cases possibly with the knife, and with the people Billy and Debbie associate with but nothing except circumstantial stuff?'

Allie sighed. 'That sounds about right.' Her desk phone rang in her office, and she went to answer it, continuing talking while she walked. 'We need to crack on with interviewing more of their people today. Someone will know why Billy and Debbie have been targeted.'

Within seconds she was back, handing out orders and they flew downstairs and into the car park. There had been another murder.

And again they knew the victim.

The call had come in from a man who'd gone to work that morning and seen his neighbour's front door open, finding him in the hall. He'd stepped inside but knew immediately that he was dead and had rung it in. The uniformed officer who had been first on scene had recognised the victim as Carlton Stewart.

Allie popped the car into gear and drove off in the direction of the Limekiln Estate, Frankie sitting in the back.

'This week is getting stranger by the day,' Perry said from the passenger seat.

'I'd say the odds of the murders being linked have gone from most likely to extremely high.' Allie quickly told them about the conversation she'd had with Kelsey Abbott.

'So we *are* looking at a drug connection?' Perry stated.

'It's got to be.'

'There's going to be repercussions soon, isn't there?' Frankie joined in. 'People were antsy when there were two murders. Now there are three, connections will be made, rightly or wrongly. Blame might be apportioned incorrectly.'

Allie raced past several stationary cars that had moved aside. 'If it is another gang getting even, we could have a blood bath on our hands.'

'Do you think it might be a loner?' He went on.

'You mean a vigilante?' Allie liked where Frankie's mind was taking him, so she encouraged him to continue. 'What's your reasoning?'

'Maybe he's lost someone through a drug overdose and wants to get even?'

Allie thought about it. His idea was a good one, but nothing she hadn't looked into. There wasn't anyone in Stoke during the past year who had died that way that they hadn't known was a habitual drug user. But then again, not everything came to their attention.

'It's a possibility,' she said. 'Either way we have to catch him quickly.'

She turned into Adam Street, a long drag through the main estate. People were already at the scene, and she parked as near as possible to the address she'd been given. Dave Barnett's car was there, and a few of the crime scene officers', plus a search team vehicle and two press vans.

'I don't like all the media,' she said, releasing her seatbelt. 'It's going to be hard enough to police the public now there are three victims, never mind field enquiries from them. We need to think about setting up a community meeting, to allay fears but also to see if anyone will come forward to talk. Frankie, can you liaise with housing to get a room somewhere for tomorrow evening?'

'Will do, boss.'

They walked to the scene, another street of semi-detached houses interspersed with maisonettes. There seemed nothing out of the ordinary. Some gardens were immaculate, others the proverbial dumping grounds. One large downstairs window was smashed, another wide open with a teenage boy and girl hanging out to see what was going on.

In front of the ground-floor flat where the crime had taken place, they showed ID and pulled on forensic gear. A tent had been erected around the entrance, which was along the side of the property and luckily not visible to the public.

A small window on the front door was boarded up, masking tape around its edges. It was weatherworn, the tape curling at the ends as it struggled to stay in place.

They stepped inside.

'The door was open?' Allie asked no one in particular.

'It was indeed.' Dave caught her eye. 'Morning, Allie. I thought twice in a week was the limit I'd see you, but we meet again.'

'Hey, Dave.' She greeted the man kneeling next to the body. 'Another fatal stabbing?'

'In my opinion, yes, but there's lots more to this one. It's nasty.'

CHAPTER THIRTY-EIGHT

Allie had had many dealings with the twenty-two-year-old man lying on the floor. But seeing Carlton Stewart's face mashed and covered in bruising was still hard to stomach. He was on his back, blood pooling around his left side coming from the wound in his stomach. Both his eyes had closed, and his nose looked as if it was broken, the swelling indicating how much pain he must have been in if he hadn't died straightway. But something was off.

'He seems to be lying a tad neat for what he's gone through,' Allie spoke to Dave. 'Has he been moved?'

'Yes, I think so,' he replied.

'So the killer beat the crap out of him, laid him out on his back, stabbed him, and then left the front door open before doing a runner?' She frowned. 'That doesn't make sense.'

'Ah, but you don't have all the magic ingredients.' Dave chuckled. 'Neither do I yet, but I soon will.'

Allie glanced around the tiny hallway for signs of a struggle. Trails of blood smeared the wall to her right. A definite handprint was to her left. How she wished it would belong to the killer, but she expected it would be Carlton's as he'd tried to keep himself upright, or get up again.

'I should be able to get samples from that,' Dave said, looking at it.

'If it's the same killer, his crimes are escalating.' Allie took in more of the crime scene. 'This is the first time he's used violence as well as a knife.'

'Debbie Mayhew was sedated before she was stabbed,' Perry mentioned. 'Maybe because Carlton is young and fit, a fight broke out before our killer was able to do the same.'

'It's got to be a man, surely, the number of times he was hit?' Allie studied Carlton's disfigured face again. 'I reckon what, ten, fifteen punches to the head to do that much damage?'

'Yes, and someone knew what they were doing,' Dave concurred. 'This wasn't a first-time fight for our suspect.'

She pointed to the room ahead. 'I need to have a quick scan around the property before we leave. Is that okay?'

'Be careful of my crime scene. Don't mess with anything you shouldn't.'

'As if I'd –' Allie turned to see smiling eyes above the mask that was no doubt hiding his grin. She'd let him off this time. 'Do you think he was murdered in the flat and then brought to the hallway, Dave?'

'From what I've seen, I'd say he opened the door, let someone in, and was attacked right here.'

'I suppose it would make sense that someone in a hurry to get away might leave it open as they left too.'

In the kitchen, Allie pulled her head back with a grimace, glad she was wearing a mask and wouldn't be able to smell the stench of stale food from the night before. A pile of dirty plates sat in the sink, the grease around the edges of the water as they'd been left to soak.

The worktops were no cleaner, full of detritus on every

available space: several cereal boxes stood in a line, used mugs waiting to be washed, and a stack of newspapers that looked ready to topple over. She had a quick shuffle through everything she could see, but there was nothing hidden.

She popped her head in the bathroom and decided to leave that to the search team. In the bedroom, the bed was unmade, the duvet scrunched up at its centre. Cheap sets of drawers stood either side, and it was here she headed for. She grimaced when she found a half-empty pack of condoms and a tube of flavoured lubricating jelly in the top drawer.

Boxes were stacked in the corner, another place to have a good root through. There would probably be some stolen items among them, but for now that wasn't what she was here for.

She was about to check in the wardrobe when a carrier bag shoved down the side of the bed grabbed her attention. Inside it were cash and a notebook.

She picked it out and leafed through its pages. Everything was split into columns. There were lists of names, amounts of money by the side, similar to the one found on Billy Whitmore on Monday. Ten pounds, twenty pounds, fifty pounds with ticks next to them. Some had gaps where she assumed payments might have been missed.

The two books had to be linked somehow.

She spotted a few names she knew, phone numbers too, and immediately thought this was a job for her right-hand woman. Sam could also analyse the handwriting to see if it was the same as in the book they'd found on Billy.

Allie got out her phone and took photos of some of the pages. Like the first, the notebook was worth taking back immediately, but she couldn't risk contamination. She shook out an evidence bag from her pocket and popped the book inside.

Once she'd scanned the rest of the room, she stepped

back into the hall. Going through everything would take too long, and besides, it wasn't her job. She could miss crucial evidence and she didn't want that.

Although she did have one person in particular she was interested in talking to again.

'Could we have this fast-tracked for prints, please?' She held up the evidence bag so Dave could see. 'It could become vital if someone from the team knows any of the names, and this one does look drug-related.'

'His dealing book?' Perry piped up from behind her.

Allie nodded. 'Which hopefully will help us to understand why three known drug associates have been wiped out in less than four days.'

Christian arrived and she acknowledged him with a nod.

'My, my, I do have my work cut out this week,' he teased before stooping down to view the body. 'I think I should have stayed where I was. It was much quieter. Mind, it was in the back end of nowhere and boring as hell.'

'Out of the frying pan and into the fire,' Allie said. 'And of course, we have one advantage. I'll be treating you to an oatcake breakfast once the case is solved.'

CHAPTER THIRTY-NINE

Allie knocked on the door of Mandy Stewart, Carlton's mum's, home in Randall Grove. She was dreading breaking the news of another death on the estate. The accusations of the police doing nothing were already doing the rounds and although she sounded callous, she didn't want to be here any longer than necessary. It was more down to her wanting to be hands-on in finding the person who had already murdered three people.

'I'm not sure how this one will go, Frankie,' Allie told the young detective standing by her side. 'On the occasions we've met, Carlton's mum has either been nonchalant or extremely dramatic. I wasn't informing her of her son's death though.'

The door was flung open before Frankie had the chance to reply. A middle-age man stood in the hallway, barefoot wearing a pair of trousers and a hurriedly pulled on T-shirt.

'Yeah?' he grunted, not even bothering to cover his yawn with a hand.

'DI Shenton and DC Higgins. Is Mandy in?' They showed their warrant cards.

'Who?' The man frowned.

'Mandy Stewart.'

'Oh, her. She moved out last year.' He glared at them. 'So you don't want me?'

'Well, I'm not sure because I don't know who you are.' Allie smiled sweetly, hoping the sarcasm wasn't showing in her tone.

'*I'm* the new tenant, I've just come off a night shift and *you've* dragged me out of my bed.'

'Sorry about that, sir.' She wasn't. 'You don't happen to have a forwarding address for her? It would help us greatly and –'

'No, I don't. So piss off and leave me to my sleep.'

The door slammed in their faces.

'He's a real charmer, isn't he?' Allie smirked at Frankie. 'I would have apologised again for waking him if he wasn't such a knob. We're not bloody psychic.'

'But we still need to locate Mum,' Frankie replied, turning to leave.

'Yes. Why don't you stay here, do some house-to-house, see if you can find out anything from the neighbours?' She opened the gate and they stepped back onto the pavement. 'It's worth a shot and I'll come back for you when I'm done.'

She left Frankie walking to the next house and made her way to Forest Avenue. DC Joy had been allocated as family liaison officer for all three murders now, so she was no longer spending the days at Billy Whitmore's property.

Allie had rung ahead to let Fiona know she was coming and that she wanted to see Riley.

The door opened, and she was shown into the living room by the very woman. Allie wondered if Fiona ever moved from the armchair by the fire, then chastised herself inwardly for her pettiness.

Riley sat down on the settee. Allie decided she would sit next to her.

'Riley,' she started. 'Is it right that you've been seeing Carlton Stewart?'

'Yes.' Riley almost shrank into herself.

'Whatever he's done is nothing to do with her,' Fiona snapped. 'I told her he was a wrong 'un, and she wouldn't listen.'

Allie held up a hand. 'Riley, I hate to be the bearer of more bad news, but Carlton has died.'

'What?' Riley's brow furrowed, her eyes filling with tears. 'He can't be. I only saw him yesterday.'

'I'm so sorry,' Allie spoke softly.

'How?' Riley whispered. 'When?'

'We're looking into that at the moment. But we found him badly beaten in his flat. He's also been stabbed.'

'Dear God.' Fiona clutched her chest. 'Like Billy, and that Debbie?'

'He was at home?' Riley burst into tears. 'I told him something like this would happen.'

'What do you mean?'

'After Billy was killed, and then Debbie, I was worried about him.' She stopped, her gaze flicking around everywhere. 'Who would *do* that to him?'

Fiona was quiet, unable to take anything in, Allie assumed.

'Riley, I need to ask you a few questions,' she went on. 'We need to know exactly what time you last saw Carlton.'

'It wasn't her, if that's what you're getting at.' Fiona cried. 'I might have known you'd think that. And you of all people know us. We're not like that!'

Allie turned to her abruptly. 'Fiona, I *do* know you, but I *don't* know what you get up to all the time. Quite frankly, it's insulting for you to think otherwise. I have helped you in the past and I'm always happy to assist you going forwards, but if I find out that you, or Riley, have done anything unlawful, then I won't do a damn thing again. I am not your friend. I am a police officer. Do you understand?'

Fiona said nothing, but her eyes went down, and there was a slight nod.

Despite it being cutting, Allie knew Fiona had taken to heart what she'd said. Allie might give the sense of being a pushover because she had a kind demeanour, but *when* pushed she'd always show who was boss.

'Riley, go on,' she said to the younger woman.

'My shift finished at half past three, and I went straight to his flat.'

'Was that the last time you had contact with him?'

'I sent a few WhatsApp messages.'

'May I see them?'

Riley picked up a phone from the coffee table, opened the app, and passed it to Allie.

There were six messages last night, three from Carlton and three from Riley. But then that was it. Nothing since.

She scrolled through a few more to see if they regularly messaged each other. Most of them were sent by Riley, but there was nothing immediate she could see that was wrong.

'Why no messages after these?' she answered.

'There are more on iMessage. We use both.'

Allie clicked on the messages tab and found several sent by Riley to Carlton, but they remained unanswered. She glanced up in confusion.

'We had a row,' Riley clarified.

'About what?'

'Nothing, really. He's a bit moody and could often ignore me for a day or two. I hated it when he did that. But I didn't think it was because he was... dead.'

'How long were you together?'

'Six weeks.' She sobbed.

Allie wished she could stay longer and murmur

comforting things, but she really needed to get on with the job at hand. They had to find someone to identify Carlton.

'Once again, I'm so sorry for your loss, but I need to contact Carlton's family. Do you know where his next of kin moved to? His mum used to live in Stoke, but she's not at the address we have on record for him.'

'She's in Manchester.'

'Do you know where?'

'No.' Another sob.

'What about any other relatives?'

'I only know of his nan. She's in a home.'

'Do you know the name of it?'

Riley shook her head.

Allie sighed inwardly. It made their job time-critical as they had to be mindful that a relative might hear the news about Carlton's demise before they'd had the chance to tell them.

But equally, they had to give out a name so that the public would help rather than hinder them with speculation. It was a difficult call, one that wouldn't be hers, thankfully.

She needed to contact DCI Brindley.

CHAPTER FORTY

Perry had made a start going door to door to the three flats in the same block as Carlton Stewart. The upstairs flat was unoccupied, the two the other side tenanted.

He knocked on the downstairs flat first. An elderly woman appeared, and he flashed his warrant card.

'Is it true that Carlton is dead?' she asked, letting him in.

'I'm afraid I can't confirm that until the family have been told, but we believe so,' he replied.

'Oh, that's terrible news.'

They went into the living room, and she sat down, in an armchair by the window, urging Perry to do the same across the room.

He glanced around, seeing a home filled with love and warmth, lots of colour. Several photos of family were on the walls, and a recent birthday card propped up behind the clock on the fireplace. There was a hint of baking in the air and his stomach gave an involuntary grumble. He cleared his throat trying to mask it.

'What happened?' the woman asked when she'd settled.

'I'm unable to tell you that at the moment either,' he told her. 'We're still making enquiries.'

'But someone killed him.' She clutched her chest. 'They might come back and hurt me too.'

'Mrs...'

'Hardy. You can call me Trisha.'

'There's no need to worry, Trisha.' Perry put on his best soothing voice. 'This is a fatal attack so there'll be an extra police presence for some time. Please try not to worry too much.'

She exhaled dramatically. 'It used to be a lovely area to live in, but over the past few years, this street has gone down bank. It's the same as a lot on the estate. I blame the council for not checking out the troublemakers before they move them in. But I do get their point when most of them have tiny children too. Everyone needs somewhere to live. It's such a tragedy all round.'

Perry let her get her thoughts out before he spoke again. It was time-consuming to sit and listen, but he also knew to build a rapport, he had to give her space.

He took out his notebook and pen to hurry her up. 'Did you know Carlton well?'

'Not really. I thought he might run me the odd errand when he moved in but no such luck. Mind you, I can take care of myself. I'm quite nimble for my age.' She patted her permed hair. 'I'm seventy-four.'

'Never!' Perry humoured her. She did look good for her age, being well turned out, her attire immaculate, right down to her slippers.

Trisha giggled. Then her face dropped. 'We shouldn't be laughing when someone has been killed next door.'

'It's perfectly fine.' Perry smiled to ease her guilt. 'When did you last see Carlton?'

'Yesterday morning. He left on foot and then came back

with a carrier bag of shopping. Then his girlfriend arrived about half past three. The children were coming home from the high school, that's how I know. I heard them shouting.' She rolled her eyes. 'These walls are like paper, even with my ailing ears.'

'And did you see anyone coming to the flat once Carlton got back?'

'Yes, there were two men. The first came about sixish. There was shouting then too. I think he was there about ten minutes.'

'Was he a regular visitor?'

'I've seen him a few times.'

'Can you describe him?'

'He was a small, stocky fella, and he had a hat on, so I don't know if he had hair or not.' She smiled. 'I don't get out much, but I can see a lot of the world from this chair.'

Perry took down all the details. Although the description was so basic they'd have trouble proving anything, it was a good start.

'He came in a car,' Trisha went on. 'It was a white BMW. I know because my son has one like it.' She pointed to a photo on the wall of a teenage boy in school uniform. 'That's him, there. Richard. He lives in Weymouth with his family. I have two grandchildren that are doing incredibly well.' She gave a sigh. 'They ring every week, and I see them a few times a year. But it's such a long way to travel. I've been thinking of moving there myself. Maybe this was a sign.'

'Perhaps,' Perry said, unsure what else to say. But he was interested in the car. 'You say it was a white BMW? Did you see the registration plate at all?'

'My eyes aren't what they used to be, lad, but I think it had the number twenty in it, if that helps.'

Perry thanked her. 'And the other man you mentioned?'

'Well, it was dark when he arrived. He was there no longer than a few minutes.'

'Might you be able to recall anything about him?'

'He was similar, a bit older perhaps. He wore a dark coat and hat. I think he was on foot because I didn't see him get in or out of a car, although he could have parked further down the road, out of my line of sight.' She paused, messing with the cuff on her jumper. 'I expect he might not have got an answer from Carlton now.'

'That's likely so we'll try to eliminate him from our enquiries as soon as possible.' Perry nodded his thanks. 'We're trying to locate his family. You don't happen to know any of them, do you?'

'I think his mother moved out of Stoke, although I don't know where. When he first came here and I tried to make conversation, he said his nan was in residential care. She had a stroke before Carlton arrived here.'

'Did he mention the name of the home?'

Trisha paused while she thought about it. 'I'm sorry, I can't remember. I know it had a nice name. Something to do with flowers.'

Perry wrote that down and then left. Trisha had given him a couple of leads to follow, but he needed more than that. He carried on to the next property.

CHAPTER FORTY-ONE

Allie was in her car when she took a call from Frankie.

'I've spoken to Mandy Stewart's neighbour two doors down, who told me Carlton's gran is in residential care, but she couldn't recall the establishment. After I knocked on a few more doors, a woman there said she was named Trudy and had moved into the Lily Elizabeth Residential Home.'

'Oh, good work.'

'The neighbour doesn't know where his mum is now, though.'

'I've been told she's in Manchester. We need to get on to that. If we can't find anything, we'll have to put out an appeal for next of kin during the press conference this afternoon.'

'Do you want me to make my way back to Adam Street? It's only a twenty-minute walk?'

'You're a diamond, thanks. Maybe you can find out a few more updates before I go to see Jenny later too. I'll let Perry know you're on your way.'

'Right, boss.'

Lily Elizabeth Residential Home was three miles from where she was. She rang ahead to let them know she was on her way. It would take a good half hour to get there in the traffic, so she set off immediately.

On the way, she tried to compartmentalise her feelings.

'They're memories, that's all,' she chastised herself. She could deal with those later: this wasn't about Karen. It was about telling a grandmother that her grandson had died.

Instead, she tried to concentrate on working through some of the nuances of the cases. Billy Whitmore was an addict, so too was Debbie Mayhew, and Carlton was a dealer. Drugs were the relevant connection.

Maybe they should dig deeper into their known associates. Although how they would do that was beyond her. There wasn't a list of people they would *like* to know of, only the ones they knew, and lots of them had been spoken to already. No one was talking. Through fear or ignorance, she could never be sure.

The sign for the establishment was upon her before she had much time to think. In large letters, it claimed to have forty-seven rooms built to accommodate dementia patients.

A rush of emotion swept over her after she'd parked, and she pushed back tears that were burning her eyes. Over the phone, she'd asked about Mrs Stewart and had been told she'd suffered a stroke, and although she would be able to tell what they were saying, she had lost the ability to speak back to them.

Allie's sister, Karen, had been the same. Karen would have been fifty-one now, and Allie often wondered how things might have been if she was still alive.

After a deep breath, she headed into the building, stepping into a large and airy reception area. Allie loved it immediately for its sense of pride and lack of the smell that was often associated with this type of establishment.

On a noticeboard to her left were several "thank you" cards and a few drawings that had been created by little hands. The carpet underfoot was pale green, clear mats in the places that saw the most action. The cream walls were lined with framed pictures, each bursting with a riot of colour. If she wasn't mistaken, they had been painted by a local artist.

Allie went to the reception desk, introducing herself by showing her warrant card.

'Could you sign the visitor's register, please, and I'll get someone to show you to Trudy's room?' the receptionist asked her.

Once that was done, Allie sat down to wait. There was a new email from Dave Barnett with some interesting information. He'd found Carlton Stewart's fingerprints on the inside of the living room door frame where Debbie Mayhew had been murdered.

So he *had* been to visit her before she died. If it was him who had killed Debbie, they might never find out now. But it was more likely there was someone separate after all three killings.

It was a minute later when someone said her name. She looked up from her phone to see a young woman in a pale-blue uniform walking towards her.

'Hi, I'm Sharon. I believe you need to see Trudy Stewart?'

'Yes, thanks.' Allie shoved her phone in her pocket and followed her through a door she was holding open.

'Nice place,' Allie complimented. 'Not like some I've visited.'

'It's won several awards for its standards,' Sharon told her, moving aside as a care worker went bustling past them.

'I have some bad news for Trudy, I'm afraid. Will she be able to understand?'

'Ah, okay.' Sharon's face dropped. 'She might not be able to communicate but she can take in everything you'll say.'

'I thought the home was for dementia patients.'

'It is predominantly – but we have a floor for other *residents* too.'

Allie grimaced as she realised her slip-up. 'Sorry, residents.'

Sharon grinned. 'Oh, I'm sorry too. It's been a long shift, and I have another two hours to go yet.' She pointed to a door ahead. 'Here you are. Would you like me to stay with you?'

'Yes, please.'

Sharon knocked on the door and went in. 'Only me, Trudy. I hope you're decent because there's a visitor for you.'

The woman sitting in the chair was in her seventies. She had the look of a houseplant that had been left with no water for a week, her thin grey cardigan matching her hair. But even so, Allie could still see a vague resemblance to Carlton. She wondered how many sleepless nights the lad had given his grandmother over the years.

'Hi, Trudy,' Allie said. 'I'm a detective inspector, my name is Allie.'

The woman groaned a greeting, her head tilting upwards to catch her eye.

Allie pulled up a chair and reached for the woman's hand. The leathery skin made her heart bleed a little, wondering how Trudy would cope with the news.

'I'm afraid I have something to tell you. It's about Carlton. I'm so sorry, but he was killed last night.'

Trudy's groan became louder, and she fidgeted. But she kept her hand in Allie's. Tears came and dropped.

'I'm so sorry, Trudy.' Sharon wiped them away for her. She turned to Allie. 'What happened?'

'He was attacked in his home. We don't have any further details yet.' She turned back to Trudy. 'We wanted to come and tell you as soon as possible and we will keep you informed of the investigation.' She looked at Sharon again.

'We need to inform all relatives, plus see if someone would be able to identify Carlton. Of course, we can do it as we know him, but we'd prefer a family member. We believe his mum moved to Manchester?'

Another groan came from Trudy. She was shaking her head.

'There is no one?' Allie hoped she was doing a good job of including her in the conversation. She didn't wish to be rude but neither did she want to tire Trudy.

Trudy shook her head again.

'I think she's saying she hasn't seen her in a long time,' Sharon said. 'I might have details of her next of kin, but she hasn't been here to my knowledge.'

'Thanks.' Allie stood up but kept hold of Trudy's hand. She gave it a squeeze before letting it go. 'We'll do everything we can to find his killer, I promise you that. And I'll come back when I have anything to tell you. Is that okay?'

Trudy moved her head slightly.

Allie left the room then, Sharon following behind. In the corridor, she turned to her.

'Could you stay with her for a while, please?'

'Of course.' Sharon nodded. 'I would have done anyway. The residents are like family to us.'

'Who do I liaise with to keep her informed of what's going on?'

'You can contact the main desk or me, if you like? If I'm not on shift, I can make sure she finds out what you've said as soon as I'm back here. Do you have a pen, and I can give you my mobile number?'

Allie wrote it in her notebook. 'And could I have a list of visitors who have been to see Trudy, perhaps over the past six weeks?'

'Sure, I can do that for you now. It won't take long.'

CHAPTER FORTY-TWO

Once she was back in the car, Allie's shoulders drooped. The only next of kin details for Trudy were the phone number they had for Carlton. That poor woman. She could imagine, but didn't want to believe, that neither her daughter nor her grandson had visited her in a long time. It was so hard to know how she'd be feeling.

Blocking Karen from her thoughts, she reached for her seatbelt, drew it across her body, and fastened it with a clunk. She'd better head back to the station to inform Jenny and get ready for the press conference.

Before setting off, she rooted out one of her favourite albums on her phone and plugged it into the sound system in the car. She needed something to sing along to – well, shout to – so she could bring back a better vibe.

The image of Trudy Stewart was playing on Allie's mind. Even if she hadn't seen Carlton in a good while, it must be awful to be told he'd been killed. Once this was all over, she would take her some flowers and sit with her for half an hour. It was the least she could do.

'A Town Called Malice' burst into the car, and she turned

it up as loud as she could bear. A car karaoke was definitely called for.

Now back at the station with a bounce in her step, Allie went to see Jenny and informed her of Carlton's next-of-kin situation and that Perry was looking into the whereabouts of his mum.

'This is really snowballing now,' Jenny said. 'I'm shocked at how quickly if I'm honest. Plus, all eyes are on us as the case widens, and it's getting nationwide interest.'

'We're doing everything we can, Ma'am,' Allie insisted.

'Oh, I have no doubt about that, but you know how the powers that be want everything solved yesterday. Do you have any strong links yet?'

'There's a slight connection with one person, Riley Abbott.'

'Fiona Abbott's daughter?'

'Yes, the eldest. She's a care worker, has visited the first and the second victims' mothers and is the girlfriend of the third. Yet... I don't know. I have a niggle about her, but I can't put my finger on it yet.'

'There'll be something there, I'm sure. A copper's gut instinct is one of our best assets. It rarely lets us down.' Jenny paused for thought. 'Does she have a record?'

'No, Ma'am. She's eighteen and clean.'

'Okay, update the team and then come to my office at two p.m. to go over everything before the press conference. I'll let the press officer know.'

'Yes, Ma'am.'

Allie went downstairs, still wondering if they should be bringing Riley in for further questioning. She didn't want the fact she'd known her for a few years to affect her judgement. But having Fiona's predicament to live with, Allie had always thought she and Kelsey got the rough end of the bargain.

Did she think Riley would murder anyone? No, she didn't.

Was it conceivable that she had? Yes, everything was possible.

At her desk, she skimmed over everything she needed to update the team on and went into the briefing room.

'I have a list of visitors to Trudy Stewart.' Allie gave her first note to Sam. 'There's only four people on it. Can you look over it?'

'Will do. I checked out the handwriting on the notebooks too, and they're written by two different people. One uses lots more capital letters than is necessary.'

'Hmm, I'm sure there's a connection, though.' Allie was thinking aloud, not after an answer. 'Both books show us names and sums of money that seem to be being collected weekly. Billy's book has names that aren't known to us, and Carlton's has names that are. Where are we with talking to people named in them?'

'There are forty-seven in total. It's going to take some time, but I'm working through them. Nothing concrete I can see yet.'

'Right, keep on to it, thanks. Oh, I had an email from Dave Barnett. Carlton's fingerprints were found in Rose Avenue, on the inside of the living room door frame. So he had been in the room, and whether or not that was before Debbie was killed or earlier, we'll never know.'

'It's not him, though, is it?' Frankie piped up. 'Unless whoever killed him gave him a good beating before finishing the job because they were annoyed he had?'

'It's probable, but I want to keep an open mind. Perry, did you get anything else from the neighbours around Carlton's flat?'

'Only that he'd been living there a few months and causing havoc with the visitors he had. A woman from number twenty-four said he'd given her some lip when she'd asked him to keep the noise down after there was a late-night party.' Perry also updated them on the chat with Trisha Hardy about the woman and two males seen before the murder.

'The female is Riley Abbott,' Allie said. 'She's a suspect until we get the post-mortem results and the time of death, and she was heard arguing with him before he was murdered. I think we should bring her in for questioning now. Sam, can you check what time her shift finished, see if it tallies with what she told me? They might give you the information over the phone if you ask nicely. If not, we can action a visit. What about the males?'

Perry brought them up to speed about the first visitor.

'Kenny Webb has a newish white Beemer, doesn't he?' she queried.

'He does.'

'Hmm... interesting. I have to do a press conference with Jenny, but I think we should bring Kenny in too. Perry, I'm sure you can deal with that?'

'I'll look forward to it, boss.'

Allie grinned. There was nothing better than irritating a low life like Kenny Webb.

'Really,' she added, 'our task this afternoon is to find the second man. Frankie, get on to uniform to see if anyone else saw him, and locate any cameras for possible images. He might have been caught leaving in a car – if we're lucky, with a registration number we can see. Either way, we need to rule him in or out.'

As the briefing came to an end, Allie gave out a huge sigh of frustration. Was this the breakthrough they needed or another cat-and-mouse chase? One way to find out.

She checked her watch: time to go and do the press conference.

CHAPTER FORTY-THREE

In her office, Allie ran a brush through her hair, and redid her makeup to at least seem like she was winning. Concealer under her eyes almost hid the bags that gave away how tired she was. There was no chance of things easing off any time soon with press and public baying for their blood.

She pouted at herself, ready for anything despite not feeling it, and made her way to the ground floor.

The press room was set out with a table and microphones at one end, sound systems hidden inside a corner unit. Two pull-up banners showed the police logos and emergency numbers to contact.

Already there were a dozen reporters sitting in the rows of chairs that filled the rest of the space. Three murders had raised everyone's awareness of the urgency to catch the killer, as well as journalistic fire to get the best lead for their own purposes. She spotted Simon, gave him a nod and then went to Jenny.

The DCI was talking to the press officer, going over last-minute things to add or remove. Jenson Wardle had worked at the station for two years now. Allie liked him immensely and smiled as she drew level with him.

'Hey, Allie,' Jenson greeted. 'Quite a case you have on your hands this time.'

'It is! How are you, and the new wife?'

'Absolutely marvellous.' Jenson's cheesy grin told her all she needed to know. He'd married his teenage sweetheart after they'd been together for ten years, having then had twin girls recently. A tall man with long arms to match, he towered over Allie. Blonde hair, not much of it.

'We'll nail the bastard soon,' she whispered, knowing they were out of hearing range to everyone.

'Always good to hear.' Jenny raised her eyebrows in a mock stern look. 'I've run through everything with Jenson. I think we'll be brief and straight to the point. I'll take a couple of questions afterwards, but I want the emphasis to be on finding Carlton Stewart's relatives more than focusing on our inability to have anyone in for questioning right now.'

'Everyone we'd like to bring in gets killed before we have the chance,' Allie said quietly, aware of even more people filling the room.

'It wasn't a criticism, more an idea of what the press will try and get us talking about. But I won't let them.' Jenny pointed to the seats. 'Shall we?'

Within minutes, Jenny asked for everyone's attention, and then began to run through the main points she wanted to address.

Allie sat beside her, glad that she wasn't having to give a talk straight to camera. She'd had media training, but it was so easy to trip up when faced with an onslaught of questions. Jenny took no prisoners, though, and Allie loved watching her annihilate anyone who tried to get one up on them.

'We believe our victim is Carlton Stewart and are appealing for his family to get in touch,' Jenny finished with.

'We've been told they now reside in the Manchester area, so if you or anyone you know has information on their whereabouts, please get in touch.

'Also, if you know anything about the crime itself, come forward. Everything will be treated with confidentiality. It's imperative that this person is caught and apprehended. The phone line is across the screen below or you can call one-one-one and be put through to my team. Another briefing will be held later this evening if further information has been gathered and confirmed.'

The cameras were switched off, and Allie relaxed with a sigh of relief. She braced herself for the onslaught to come. Even if it wouldn't be aired, it was likely to be unpleasant. She was certain some journalists thought they sat around all day drinking tea because they hadn't arrested anyone.

'Right, now that's done, I'll take a few questions from the press.' As hands shot up to catch her attention, Jenny pointed into the crowd.

'Do you think the murders are gang-related?' a man asked. 'Each victim is known to be connected to drugs.'

'We're keeping an open mind about everything at this stage in our enquiries. But we are looking into every aspect of each individual's lives.'

Clever, mused Allie. Jenny had answered in the affirmative without giving away too much.

'What about their families?'

'They've been allocated a family liaison officer who is working closely with them all, keeping them informed.'

'Are you certain there won't be more murders?' a woman asked.

'If I was, I wouldn't be in this job. I'd be on a cruise somewhere after having predicted the winning numbers for the lottery.' Jenny smiled.

Muted laughter followed. Allie liked that Jenny always

tried to inject a little lightness into the conference. They'd both known most of the reporters for a long time and it was good to see them respond well because they often needed their help. Well, most of them. She was waiting for one to pipe up with something more succinct. Right on cue, Will Lawrence from *Staffordshire Post & Times* shouted out a question.

'What happens if there are more murders? You haven't got very far. You don't even seem to have a suspect in for questioning.'

Jenny's back straightened that little bit more as she glanced around to see who had made the remark. Allie anticipated Jenny putting him down yet again.

'There have been three murders in as many days,' Jenny replied. 'We're doing everything possible to collate the information coming in whilst waiting for forensics to be run. There are a vast number of officers working each case, and I am confident we will bring things to a close soon.'

'Before or after another murder?'

'That depends on how much longer you'll be in our company, Mr Lawrence.'

More laughter filled the room, and Jenny stood to indicate the meeting was over.

Allie giggled when she saw the colour of Will's face. *Serves him right, the sleazebag.*

CHAPTER FORTY-FOUR

In interview room three, Perry was sitting across from Kenny Webb. As it was an informal chat, there were only the two of them. Even so, the formalities had been done beforehand.

'So, Kenny, I've asked you to come in to answer a few questions about some things that have come to our attention. Happy to proceed?'

There was no point in saying any more than that. Kenny knew the score, when Perry might pause the informal chat, caution him, or even stop the interview altogether and arrest him before continuing.

'Get on with it.' Kenny waved Perry's comment away. 'I've got much better things to do.'

'You have some nasty bruising appearing on your knuckles. What's been going on?'

Kenny folded his arms, hiding his hands from view. 'I had an argument with a wall.'

'A wall did that to you?' Perry sniggered. 'I think you're losing your touch.'

'I was angry. Better to hit out at an object than a person.'

'Oh, I agree. But that's not what happened, is it?'

'I don't know what you mean.'

'We found Carlton Stewart in his flat this morning. I'm afraid he was dead.'

'Yes, I've heard.'

'Was he still working for you?'

Kenny, who had been looking away, turned back sharply. 'And what does that have to do with anything?'

'Just asking. According to our witness, you're one of the last people to see him alive.'

'Well, you got that wrong, because whoever killed him is the one you're after.'

'So you didn't visit him yesterday?'

Kenny folded his arms. 'Yeah, I did. We had words, but he was well and truly alive when I left him.'

'There were no punches flying?' Perry's eyes went to Kenny's hands that were on display again.

'No comment.' Kenny shoved them under the desk.

'Oh, come on. You know better than to lie to me. What's been going on with you this week? First, we find Billy Whitmore dead, someone you know extremely well.'

'I would expect *you* know Billy as well as I do.'

'Then there's Debbie Mayhew.'

'Everyone on the estate knows her name.'

'Fair point. But now Carlton is dead too. And he works for you.'

'Where are you going with this?' Kenny sighed. 'Half the blokes in Car Wash City know Carlton.'

'Half the blokes in Car Wash City weren't seen entering and leaving the property of the deceased. They weren't heard shouting at Carlton. They didn't arrive and leave in a white BMW. Need I go on?'

Kenny sat quiet for a moment.

'Which rooms did you go in?' Perry asked.

'What?'

'I want to know where we'll find your prints.'

Perry could almost hear his brain trying to work out his options. If Kenny had only been in the hall, there would be no prints in other rooms. As Carlton was found on the floor, the logical solution might be that he'd opened the door and the fight took place there. But for now they needed to wait for the evidence.

Kenny said nothing so Perry continued.

'Let's move on. We need to establish your whereabouts last night. What time did you go to Carlton's flat?'

Kenny glared at him. 'It was about six. We had words, it might have got a bit heated, but I left, and he was fine.'

'You didn't hit out at him at all?'

'Did anyone see me?'

'That's not what I asked.'

'I might have swung a punch at him. He might have swung one back.'

'And you left him standing?'

'I did.'

'What time would that be?'

'A few minutes later.'

Perry made a note. That tallied with what Trisha had told him.

'So where did you go then?'

'Home, to the missus. Want to check?'

'If I feel it's necessary. And that's your final word on the matter?'

'It is.'

Perry sighed inwardly. He hadn't got enough to arrest him yet, and he wasn't going to get anything else out of Kenny until they had the evidence to back it up. He could perhaps put him at the crime scene if his fingerprints were found, but that would count for Riley Abbott too, even though he knew it was unlikely she would have been able to inflict the damage that had been caused to Carlton.

One thing was certain. Kenny knew more than he was letting on. And it was up to them to work out what it was.

Although it would have to wait for another day. They had more pressing work to do.

'Anything useful?' Allie asked when he got back to his desk.

'Not really, but I'm sure he isn't telling us everything.'

'I wonder if he thinks someone is setting him up. It's such a small circle of acquaintances that have been killed, and they can all be connected to him.'

'Do you think someone could be strategically pointing the murders to Kenny, so we hop over to his trail rather than their own?'

'It's possible. We still have a lot of digging to do. I'll be glad if he's frustrated that we dragged him in, though.'

Perry pointed to the notebook underneath her arm. 'Your turn next.'

Kenny pushed the door of Bethesda Police Station so hard that it ricocheted and almost hit him in the face. He marched off, his phone out of his pocket before he was across the car park. He continued to walk along Bethesda Street towards the city library as he dialled a number.

'Come and fetch me, now,' he growled when his call was connected. Then he stood waiting for his ride back to work.

The rain didn't do anything for his mood, so he moved to stand under the entrance canopy. An hour he'd been in the station, and they hadn't got anything on him. He wasn't even lying. When he'd left, Carlton had been alive. Beaten up, but still talking and breathing.

Someone must have followed him, found Carlton in a

state, and used it to their advantage. He would have been easy to finish off as he'd been barely conscious anyway.

Which meant that someone *was* setting him up to take the rap for killing him. Kenny wasn't going inside for something he hadn't done. He had to sort this out, and quick. Because when he found out who was responsible, they were going to wish they hadn't messed with him. Plus someone needed to take Carlton's place now as well as Billy's.

He cast his mind back. Had there been anyone lurking in the shadows? He couldn't recall seeing anything, but he hadn't been looking, so wound up by Carlton's revelation.

And where was his notebook and cash now? Perry Wright hadn't mentioned it, but that didn't mean it wasn't found on Billy Whitmore.

But the worst thing he could curse himself for? Trust him to leave the front door to Carlton's flat open in temper, so it gave easy access to the place. He'd thought Carlton would close it eventually.

Traffic was heavy, but finally his lift arrived, and he jumped into the car.

'All right, boss?' Milo saluted him.

'No, I'm fucking not. Get me away from here, back to the office. I need my car.'

Without another word spoken, Milo screeched off from the kerb, Kenny flicked his eyes across to the police station. Who the hell was messing with him? He had to put together the pieces of the puzzle before the whole lot landed on his shoulders.

He'd speak to Martin as soon as he could, but first he needed to pay someone else a visit. Someone who might know what had been going on.

Either way, *someone* was asking for trouble.

CHAPTER FORTY-FIVE

A small part of Allie felt sorry for Riley Abbott as she sat in interview room two. She hadn't been brought in under caution in connection with the three murders as there wasn't enough evidence. For now, it was all about establishing her whereabouts and hoping she might volunteer further information.

It was looking likely that each victim had died of a fatal stab wound, but it was the violent attack carried out on Carlton that was muddying the waters. Most people when threatened might fight back in self-defence, but nowhere near as much as his wounds suggested.

It was possible Riley could have been responsible, but Allie assumed Carlton would be too strong and hit back, twice as hard. Riley didn't seem to have any bruising either, where he might have lashed out at her, although her eyes were red and swollen from crying, so it was hard to tell.

It was also feasible that someone else beat Carlton, and Riley had found him and stabbed him while he was unable to defend himself. Allie didn't want to believe this of her, but it was possible.

Or maybe that was done by the man who'd visited Carlton after Kenny Webb? Or even Kenny Webb himself.

Before she went into her, Allie studied Riley's body language on the monitor from the obs room next door. There was a uniformed officer with her, standing by the back wall. Riley was sitting, hands in her lap, right knee jigging up and down. Her eyes kept going to the door, waiting for someone to come through it.

'Right, let's do this,' Allie said to Frankie, who was sitting in with her to take notes.

They went into the room and sat across from Riley. Allie gave her a reassuring smile before she began.

'Riley, as you know, this interview is voluntary so you're not under caution at this moment in time, but I do want to mention that should things change we will move to it being so. You'll have the opportunity to seek legal advice at any time. Do you understand?'

'Yes.' Her voice was almost a whisper, and she cleared her throat.

Allie noted she wouldn't look at anyone, just kept her eyes focused on the table.

'I know this will be hard for you, to talk about Carlton, but remember when I spoke to you earlier in the week and you said that you knew Billy Whitmore and Debbie Mayhew? Well, you also knew Carlton well.'

'Yes, but I didn't kill any of them!' Riley's face screwed up and she burst into tears. 'I'm not like that.'

'I know you've seen a lot of violence as a child and teenager.'

'That doesn't mean I'd want to harm anyone. I hated what Trevor did to my mum.'

'I can understand that, having witnessed a lot of it too. But there's going to be evidence of you in Carlton's flat –

fingerprints, strands of hair possibly.' She stopped short of saying bodily fluids.

'I went there a lot.'

'Yes, that's a fair comment. But it does seem a coincidence that you know all three victims.'

'Carlton knew Billy, and Debbie.'

'Are you saying Carlton was involved with their deaths? Did someone then kill him because of that?'

'No! I told you, he was with me,' Riley reiterated. 'He wouldn't do anything like that.'

Allie filed away what she had said for later in the conversation. 'Not even for drugs money?' she went on.

'I don't know anything about that.' Riley clamped her mouth shut.

'Oh, come on. You lived with Billy, and Carlton visited him, so you must hear, or see, what's going on.'

'I didn't.'

'A neighbour of Carlton's saw you arrive and leave yesterday. She said she heard shouting from the flat. What were you arguing about?'

'I can't remember. Something and nothing.'

'Something and nothing?'

When Riley wouldn't elaborate, Allie reached for an evidence bag she'd brought into the room with her.

'Can you tell us why we found cash and a notepad at Carlton's flat? For the purpose of the recording, I am showing Ms Abbott evidence bag number W182/1Redm22.'

Riley glanced at them but pushed them away. 'I don't know anything about them.'

'So we won't find your prints on them at all?'

Riley was slow to shake her head, a fierce blush appearing as she wiped furiously at fresh tears.

Allie sat forwards. 'We've known each other a long time

now. I don't want to see you getting into trouble for perverting the course of justice.'

'Wh-what?' Riley had the look of a five-year-old child who had lost her balloon to the sky.

'Something was going on with Carlton and Billy, wasn't it? It's okay to be loyal at times, but not when it will get you into trouble.'

'I-I don't know.'

'You never saw anything suspicious between the two of them?'

'Not enough to get them killed.'

'So tell me what you do know. They were dealing drugs, weren't they?'

Riley nodded, her shoulders dropping at the enormity of what she was about to do.

'Yes,' she said.

'Were you involved too?'

'No, I hated all that stuff. I saw what it did to Billy.'

'What about your mum?'

Riley shook her head vehemently. 'I didn't see anything.'

'Where were they getting the drugs from?'

'I don't know.'

'You were never with Carlton when he took a delivery?'

'No.'

'Nor Billy?'

'No! I've told you all I know. Please can I go home now?'

'I'd like to ask you some more questions first.'

'I had nothing to do with any of it. You have to believe me!'

'But you were up to something with Carlton, weren't you?'

There was a knock at the door. Sam popped her head around the frame. 'Can I see you for a moment?'

Allie paused the recording and left the room.

Outside in the corridor, Sam held up her phone. 'Some forensics have come back. Dave said to tell you that he'd been super quick and would like several boxes of doughnuts in thanks.' She smiled. 'We have fingerprints from Riley Abbott, which is to be expected. We also have prints belonging to Kenny Webb on the inside of the door and on the wall.'

'Oh, now that's very interesting.'

'Even more so, the ones on the notebook you found in Carlton's bedroom that you asked Dave to fast track are Carlton's, Billy's, and... Fiona Abbott's. Riley's only appear on the carrier bag.'

'I bloody knew Fiona was involved,' Allie cried, then lowered her voice. 'She had the chance to get away from Trevor Ryan and start again, and what does she do? Get in with a creep like Billy Whitmore and start bloody dealing.'

Allie went back into the room, and whether her anger showed on her face, she kept it to herself. But Riley must have sensed it as she almost cowered in the chair.

'We have some evidence that's come to light,' Allie said, 'so we need to end this chat for now.'

'It's about my mum, isn't it?'

'Why would you say that?' Allie glanced at Frankie surreptitiously.

'Carlton was the dealer really, but she and Billy sold stuff for him too.'

'And you didn't do anything with Carlton?'

Riley squirmed. 'I don't know what you mean.'

'You were heard saying that you didn't want to do any more jobs.'

'Did my mum tell you that?'

Allie said nothing. Instead, she waited as Riley decided what to say next.

'I'm going to find out one way or another what you've

been up to.' Then an ugly thought crept into Allie's head. But before she could voice it, Riley spoke again.

'I've changed my mind. I want legal advice.'

'That's probably wise as we need to caution you and hold you here for a while longer.'

CHAPTER FORTY-SIX

Fiona sat in the kitchen, the cigarette she'd smoked doing nothing to calm her nerves. It had been a shock when a police officer had turned up for Riley, asking her to attend an interview at the station. She'd offered to go along, but Riley was adamant that she went alone, and being an adult, there was nothing she could do but wait in the reception area for her anyway.

Now she was in a mad panic because she hadn't had time to go through with Riley what *not* to tell the police. Riley was a good girl, never bringing any trouble to her door during her teenage years, and Fiona worried she would crack under pressure and say things she shouldn't. Which would mean Fiona would be in trouble then too.

She ran a hand through her hair, tears welling. How had she got the family into such a mess again? What was it with her? Why was she always making the wrong moves? It wasn't as if she did it purposely. It seemed her self-esteem had been given a kicking over Trevor's treatment, something she couldn't seem to get away from even now.

She jumped at the sound of the back door opening, announcing the arrival of Kelsey home from school.

'Hey, Mum.' Kelsey smiled, throwing her bag onto the table. 'How are you feeling today?'

It always warmed Fiona's heart how caring her youngest child was. Kelsey was nothing like Riley who could be as self-centred as her mother at times.

'I'm okay,' she said. 'How about you?'

'Good now school is done.'

'Did you do okay in your test?' Fiona vaguely remembered her saying something about double maths that morning.

'I think so, but I hate algebra.' Kelsey opened the fridge and took out a can of lemonade. 'Can I have one of these chocolate bars?'

'Yes, get one for me too.' A sugar fix might make her feel better.

Kelsey sat down across from her and passed the chocolate to her. 'I'm going over to Leah's later,' she said, unwrapping her own.

'That's nice. Got anything planned?'

'Just hanging around. Where's Riley, at work?'

Fiona paused. She could either say nothing or tell Kelsey what was going on. She opened her mouth to come clean and then decided against it.

'She's working an extra shift. She's a bit like you, wanting to be away from her old mum while things are tough.'

'It's not that, Mum.' Kelsey shook her head. 'It takes my mind off things. It's going to be horrible having Billy's funeral when he can be buried. Mind you, everyone at school is talking about the murders, so I can't get away from it anywhere.'

Fiona leaned across the table and gave Kelsey's hand a squeeze. 'It'll all work out fine,' she reassured her, before biting into the biscuit bar. 'We'll be okay – you, me, and Riley.'

'I know.' Kelsey stood up. 'I'm going to get changed out of my uniform.'

As Fiona sat on her own again, she realised her family needed to come first. Perhaps with Billy gone, there was another opportunity for her to start again. This time she didn't want to mess up.

It was eight p.m. before Allie got to speak to Riley again. She'd been on the phone to Carlton Stewart's mum. Mandy Stewart had told her how her son had all but ruined her life. He'd been rotten to the core were her actual words, and even though she said he could move to Manchester with her, she was glad he'd stayed behind.

It must be awful to have a child that was so out of control, even now Carlton was a grown man. Allie grimaced, wondering if she and Mark would end up with someone similar. A tearaway teen who'd let them know what he thought of them interfering, of being removed from his home for bad behaviour.

She shook her head – mustn't dwell on what might not be. She needed to stay in excitement mode, at least until she'd made her mind up.

The duty solicitor had taken a while to arrive, but now he was here, they got straight to it. Patrick Cunningham was someone Allie liked on some days but not on others. If he was in good spirits, he'd be excellent to work with, but often he'd come in and lower the mood in a room in seconds.

Today, though, their luck was in. He sat across from them with a smile on his chubby face, a button on his white shirt about to ping off in the effort of holding in his bulldog neck.

He must have put on a fair few kilos of weight since she'd last seen him and it didn't suit him.

'I've advised my client to work with you until I see fit to do otherwise,' he informed her, alone this time doing the interview.

'Excellent, thank you.' Allie's voice was laced with sarcasm. That was part of his bloody job. Her attention turned to Riley. 'Are you ready to talk now?'

Riley nodded.

'For the purpose of the recording –'

'Yes, I'm ready to talk.'

'Right then, let's start again. Who was Carlton Stewart working for?'

Riley bit her lip, lowering her eyes again. 'He'll kill me if I say anything.'

'It was Kenny Webb, wasn't it?'

Riley gave a defeated look.

Allie held her gaze. 'I think there's been far too much death on his patch right now for him to worry about you.'

'You've been talking to him?' Riley's voice went up a notch, the shake in it clear.

'We have. Whatever you say, we probably already know. So I think it's time you were honest with us. Was it Carlton who murdered Billy?'

'No.' Riley shook her head.

'Did he get access to Irene Mayhew's property because you stole a key perhaps and gave it to him? And then when Debbie found an intruder, did Carlton kill her so she couldn't identify him?'

'No, that's not what happened.' Riley sat forwards. 'He wouldn't do that.'

Patrick put a hand on Riley's arm and glared at Allie. 'My client can't possibly know what someone else did unless she was there.'

'I am trying to establish that,' Allie replied.

'Then change your questioning to suit or I'll advise Ms Abbott not to reply.'

Allie's temper rose, but she pushed it down for now.

'How do you know Carlton isn't capable of these crimes?' she persisted.

'I just know. He was kind and gentle to me.'

'That's because you've only known him a matter of weeks.' Allie opened the file she'd brought with her, slid out a photo, and put it on the table with a bang.

'For the benefit of the recording, I am showing Riley Abbott a photograph. *This* is what Carlton was capable of.'

CHAPTER FORTY-SEVEN

The photo was of a woman in her late teens, her features barely visible. Her hair was matted with blood, coming from a large gash above her eye, her face a mass of bruising, old and new. There were pressure marks on her neck where hands had squeezed it.

'That wasn't done by Carlton.' Riley flinched and sat back, as if to distance herself from it. 'He wasn't like that.'

'He never got the time to show you.' Allie pointed to the image again, trying to keep her temper in check. 'After all that happened to your mum, I'm surprised you'd want anything to do with someone who beats women.'

'I didn't know!'

Allie picked up the photo, slid it back into the folder, and placed it to one side. 'So are you ready to tell me what's been going on with you and Carlton?'

Riley turned to Patrick.

'Do you want to stop for a chat?' he asked, glancing up from his notes.

'No, I want to talk. Is that okay?'

'I must advise you to –'

'I gave Carlton addresses of clients I visited,' she blurted out. 'People who lived on their own. He checked out the properties and if he thought he could get in and out easily, he robbed them.' Riley looked up, eyes pleading. 'He only did it when they weren't in, though.'

'That doesn't make it right.' Allie's eyes widened. 'Do you have any idea how traumatising it would be for someone vulnerable to have their home ransacked? It's unsettling and damaging to their mental wellbeing. Some of them don't even recover.' Allie shook her head. 'I'm surprised at you, Riley.'

Tears trickled down the young woman's face, and she wiped at her cheeks. 'I did it for the money. I was scared that if Mum started dealing all the time, that she'd go to prison if she was caught, and I didn't want us to be split up. She'd just started, I swear,' she backpedalled. 'She said it was a quick way to earn a few quid and that she wouldn't be doing it forever.'

Now they were getting somewhere. 'Was it Carlton or Billy who got her the gig?' Allie asked.

'Carlton. She's only been doing it since I started seeing him. She'll stop now.' She swallowed a sob. 'Please don't take her away from me and Kelsey.'

Allie's stomach rolled over at the thought. Riley was eighteen and already going into a life of crime. Kelsey was fourteen and living through all this shit might mean she'd do the same.

It was so maddening. Kelsey was such a level-headed kid, and Allie didn't want to see her going the same way as her sister and mum.

This was all down to their mother. Fiona had a lot to answer for.

.   .   .

Riley had been taken to a cell. She sat on the thin mattress of the hard concrete bed, wondering when she'd be able to go home. Her mum was going to kill her when she found out what she'd done. But even though he was dead, she couldn't let Carlton take the rap for everything, despite coming to terms with what he'd been seeing her for.

Her mum was in trouble now, though. Was she more involved than she'd been letting on?

Riley thought back to the day before Billy had been killed, the argument because she'd found out about the drugs. She'd said it was too risky, that Billy might bring the police to the door if he got caught. It was then she'd found out her mum was dealing too.

Riley had pleaded with her to stop. She had Kelsey to think about, not just herself. But Mum had been adamant that if she got caught, she could blame it on Billy.

Riley visibly jumped as someone in the next cell gave out a high-pitched scream. Outside it was raining, and in between cries of injustice, it beat like a drum as it came down heavy.

Grief over losing Carlton had made her numb. She'd cried a lot since it had happened, but part of her didn't believe he was gone yet. Neither was she ready to accept what he'd done.

There were tears of pity for herself too. Apart from a shoplifting caution when she'd been sixteen, she'd never been in trouble. She hoped the police would caution her because they didn't have that much evidence against her, not now Carlton had died.

She hadn't known about that girl, though, the one in the photo.

She couldn't get over what Carlton had done to her. She had been *battered*. It must have hurt her so much. It reminded her of what Trevor had done to her mum.

How had she not known Carlton was a monster? Did she

have a lucky escape after all? Because he had been using her. She could see that now.

A tear fell down her cheek, quickly followed by another. She had never felt so alone. But whatever happened next, she'd look after Kelsey. Her sister deserved better, and it was up to Riley to make sure she was okay.

The cell door opened. DI Allie Shenton appeared in the doorway.

'Come on, let's get you home.' She beckoned her out.

'I can go?' Riley shuffled to her feet and was across to the door in seconds.

'You're being released pending further enquiries. We need to gather more evidence but we're also sympathetic to you suffering the death of someone close. I know Carlton's murder in particular must have hurt you so much, never mind Billy's. The duty sergeant will give you your things, and then I'll take you home.'

'I can manage.' Riley slipped her shoes on. 'I don't want to go anywhere with *you*.'

Allie sighed. 'I'm taking you anyway.'

'I said I can manage!'

'And *I* won't take no for an answer.'

Riley huffed and pushed past rudely. At least she was getting out of here.

CHAPTER FORTY-EIGHT

Allie went upstairs to find her team still at their desks.

'Haven't you guys got homes to go to?' she said as she walked towards them.

'I'm still working my way through the list of names in the notebooks,' Sam told her.

'Me too,' Perry said.

'Me three.' Frankie yawned.

Allie retrieved her belongings from her office and came out. 'There's nothing that can't wait until tomorrow. You all look as knackered as I feel.'

Perry stretched his arms into the air. 'I wouldn't say no to an earlier night.'

'Good. Home, now. All of you. Let's start early tomorrow, refreshed.'

They took a bit of persuading, but they left the station together. Allie went to collect Riley who was waiting for her in the custody suite. Now in the car, there was a stony silence.

Allie didn't blame the girl for not speaking to her, but it was hardly her doing. Perhaps once she'd had a long hard think about everything, and the fact she may come away with a criminal record, she'd understand why.

They were almost at the Limekiln Estate when her phone rang. Allie pulled over to answer it.

'Kelsey? Wait a minute. Slow down, I can't catch what you're saying. Have you rung for an ambulance? Okay, good. I'll be there in minutes; I'm round the corner. Okay?'

Allie disconnected the call.

Riley stared at her. 'What's going on?'

'That was Kelsey. She's found your mum in a state.'

Riley gasped. 'But you mentioned an ambulance. Is she okay?'

Allie didn't want to alarm her, neither did she want to mislead her. And they were only a minute from their destination.

'It sounds like she's in a bad way.' She pulled away from the kerb.

'It's him, isn't it? That Kenny Webb. He's hurt her because he found out I spoke to you.'

Silence fell between them as Allie wondered if it *was* her fault. Could Kenny be responsible, being pissed off after they'd brought him in earlier?

But why would he hurt Fiona? Had he wanted information from her and she either didn't know anything or refused to give it to him?

The door to the house was wide open when they arrived, and they rushed inside.

'Mum?' Riley shouted.

'She's bleeding so much,' Kelsey cried, relief evident that someone else was here. Her mobile phone was on the floor, on speakerphone to the emergency services.

Allie took over the call and disconnected it once she'd spoken to the operator.

'She told me it would be okay,' Kelsey said as Riley hugged her close. 'That I had to talk to Mum to keep her awake.'

'Well, you did a great job of that because I can see her eyes are opening a little.' Allie slipped on a pair of latex gloves and touched Fiona on the shoulder. 'Fiona, it's Allie.'

Fiona tried to focus on her. There was a deep gash on the side of her head, her right eye was swelling, and her top lip and nose were split. Blood was everywhere but luckily slowing to a trickle.

'Hi, there.' Allie smiled. 'You look like you've been in the wars. Don't worry, help is on its way. The ambulance is here now. And Kelsey has done such a good job of taking care of you in the meantime.'

There was a noise behind them, and a male and female paramedic came in, the male knocking on the door to announce their arrival.

'DI Shenton,' Allie introduced herself. 'Patient is breathing, and I haven't moved her because she's mostly unresponsive.'

'Gotcha.' The man nearest to her knelt beside her. 'I'm Gavin. That isn't Stacey with me, but her name is Susi.' He grinned at Susi, who rolled her eyes at him, and then turned his attention to Fiona. 'Hello, meducks, what on earth have you been up to?'

Allie stepped away, removed her blood-stained gloves, and wrapped them inside each other in case they were needed for evidence later. She took a moment to realise that Gavin's joke about a popular TV series in the 2000s was to put her at ease too. It was good of him to do that. She must remember to thank him.

'Can you tell me what happened?' Gavin asked Kelsey.

'I've been out with my friends and when I got back, I found her like this,' Kelsey replied, in bits and spurts as she struggled to get her breath through her sobs. 'I-I thought she was dead at first.'

'Well, she's not and she's not going to die on our shift either,' Susi reassured her.

'I've been calling you, Riley.' Kelsey frowned at her sister. 'But you weren't picking up. Where were you?'

'I'll tell you later,' Riley replied. Then she glared at Allie with a hate she didn't deserve.

Allie decided to ignore it. 'Do you know who did this, Kelsey? Did your mum say anything to you?'

Kelsey shook her head. Then she too glanced at Allie with flashes of anger before turning back to her mum.

It stung to see both girls so hostile towards her, so Allie left the room.

While the paramedics attended to Fiona, she stepped out of the house, her hands clenching in and out of fists. She wanted to punch something to rid her of the anger that was bubbling up inside. Instead, she took a few deep breaths to calm herself down.

'What's happening to my family again?'

Allie spun round to see Kelsey in tears. She took the girl in her arms and held her while she cried. It was the least she could do.

A few minutes later, Fiona had been assessed enough to be transferred to a chair. She was wheeled along the pathway and into the ambulance. A small crowd had gathered, and the doors were closed quickly on prying eyes.

'Is your mum okay, Riley?' a woman queried.

'She's fine,' Riley snapped, clearly unable to cope with the attention. 'She fell down the stairs.'

There were a few mutters, and arms folded, but people began to move away.

'If there's anything I can do to help,' the woman added. 'You know where I am.'

This time Riley said thank you.

'We'll need a witness statement from you,' Allie informed Kelsey. 'I'll get someone to call and see you tomorrow.'

'Why don't you leave us alone?' Riley pushed past her and opened the door to the ambulance. 'You're not family, so don't pretend that you're trying to help us.'

Allie said nothing, letting the girl have her say. Riley was angry, and part of what she'd said was true. But Allie was doing her job now. She would have done the same for anyone else who needed her help. It was nothing to do with the young girl she had grown so fond of. Was it?

Or was it guilt because this *could* be down to them? If Kenny Webb had thought Fiona was involved in any way with the recent spate of murders, he could have attacked her. The same way he might have beaten Carlton Stewart to death before stabbing him.

Yet it didn't seem like something that Kenny would do.

But he would get someone to do it for him.

Riley stepped inside the ambulance, leaving Allie with Kelsey.

'Do you want to come to the hospital with me?' Allie asked. 'There's only room for one of you in there.'

Kelsey nodded.

'You don't have to do that,' Riley snapped. 'I'll get us both a taxi.'

But Kelsey spoke out. 'I want to go with Allie.'

Riley sighed. 'Fine. I'll meet you there.'

The door shut with a clunk for the final time, and as the vehicle pulled off, quiet dropped on the street.

Allie watched Kelsey wrestling with her emotions. Something didn't add up with that family – with Fiona, with Billy, with Carlton, with Riley. And somehow Kenny Webb was involved too. But Kelsey was the innocent victim, Allie was sure of that.

So forgive her for safeguarding someone she'd known since she was ten. Someone who she wanted to protect from the life she was growing up in.

Someone she was perhaps too fond of.

CHAPTER FORTY-NINE

Lisa had been delighted that Perry was coming home early. There was a surprise waiting for him when he got there too.

'Daddy!' Alfie ran to hug his legs as soon as he opened the front door.

'Hey, buddy.' Perry bent over to pick him up, relishing the smell of a freshly bathed child and the feel of his skinny frame in his arms. He kissed him loudly on the cheek. 'Have you missed me?'

'Yes. Lots and lots.' Alfie threw out his arms. 'This much!'

'Me too.' Perry grinned. It was so good to see his son.

'Mummy said I could stay up for fifteen minutes when you got home.' Alfie wriggled from his grip, took his hand, and pulled him into the kitchen. 'You can help me to finish my Lego.'

'That wasn't part of the bargain, young man,' Lisa chided as she leaned in for a kiss too.

But Alfie took no notice, and before long, Perry was at the kitchen table with his head in a bucket of colourful bricks, liking the sound of his son's giggles.

'Not that way, Daddy.' Alfie took the brick from him and

slotted it into the right place. He quickly followed it with another and pretty soon there was a red wall appearing.

'It's been a long day.' Perry laughed at being shown up by a six-year-old.

'Come on, Alfie,' Lisa ordered a few minutes later. 'Time for bed.'

'Aww. Can I stay up a bit longer? *Please,* Mummy.'

'Nice try. You've already been up for an extra hour. Say goodnight to your dad.'

'Night, Daddy.' Alfie dropped from his seat and gave Perry another hug.

Perry kissed his forehead. 'Night, buddy.'

Alfie disappeared with Lisa, and Perry sat back with a huge smile on his face. A few minutes with his boy, with his family, was enough to calm him, soothe his mind, and take away all the stress of the day.

It had been another full-on shift of investigating, and yet they still hadn't got a suspect. There were a few persons of interest, but nothing they could call a good lead. Frustrating wasn't the word. It was more like infuriating, but he knew in this job, one single thing could turn a case on its head. They simply hadn't found what it was yet.

Once they'd eaten dinner and wine had been poured, they relaxed in the living room. Lisa was snuggled in to him, his arm around her shoulders while they watched TV. Or rather, while she did. His mind was still on the case.

He doubted he'd get to sleep tonight with so much racing through it. Three murders in four days and the possibility of another anytime because they hadn't got anywhere.

He thought back to the victims, all known to them for drug-related offences, wondering how their parents felt. Did they despise the shame they brought to their door? Irene Mayhew and Gladys Whitmore still spoke highly of their children, despite their downfalls. He expected Carlton

Stewart's grandmother would too if she had the ability to speak.

He ran a hand idly along Lisa's arm. 'Do you ever feel a disappointment to your parents, Lise?'

'Well, I know they wanted me to be a doctor and marry a rich man, neither of which I did.' She smirked. 'But I think they know I'm happy, and that's what really matters. What's brought that on?'

'I don't know.' Perry yawned loudly. 'I know I neglect you at times because of my job but I also think Mum would like to see me – us – more.'

'You can't do everything, Perry. Besides, your mum is independent. If she wanted to see you more, she'd hop in her car and drive over, you numpty.'

'I know. It just astounds me that some folk are cruel to everyone they meet, and if that includes their family, they're not bothered. And yet some are nasty bastards, but if you say anything to, or harm, *their* family, they'd kill you for it.'

'Wow, that's deep for this late in the evening.' Lisa turned towards him. 'I hate how the job gets to you at times.'

'Sorry.'

They sat in silence, watching the TV aimlessly.

'So you're no nearer to catching him?' Lisa asked then.

'Nope.' Perry sighed. 'It's a tough one. We've only come home early because we're so knackered.'

'Well, a bit of time with your boy, *and* me, and you'll get lots of ideas now. It's good for the mind to take a break. I bet you wake up in the morning and have an epiphany.'

Perry laughed. 'I hope so.'

'It's good to have you home, though, although you do look absolutely exhausted.'

'Hey, this old man can still give you a run for your money.'

'Ooh, what did you have in mind?' Her hand slid over his chest.

'Nothing like that! Mind you, it might make me sleep.'

They settled again, and Perry tried again to switch off. He was in his best place now. His time was his own, to spend with his family. And yet it was what *he* hated about the job too – the inability to stop thinking about it. The victims who shared his mind until they were laid to rest. The man who was out there eluding them. The public on their backs for not catching him yet, despite it only being four days since Billy had been found.

He concentrated on the TV, his thoughts returning to his mum. He would get Lisa to send her some flowers. Better still, he'd take them to her himself. She would like that.

CHAPTER FIFTY

At the Royal Stoke University Hospital, Allie went in search of coffee and then found a quiet spot to sit alone for a few minutes. Along a corridor lit by emergency lighting, she found an alcove. Here, considering the time of night, the place had a calm about it. She suspected that was because she wasn't in the thick of things.

The last hour had drained her, and really, she should go home and get some sleep. But she couldn't leave until she knew Fiona was okay, the girls too.

Finally, she went to A&E and located Fiona in a cubicle, lying on a trolley bed. There was no one attending to her now, but there was a blood pressure monitor next to her, and a padded bandage around her left wrist. A sling was holding her right arm.

The damage to her face had worsened, both eyes swollen due to a probable punch to her nose. Her hair was matted in blood from the cut to her head.

'Hey.' Allie smiled. 'How are you?'

'Why should you care?' Fiona looked at the bed. 'It's your fault it happened.'

'Can't see how you work that one out. I'm not the one who's committed a crime.' Allie had her attention then. 'Where are the girls?'

'Kelsey's gone to get a drink, and Riley needed some fresh air.'

Allie took the opportunity to have a good talk with her.

'I know about the notebook and the money. I know about the drugs you were supplying. I was on my way to question you about them when I got a call from... the control room.' Allie didn't want to drop Kelsey into anything by mentioning it was from her. 'You've taken a right beating. Are you going to tell me who did it?'

'I fell,' Fiona muttered.

'Don't play games. You know we had Riley in for questioning this afternoon. Why weren't you there for her? She needed you.' Allie explained a few things about what had happened. 'But I think you knew that already, didn't you?' she added at the end. 'Riley said she was with you on Sunday evening but during our chat she slipped up and said she was with Carlton.'

'She's telling the truth. She was with him.'

'So where were you?'

'I was at home. I didn't want you to know she was seeing him. She's a good girl.'

'So you have no alibi?'

'I don't need one. I didn't do anything wrong.' Fiona winced as she tried to shake her head. 'What's going to happen to Riley?'

'She'll be interviewed again, and then we'll charge her if we have enough evidence.'

'What for?'

'Perverting the course of justice, inciting burglary, offering information that was used to ascertain stolen goods.' Allie used her fingers to count on. 'Those are what I can think of off the top of my head.'

Tears dripped down Fiona's cheeks. 'I'm sorry.'

'You don't exactly set a good example, do you? Why are your fingerprints all over the book and money found in Carlton's flat?'

'I asked him to keep them safe for me.'

'From who?'

Fiona said nothing.

'You need to tell me,' Allie insisted. 'It was Kenny Webb, wasn't it?'

Still she said nothing.

'Look, if you don't tell me who it was, then I can't protect you. What happens if he comes after you again and Kelsey is home? She's a good kid and would want to protect you. What if he turned on her too?'

'He wouldn't hurt a child.'

She huffed. 'But he's okay punching a woman and doing enough damage so that she needs medical treatment via an ambulance? I'm not so sure he'd care how old she was. And after what you went through with Trevor? You're going to scar that girl for life.'

'I'm sorry, all right!'

'You need to tell her that.' Allie sighed. 'It *was* Kenny, wasn't it?'

Fiona shook her head. 'I don't know who attacked me, but Kenny did come to see me.'

Finally, she'd said his name. Allie was getting through to her.

'What did he want?'

'That cash you found on Billy belonged to him, and he wanted it back from me. I told him I hadn't got it, and that's when he started shouting in my face. I've never seen him so angry. I was so scared, I wanted him to get it over with and leave me alone.' Fiona's nose was swelling, and she was having trouble breathing through it. She sniffed loudly. 'When he left, I thought it was all over. But then a few minutes later, the doorbell went again, and when I answered it, two men in balaclavas came in and... did this to me. I thought they were going to kill me.'

'Did you recognise anything about either of them?'

'No.'

It was hard to see Fiona so upset when all Allie wanted to do was give her a lecture. Instead, she moved closer to the bed.

'It's a good job they stopped when they did,' she said. 'As soon as you're fit, I'll need you in the station to make a statement about what's been going on.'

'No, I can't.'

'You don't have any choice in the matter. Don't you realise I may have to refer this to social services?'

'Allie, please!'

'Kelsey's fourteen, and she's seen way too much in her short life.' Allie paused while she let Fiona take that in. 'It's about time you put her first. A bit of dealing isn't likely to land you with a sentence, but if you continue then we'll have no choice.'

Fiona nodded, seemingly beat. 'What has Riley been doing?'

'I'll let her explain. But what she's done might get her a caution this time as we don't have much proof, especially now that Carlton is dead. However, we will investigate things further. So for now, think yourself lucky that you're all going back to the same house tonight. It could have been so much different. Riley could be locked in a cell. You could have ended up having to stay in here, or even worse. Where would that have left Kelsey?'

Fiona wiped gently at her eyes.

The curtain was pulled back, and a man in a blue uniform came to join them. 'Hi, Fiona, isn't it? I need to take your blood pressure again before you go off for X-rays. Then we can get that gash on your head sorted.'

Allie turned to leave. 'I'll send someone out to see you and Kelsey tomorrow. Hope you get on okay tonight.'

She walked back along the corridor. Of course, she wouldn't refer anyone to social services unless she had to. She didn't have enough evidence that a minor was being ill-treated or in severe danger or threat to life.

Yet she did want to speak to Kelsey before she left, if only to put her mind at ease.

CHAPTER FIFTY-ONE

Everywhere Allie looked there were people. A man with a lump on his ankle the same size as a tennis ball sat with one shoe on. A child two rows back with a patch over one eye was kneeling on the chair and laughing with the young girl behind him. An elderly lady and what looked to be her daughter were reading a book apiece to while away the long waiting time flashing up on the digital display.

Yet there was a general sense of calm within the panic, the crying, the odd scream, and the muttering of conversations behind curtains.

She finally spotted Kelsey. The man next to her had a large piece of gauze held over his arm. Allie waved to get Kelsey's attention and then pointed towards the exit. A minute later, they were outside, the dark a welcome relief from the artificial lighting.

'Jeez, it's so hot in there, isn't it?' Allie flapped a hand in front of her face. 'It isn't nice out here, but at least I can cool down for a minute. Where's Riley?'

'She's gone for a walk around the grounds to clear her head.'

'Right. And how are you feeling?'

Kelsey shrugged. 'Is Mum going to be okay?'

'Yes, I think so. She's having her X-rays, so they should know soon if there's anything to worry about.'

'Do you think there is?'

'Well, I'm no doctor but I think a lot of it looks superficial.'

'Good, because I want to go home.'

Allie said nothing, watching an ambulance come into a bay beside an abandoned parked car.

Kelsey had obviously realised what might have happened if things were worse. In some ways, she reminded Allie of herself at that age. All over exaggerated confidence with a lack of street cred to back it up. Kelsey was more worldly-wise than most teenagers her age, yet she was still a child, who needed a grown-up to care for her. To shower her with love. To show her what was right and wrong. To nurture her towards a bright future.

'You might have to stay here for a few hours, but I expect you'll be home by morning.' Allie glanced at her watch: it was nearing midnight. She'd have to leave soon. 'Would you like another drink and a chocolate bar before I go?'

'No, thanks.'

'Why don't you check on your mum then, see if she's back?'

Kelsey nodded. 'Will I see you soon?'

'I would think so.'

They shared a smile.

After having several X-rays, Fiona was in her bay again, wondering where her girls were. She wanted her family with her. No doubt Allie Shenton would still be around some-where, though.

If it weren't for Allie, Fiona often wondered if Trevor would have gone too far one day and killed her. She had a lot to thank her for, and she was okay for a police officer, having helped her out a lot over the past few years.

And yet she must seem like the most ungrateful bitch she'd ever known. Trouble with a capital T. Or was it gullible with a capital G?

Nevertheless, it was hard to say thank you, especially as she'd been the one to get herself in the same mess once Trevor was out of her hair.

What was it with her and untrustworthy men? She stood to lose so much. And even if Billy might have been a bad lot, he'd never laid a finger on her, nor the girls, and she'd felt pretty safe living under his roof.

Until today.

She'd lied about Kenny Webb. He'd frightened the life out of her when he'd banged on the front door, and she'd had no choice but to answer it after he'd threatened to put her windows through.

He'd screamed at her and slapped her face to get her to talk. And once she couldn't tell him what he wanted to hear, he'd laid into her. She had never taken a beating like it for years.

Memories of what Trevor had done to her came flooding back. The push at the top of the stairs when she'd dared turn away from him. The broken arm because he'd yanked it up her back. The fractured fingers after he'd stamped on them. The endless bruises from one thing leading to another.

As the images ran through her mind, she strained to cry with eyes that were so swollen she was having to squint. Tried to sniff through a nose that had been broken. She couldn't even hug her children because her arm was in a sling, the other hand bruised and throbbing.

So even if Allie hadn't said anything to her, she knew she had to change. She couldn't go on like this, not again.

The curtain opened, and Fiona braced herself for another round of poking and prodding. But it was Kelsey returning. She smiled, then grimaced as her lip split a little more.

Kelsey stood at the end of the bed.

'Where's Riley?' Fiona asked.

'She went for a walk. I've messaged her and she's coming back. Are you okay?'

'Yes, the X-rays are clear. I'm going to be sore for a few days and I have to wear this sling for two weeks.' She raised her elbow slightly and then lowered it again. 'My head is okay too. I'm waiting for a couple of stitches in the cut, and then we can go home.'

'Your head will never be right.' Kelsey's tone was harsh, but she smirked.

Fiona pointed to the chair, and as Kelsey sat down, she wanted to reach to her. But it was too painful. An impression of the sole of Kenny's boot was scratched into the skin on the back of her hand, and she remembered the pain when he'd laid into her.

'Kelsey, I'm so sorry,' she said.

'It wasn't your fault.'

'Yes, it was. Since we moved in with Billy, I've been really selfish, thinking of myself. Sometimes I get scared I can't cope on my own, and I forget I have you and Riley. Things are going to be different from now on.'

When Kelsey said nothing, Fiona couldn't blame her. The poor kid had heard it all before. How would she think this time was going to be better?

'I *am* going to get help,' she insisted. 'I promise, duck.'

Kelsey lay her head on her mother's legs. They sat in silence for a few minutes until the curtain swished again. Riley was back.

Relief washed over Fiona now her family were all together. Angry, perhaps, but in one place. She had to keep it that way.

'Where have you been?' Kelsey asked Riley.

'Sitting on a bench by the car park. I had a lot to think about.' She avoided her sister's eye. 'How are you, Mum?'

'Hurting like hell, but I'll be fine.'

'It was Kenny, wasn't it?'

Fiona paused. She had to be honest but try not to worry them at the same time. She nodded, closing her eyes momentarily when pain shot across her temple.

'But I'm not telling Allie, and I don't think you should either. It'd be more than my life's worth to say anything about him.'

CHAPTER FIFTY-TWO

Allie ran across the grass. Her breath was ragged, her chest hurting with the effort of trying to get away.

She tripped, jarring her wrists, and shouting out. But she pushed through the pain and continued to run.

She wasn't sure if her body would cope with going much further. It was getting harder and harder with every step.

Looking over her shoulder, she could see him gaining. She was almost out of danger.

She caught sight of the road ahead, lights in houses and on passing cars, and screamed out to anyone to hear her. But her voice was carried away on the wind.

Then his hand grabbed at her shoulder, and she flew to the left, falling onto her front. She turned over and tried to get up, but he was all over her.

He straddled her, grabbing her wrists as she kicked out.

She screamed again.

It was the worst thing she could have done. Because he punched her to ensure she stopped.

She didn't.

He punched her again.

A balaclava hid his features. She'd never be able to identify him. If he didn't kill her first.

His hands went around her neck, and she tried to pull them away. He was too strong. She clawed at his face, but there was nothing there to scratch at, mark him.

There was no doubt it was a man. She could tell by his strength, his determination to start what he'd finished.

She tried to take in air, but it was useless. Her arms were growing weak, her legs kicking out to get him off her slowing.

Her vision started to fade. Darker, darker. She wasn't going to make it.

'Allie. Wake up.' Mark touched the base of the bedside lamp to switch it on.

'No!' Allie came to with a rush of adrenaline, almost hitting out at him until she realised where she was. 'What time is it?'

'Nearly half past two.'

She could hear the annoyance in his tone, but equally there was concern too.

She took a few deep breaths to slow her heart. 'Sorry, I had the nightmare.'

It was the one she'd had for years after Karen had been attacked, and the man who'd hurt her was still on the loose. It was always her running, always him unrecognisable when he pinned her down. It hadn't changed, even when they'd caught him, and she now knew what he looked like. She still got it when she was stressed.

They lay on their backs for a moment. Allie's breathing slowly returned to normal. She wanted to sleep. She *needed* sleep because she had to be in the office early again. There was so much to do; to piece together, to collate and gather.

Last night at the hospital had worn her out. Before her nightmare, it had taken her ages to drop off. All she could think about was the Abbott family. Kelsey's angst when she'd first seen her, kneeling next to Fiona. The expression on her face when she realised that her mum might not make it.

Allie had broken her promise.

When they'd arrested Trevor Ryan and, with the help of the city council, got the family into secure accommodation, she'd said things would be better from now on. Of course, it wasn't Allie's fault that Fiona had got mixed up in Billy Whitmore's affairs, but she felt responsible somehow.

In a way, she knew this was one of the reasons why she hadn't thought of fostering children. She'd get too attached, never wanting them to return to parents if they were on a break.

Never wanting them to be adopted by someone else after they'd stayed a while.

Never wanting to let them go back into the horrible worlds they'd come from.

She ran a hand through her hair and sighed with resignation. *Was* it her fault? But then again, her work had to take top priority. It was selfish, but still.

Which left her with a bigger question. Would she dare to be a mum, even in a temporary situation?

'Shall I make a cup of tea?' Mark offered.

'No, you stay here.' Allie sat up and swivelled her legs over the side of the bed.

'You've barely closed your eyes.'

'I doubt I'll be able to settle for a while.'

'If you're sure.'

His hand ran across the base of her back before it dropped. She was certain he'd be asleep again before she'd slipped out of bed.

In the kitchen, she wondered whether to have a mug of tea or hot cocoa. Then she sniggered as she filled the kettle. Perhaps half a bottle of whisky might be better. And where was her emergency chocolate when she needed it? Reaching for the biscuit tin, she took a handful of gingernuts from it.

She pushed her mind back to Operation Moorcroft. Three murders were a lot for them to process. Was their killer relying on them not having the evidence back to find him until it was too late?

Was he planning his next kill right now, while she sat here thinking about him? After all, they had no idea where to look, how to tell if the public were in danger. It had only been four days since Billy Whitmore lost his life, but even so, it was infuriating they had no one in custody yet.

It was up to her and the team to locate the killer. So far, they had an image of a man they might want to talk to, a mixed-up teenager, and perhaps Kenny Webb. Nothing concrete and nothing final.

She glanced at the clock and stood up. Maybe she should at least try and get a couple more hours of sleep. A deep stretch followed by a yawn and she went back upstairs.

She hoped she didn't arrive in work tomorrow and find another murder on the estate. Because if she did, she'd feel personally responsible.

CHAPTER FIFTY-THREE

FRIDAY

Allie's first port of call was to see DCI Brindley. She jogged up to her office and knocked on the open door to catch her attention.

Jenny beckoned her in. 'How're things progressing? I have a press release to do this morning. Any new information I can share?'

The DCI would know a lot of what had happened the day before, but Allie briefed her on the rest. She was mortified when she finished with a yawn, doing her best to muffle it with her hand.

'Sorry, Ma'am. It was a late night.'

'Any reason?'

Allie told her what had happened to Fiona Abbott, the trip to the hospital, and the rationale why she thought Fiona had lied about Kenny Webb.

Jenny removed her glasses and pinched the bridge of her

nose. 'And you thought the Abbott family took precedence over Operation Moorcroft?'

'No, Ma'am.' Allie frowned. 'My team had all gone home as there was nothing further we could do until the morning, and they were exhausted. I was about to leave when the call came through.'

'Really, Allie, I expected better of you.'

'I went in my own time, Ma'am,' she reiterated. 'They're a family in crisis.'

'And you're no longer a social worker so that doesn't make it right. If you have concerns, you can report them to the necessary service. For now, I need you to keep your head firmly in the case we're working on.'

Allie went to speak, to defend her actions again, but refrained. She wanted to rant, to say how unfair Jenny was being, but equally knew it would be best kept to herself.

'I'll be joining you for the team briefing this morning,' Jenny added. 'In about fifteen minutes.'

'Yes, Ma'am.'

Allie left the room, her shoulders dropping when she was out of sight. Sometimes in this job, she couldn't seem to do right for wrong.

She hated being dismissed like that, but she stood by her decision to help the Abbott family. After all, that was what her *job* entailed.

In the main room, Perry was sitting with Frankie while they studied something on the computer. Sam was listening to someone on the phone.

'You okay?' Perry asked when he clocked her face.

'Jenny's just come down on me like a ton of bricks,' she spoke quietly. Running her fingers through her hair, she made a fist and pulled at it. Then she regaled her woes to Perry, Frankie and Sam listening in now too.

'I thought I was helping,' she finished. 'But obviously not.' Her shoulders rose as she took a deep breath.

'You care too much,' Perry spoke matter-of-factly.

'And is that a crime now?' Allie's brow furrowed.

'No, but you need to be careful. Don't get too close.'

She was about to give Perry some lip but then realised it wasn't worth it. Nor was it fair. Because he was right. Then Sam came to her defence.

'We all know it's hard to switch off in this job.' Sam raised a hand when Perry was about to speak again. 'Our role is to protect the public and, whether we like it or not, some of them get under our skin, especially if they keep appearing on our radar.'

'I suppose,' Perry relented.

Frankie hadn't said a word, listening with an open mind, she hoped. However, Allie needed to nip the conversation in the bud. It was something she and Perry would never agree on. He often thought she was too sentimental, letting her feelings get in the way too much. She knew without her emotions she wouldn't be able to do the job to the best of her abilities. And she would never apologise for it.

But she and Perry were friends more than work colleagues and, although she valued his opinion, he also respected when she didn't agree with it. She smiled at him, glad to see it returned.

She stood up. 'Let's get on with the day. Shall we move to the briefing room and go through what we have so far? See if anything comes up that we've missed?'

The four of them settled around the large conference table before everyone else joined them.

'Okay,' Allie started. 'Billy Whitmore, Debbie Mayhew, and Carlton Stewart were all known to us as drug dealers or users. As far as we know, Riley Abbott has connections to all three but no real motive – or none that we know of. It's clear to me that Carlton used her to get information about vulnerable people she visited and then he robbed them.'

'I always thought he was a nice guy.' Sam rolled her eyes in jest.

'Do you think someone will come after Riley next, especially now her mum has been attacked?' Frankie commented.

'I hope not,' Allie said. 'I couldn't sleep last night for thinking about her.'

'Neither could I,' Sam said. 'Everything was running through my head.'

'I had the nightmare.'

'Ouch.'

Allie had confided in them all about it over the years, saying she couldn't understand why she still got it, not now Karen's killer had been caught.

'I did get to see Alfie, though.' Perry grinned. 'Lisa kept him up.'

'Aw, how's my favourite little person doing?'

'Mighty fine and still like a whirlwind.'

Allie loved to see Perry so content. Family time was important and she was glad she'd sent them all home last night, rather than them staying for a couple more hours.

Then a thought popped into her head.

CHAPTER FIFTY-FOUR

'If we put aside the drug connection for a moment,' Allie said, 'do we think it's anything to do with the fact that Fiona isn't treating her daughters well? Perhaps whoever attacked her wasn't linked to Kenny after all?'

'You don't think it's drug-related now?' Frankie queried.

'Possibly not. Maybe it's because of how they are being with each other.' Allie paused. 'Could our killer be getting revenge on family members who haven't been looking after their own? Billy Whitmore made his mum leave her home to make way for Fiona and her children to move in.' While other officers came into the room for team briefing, she raced to the digital screen, bringing up images of their victims. She pointed to the middle one.

'Debbie Mayhew was abusive to her mum. She'd beaten her on several occasions, stolen her money, and caused a general nuisance, insisting on staying at the property when Irene didn't want her there. Irene was scared of her own daughter.'

There was a buzz around the room as everyone caught up with her assumption.

'And then there was Trudy Stewart,' she added. 'Although not his mother because Mandy Stewart moved out of the area and left him behind, she's Carlton's grandmother. The care worker at the residential home said he hadn't been near the place. Was our killer getting revenge for Carlton leaving her lonely?'

And just like that, everything they had been working on since they'd found Billy Whitmore fitted into place.

'So what do we have outstanding?' Allie asked.

'I emailed Lily Elizabeth Residential Home to ask them to go back further for a list of visitors for Trudy,' Sam told her. 'I'll call them as soon as we're done here.'

Frankie startled everyone when he banged the palm of his hand on the table. 'We've been hellbent on it being drug-related that we've missed the obvious.'

'No, we haven't.' Perry shook his head. 'Sometimes it's ruling people out rather than ruling them in that gets the job finished. Everything we've done has led us to this point.'

'Perry's right,' Allie concurred. 'Sam checked out a ton of people from the two notebooks we found to cross them off our list. Plus she waded through hours of camera footage. The rest of us have spoken to the relatives and revealed tiny details that fit together to solve a larger puzzle.

'We've handled umpteen calls from the public in response to the press releases. We've had forensics backing up everything we've done. All this in four days for three murders. Not a minute of that time was wasted.' Allie glanced at Sam. 'Go and make that call to the Lily Elizabeth now.'

While she was out of the room, Allie ran through some outstanding actions. There was so much to do and think about. She was about to speak again when Sam came bursting back in, a piece of paper held high in the air.

'I've received an email from a resident in Adam Street. Someone caught a man on their security camera. It matches the description that Carlton Stewart's neighbour gave to Perry. It's the right time and place. I think this could be him.'

Allie took the paper from her. The image was black and white and showed him walking along the pavement, hands in the pockets of a dark coat. A woollen hat covered his head, light hair at the sides of his face which was barely visibly but clean shaven. He was of medium height and build.

She took in a deep breath. Could this be their man?

She put it on the table and twirled it round so everyone could see it.

'Then I rang the Lily Elizabeth and found out that Trudy received four more visitors over the past six months,' Sam went on. 'One was from social services, another was a speech therapist, and a third was an elderly woman who visited when Trudy moved in but hasn't been since.' She paused for drama. 'The fourth was a man, who came once a month until about six weeks ago. The woman I spoke to gave the same description as him.' She tapped the image twice.

Allie's eyes widened. 'Do we have a name?'

'Sadly, no.' Sam sighed. 'They couldn't tell from the scribble, and when I asked them to email me a photo of the signing in sheet, all I could make out of the surname was it begins with B and the next letter is an E.'

Allie glanced around the room. 'You see, I don't want any of you to think that what we've done so far has been for nothing. *Everything* that has happened has led us to this.'

'Which is what?'

Allie looked to see Jenny standing in the doorway. 'We have a suspect, Ma'am.'

Jenny listened to all the details Allie had set out to the team, nodding at her when she'd finished.

'Okay, we need to find this man. What's your plan of action?'

'Thanks, Ma'am.' Even though she was sure she'd done

nothing wrong, Allie was pleased she seemed to have been forgiven for her actions from the night before. But now was not the time to think of herself.

She turned to her team.

'Frankie, can you show Trisha Hardy the image we have, to confirm it's who she saw visiting Carlton?'

Frankie stood up. 'I'll go now.'

'Ta. Perry, you can speak to Gladys Whitmore, and I'll go and see Irene Mayhew. We'll show them all the image and see if they recognise him.'

'I can check the council-owned properties,' Sam said. 'See if any repairs have been done lately, and if so, by whom. It could be an inside job.'

Allie nodded. 'I want you all to call me when you have details. Time is of the essence, but I don't need to tell you that.'

As officers left the room, Jenny picked up the image and studied it before passing it back to Allie.

'Get this on every social media platform we can, and the camera footage too. Run with the image if the neighbour isn't in. We can eliminate him if necessary. Either way, I want him found.'

'Yes, Ma'am.'

Allie was already reaching for her phone. Her team was gone, rushing in various directions. Adrenaline flooded her at the thought they might be close.

The call she made was answered.

'Hey, Simon, I need your help.'

CHAPTER FIFTY-FIVE

He took a mug from the kitchen cupboard. He added a tea bag and a spoonful of sugar. As he waited for the kettle to boil, he stared through the kitchen window.

The rose bush he'd planted shortly after his mum's death was in the perfect spot. It was a shame Muriel wouldn't see it flower, but at least she wasn't having another bad day.

From the moment he'd moved in with her, things had dropped off with the help she needed. He had been left with more and more to do. When he'd been working, Muriel had been a priority as there was no one else to help. Over the months before she'd died, things had slipped even further. He'd tried so hard not to get irate.

Unless he'd moaned to the receptionist at the doctor's surgery, which he didn't like doing, he'd always had to wait. He wished he'd been able to get more home help, but even that hadn't been allocated to Muriel in time.

Broken promises, that's all he'd ever got. Someone from the housing office said they'd get in touch with social services for extra help. Social services said they had a waiting list and asked him to get in touch with a local care team. The local care team had no vacancies either, so he was left with it all.

He could easily lift Muriel out of bed because she was so light. At a push, he'd help her with a cardigan and put her in a chair by the window, but he'd drawn the line at personal care. It would be degrading for them both.

Luckily, their neighbour, Doris, had been a nurse and had offered to take care of some of the duties. He'd paid her, of course, even though it had taken weeks before she would accept anything.

He didn't know what he'd have done without her, especially when Mum suffered her third stroke which took her speech away completely.

Once the tea was ready, he moved through to the living room, where the news he'd recorded the day before was on pause. There had been a briefing about the murders, a woman giving a press conference inside Bethesda Police Station. He pressed 'play' to watch it again.

Her name and rank came up below her image. Detective Chief Inspector Jenny Brindley. She was a similar age to him, mid-fifties or thereabouts, with short brown hair and warm eyes set in a face that was trying to show empathy over the murders of some degenerates. She seemed more like a school headmistress in her uniform, or a lawyer type.

There was a younger woman beside her, long dark hair and a similar demeanour. Her name wasn't on display, although it had been said at the beginning and he'd missed it. Shenton, he recalled.

They were showing an image of him in Adam Street. He recognised the house on the corner. Things were coming to an end for him now.

He thought back to when it had all started. Left to fend for himself when he'd had to move in with Mum, it had brought back painful memories of his childhood. His older brother, Graham, had *always* been after getting one over him. He'd made his life hell when they were growing up.

In their parents' eyes, Graham could do no wrong. Yet to him, it seemed quite the opposite. Where he studied hard, Graham flunked every exam he took.

Where he stayed in as he didn't have an interest in partying, Graham would be out until all hours of the morning.

Where he wasn't interested in girls, Graham got his childhood sweetheart pregnant at eighteen.

Graham was practical to his brother's theoretical and became a brickie, setting up his own business.

He became an accountant for a good many years until the firm he'd worked at since he was sixteen went into liquidation and he found himself unemployed for the first time since he'd left school.

After a few temporary jobs, he found a permanent position on the refuse lorries, working for the local council. It had seemed like a bad move at the time, but he soon found out that he really enjoyed it. He was part of a team of four, doing the same rounds on a weekly basis. So having to finish broke his heart, but Mum had to come first.

DCI Brindley was still taking questions about the murders. He should concentrate, to make sure he hadn't done anything that might lead them to him sooner than he wanted.

'We are doing all we can to apprehend the suspect,' the woman concluded. 'There will be further briefings tomorrow.'

He sat back on the settee for a moment. He'd better get ready soon.

For he was certain it would only be a matter of time now before the police came calling.

CHAPTER FIFTY-SIX

Perry was in Gladys Whitmore's living room.

'How are you?' he asked first, once they were both seated.

'I'm bearing up, but it's the limbo. The not knowing what happened to my Billy. Being unable to have a funeral for him. I know a lot of people think he was a wrong 'un, but he was still my son.'

'He was.' Perry smiled. 'I wanted to talk to you about visitors to your property. I was wondering if you could cast your mind back over the past six months. I have a photograph I'd like to show you.' He got out his folder, retrieving the image of the man who'd been caught on film.

'Blimey, lad, that's asking a lot. I can barely recall what I had for my dinner yesterday.' Gladys pushed herself to her feet. 'Now, where did I leave my glasses? The last six months, you say?'

Perry didn't need to reply as she'd already left the room. She was back in a short while with a small diary, which she handed to him.

'I thought this might help. I write everything in there, so I can't forget something important.'

While Gladys sat herself down again and put on her glasses, Perry flicked the diary back six months. He scanned the appointments – doctors, dentist, hairdressers, hospital. He stopped.

'You had a new TV delivered before Christmas?' he asked.

'Yes, from Curry's. Two men came. I paid for it to be fitted too, save me faffing about getting all the channels set up.' She pointed to the set. 'It's so big! I can see a lot clearer than I could on my old TV.' She looked at the paper Perry had given to her. 'Oh, yes, I *do* know this man.'

Perry's head went up. 'You do?'

'He's one of the bin men.'

'Do you know his name?'

'I did but I can't think of it. It might come back to me.' She stopped to think but shook her head. 'I only knew him to chat to once a week, but he always looked out for me. He got quite worried because I was on my own, no matter how many times I would tell him I was fine. I think he thought I was vulnerable. Well, sure I am, but aren't we all at this age?'

'When was the last time you saw him?'

'I can't remember – before I moved, I think. That's why I forgot to mention it. I asked the driver of the lorry when I hadn't seen him for a few weeks, and he said he'd retired. I think he had something wrong with him – cancer perhaps. Shame, because I always liked to have a natter with him. He used to make me laugh. Oh, what was his name?' Then she frowned. 'What does he have to do with anything?'

'We need to speak to him, to eliminate him from our enquiries.' Perry kept his tone easy, smiling at Gladys.

'Oh, I hope he isn't in any trouble.'

'You've been most helpful.' Perry put away his notebook and stood up, choosing not to reply. 'Thank you for your time. We'll keep you updated on any new developments about Billy.'

Before he was back in his car, Perry was on his phone updating Allie. 'He's not a binman now, though, so that might narrow it down. It seems he retired on ill health.'

'Great, thanks. I'm in Rose Avenue now,' Allie told him. 'I'll mention this to Irene. Oh, and keep your phone handy. I have a feeling I may be needing you.'

When Allie knocked on Irene Mayhew's front door, she was glad when there was no one home. She'd been hoping that Mary Westbourne would still be looking after her. She jogged along Rose Avenue to see.

Mary answered the door and invited her in. 'Irene is in the living room.'

'Thank you.' Allie followed her in.

Irene got to her feet when she saw her. 'Do you have news?' she asked, almost a whisper.

Allie had heard that tone so many times before. She could tell Irene wanted to know, but equally didn't want to. Because there would be more pain coming. Even when she or her team told someone that a loved one's killer had been caught, the grief often overwhelmed them again. It was heartbreaking to watch it play out.

'I have a photo I'd like to show you.' Allie sat down, urging the women to do the same before getting it out. 'Do you recognise this man at all? We believe he was a binman in this area.'

Irene looked at the photo and nodded. 'That's Michael. I haven't seen him in a while, though.'

The hair on Allie's neck prickled. Michael with a surname beginning with B E. They were another step closer.

'Could I see?' Mary asked.

Irene passed the paper to her.

'Yes, that's Michael. Is he —'

'Did he visit you regularly?' Allie interrupted, knowing it was rude, but she didn't want Mary to finish her question.

'He always helped me with the bins, and I used to chat to him.' Irene paused. 'He did come inside once. I was joking with him about needing a man around the house to do odd jobs. He asked what I wanted doing. I was after a plug changing and a shelf putting up. Anyway, Michael came one Saturday morning and did the two jobs for me. He wouldn't take any payment either.'

'And was Debbie there?'

'No, thankfully.'

Once she was back in the car, Allie rang Sam.

'I was about to call you,' Sam said. 'The phones have gone mental since the photo went out. Simon added it to the *Stoke News* Facebook page, and we popped it onto ours. We have a name.'

'Michael...'

"Ah, you beat me to it.'

'Not completely, that's all we know. Irene and her friend recognised him.'

'Well, his surname is Benedict. I suppose you know he was a binman?'

'Yes, he retired due to ill health. Call Refuse Collection. See if they have an address of the previous employee.'

'On it.'

As soon as she called off, the phone went again. This time it was Frankie.

'Trisha Hardy has confirmed the man in the image was the same as the one who visited Carlton Stewart, boss.'

'We're getting closer, Frankie,' she said after updating him of everything else she'd learned. 'Stay on standby and await my instructions.'

CHAPTER FIFTY-SEVEN

Allie Googled *Stoke News* and typed in the name Benedict. It seemed familiar to her. Sure enough, the name popped up on a report. She scrolled down to read. Graham Benedict had been missing for six months, disappearing one lunch break. His car had been found at his depot, but there had been no sightings of him since.

Another call came in from Sam.

'Give me good news,' Allie cried.

'Don't I always?'

The excitement in her voice flipped Allie's stomach.

'Michael Benedict was based in the Tunstall depot, and some of his route covered all three addresses of our victims or their relatives.'

'So Mary, Gladys, and Trudy would have known him?'

'Yes. Apparently, Michael was always watching out for the oldies.'

'And he retired on ill health?'

'He did, due to late stages of lung cancer. It was six months back.'

'Would they give you an address? If you need a warrant, I'll get Jenny to push it through.'

'Already have it. The guy I spoke to was distraught about what had happened. He used to pick him up and drop him off each morning. He lives at twenty-seven Clifton Street, Bradeley.'

'Call Frankie and Perry, get them to meet me there.'

'On it, boss.'

The traffic was light due to the time of day, but there were so many bottlenecks and narrow streets to negotiate that it was still taking her an age to make headway. Whilst driving, she thought about Michael Benedict. He certainly didn't seem like an average serial killer. Then she scoffed and got her brain back into gear. What a stupid thing to say. Benedict looked to be in his fifties or sixties, was dying of lung cancer but seeking revenge. He'd obviously done his homework during his chatty sessions, finding out who was vulnerable and who wasn't.

It was going to be an interesting interview once they had him in custody.

As she raced down Ford Green Road, she was minutes away from her destination. Just before Rose Avenue, Allie spotted Perry and flashed him out in front of her. They turned left towards Bradeley, and she switched off the sirens, radioing for Perry and Frankie to do the same.

In a matter of minutes, they were outside another bungalow on a private housing estate. Allie checked the clock on the dashboard. It was half past midday, yet the curtains were drawn at both windows visible from the road.

They piled out of their cars and met on the pavement.

'We'll take the front,' Allie said. 'Perry, you go round the back.'

In single file, they marched along the path.

Allie knocked hard on the door, a proper copper's rap.

She and Frankie waited, but there was no reply. She stooped level with the letterbox. A black draught excluder snapped at her fingers, blocking her vision. Pushing it aside, she shouted.

'Mr Benedict? Michael. It's the police. Can you come to the door, please?'

No answer. She tried again.

'Michael, in light of your curtains being drawn, we will have to assume that you are unable to get to the door and we will have to force our way in. If you can't move, can you make a noise instead?'

Still no answer.

Perry popped his head around the side of the property. 'Boss, the back door is unlocked. I can see a knife on the kitchen table. Looks like there's dried blood on it.'

They quickly followed him. Allie knocked on the door, pushing it open wider.

'Michael, it's the police. My name is DI Shenton. We're coming into the property now. If you have anything that might harm us, please put it down and step away.'

With no movement or sound, they went inside. Apart from the knife, the kitchen was clear, so too were the living room and bathroom.

Two bedroom doors remained shut. Allie was about to tell Perry to try one while she tried the other when a voice rang out.

'I'm in the front bedroom. You can come in, if you like.'

'Make sure no one else enters the property,' she told Frankie.

'Yes, boss.' He disappeared from the hallway.

Allie glanced at Perry and pointed to the other side of the door. He moved into position. With a huge jolt of adrenaline pushing her forwards, she pressed the door handle down and braced herself. Although Michael's tone was calm, she wasn't taking any chances.

But no one came rushing at them.

A man was sitting in a chair by the side of the bed. He was hugging a teddy bear, staring straight at them.

'It was my favourite toy when I was a child,' he explained. 'I didn't realise until Mum died that she'd kept it all these years.' He stood up, putting the bear on the bed.

'Michael Benedict?' Allie stated his name, although she recognised him from the image.

His demeanour offered nothing about the hideous crimes he'd committed. He was like a man you'd walk past in the street, someone who'd give you no trouble.

He smiled, almost affable. 'Yes.'

'Sir, you need to come with us.' Allie's tone was quiet. 'Michael Benedict, you're under arrest for the murders of Billy Whitmore, Debbie Mayhew, and Carlton Stewart.'

While Perry cuffed him, she read Benedict the rest of his rights. Then Perry led him out of the house and into a car.

Allie relayed the outcome of the situation to the control room and took a deep breath as she came out of the bedroom. She wanted to pull back the curtains in every room, let the sorrow of death leave the property, but knew she couldn't touch anything until forensics had been all over it.

But she did want to have a quick scan around while she was here.

Flicking on latex gloves, she popped her head around each door. The bathroom had been made into a wet room, presumably to make things better for his mother. There was a second bedroom, which she assumed to be Michael's. A pile of clothes had been ironed and placed neatly folded on the bed. Toiletries on the dressing table, slippers underneath it. The duvet cover and walls were grey, in comparison to the pink and lilac flowers in his mother's room.

The living room was next. All that was in there was a welcoming room. It seemed no different than many homes she'd been to, inviting and warm. Apart from there were no family photos. A lone image of an elderly lady sat in a frame on top of a side unit. Allie assumed it was Michael's mum.

Finally, the tiny kitchen they'd come in through. So clean, obsessively tidy: almost as if Michael never ate in there.

The knife on the table was covered in remains of dried blood. It had to be the murder weapon.

Relief rushed over her, but it was mixed with sorrow. They'd got him, their killer, yet somehow, she didn't feel the same satisfaction as usual.

CHAPTER FIFTY-EIGHT

At the station, there was a buzz in the air. Allie sat in Jenny's office as she retold her what had happened that morning.

'Well done,' Jenny congratulated. 'It was a great team effort you watched over.'

'Thank you, Ma'am.' Allie nodded. 'We'd already interviewed people who we could go back to with more evidence, and that's when our previous workings became vital. We found him quickly because we work well together.'

'And yet...'

Allie paused, then said what she was thinking anyway.

'Would it seem wrong if I felt sorry for him? I'll find out more when we interview him, but he seems to have gone to so much trouble to link himself to the murders and make sure we catch him.'

'Is that because he has a guilty conscience?'

'I think it's more to do with him dying.'

Jenny's brow furrowed.

'He has terminal cancer. I thought he was weak, but he must be strong in some ways. He used a knife to stab Billy Whitmore, which would have taken some force, and yet he used sedatives to ensure he had enough strength to do the same to Debbie Mayhew. But then there was the attack on Carlton Stewart before he was murdered.'

'Perhaps he finds it harder to harm a woman?'

'Perhaps.'

'He left the knife out for you, I gather?'

'He did. I'd like to find out his reasoning behind it all if I can tease it out of him. The families of the deceased deserve to know if possible.'

'I'd like to do the press conference once he's been charged.' Jenny nodded. 'Go and do your stuff. Well done again. Great job.'

'Thank you, Ma'am.'

Outside in the corridor, Allie nipped to the ladies before rejoining the team. Inside a cubicle, she reached her phone from her pocket and rang the one person whose voice she needed to hear.

Mark answered after three rings. 'Hey.'

'Hey, you.' Her voice broke.

'What's wrong?'

'Bad morning.' She closed her eyes momentarily.

'Oh?'

'But we got our man.' Allie burst into tears.

'That's fantastic, isn't it?'

'Yes.'

'So why are you crying?'

'I'm not,' she fibbed.

'I can hear you.'

'Relief, I guess.' She laughed now, the initial release over. 'As well, I-I needed to hear your voice.'

And she did. That was all it took to ground her again. To realise that there were genuine people out there.

'I'm so proud of you,' he said.

'Oh, don't.' She wiped at her cheeks. 'I'll start crying again if you carry on with that talk.'

After taking a few minutes to chat to Mark, Allie felt calm again and went back to the floor below to join her team. Frankie wasn't at his desk, so she assumed he'd gone on a food run to the canteen as none of them had eaten in a while.

She popped into her office and opened the drawer where she kept the chocolate. It was a sorry state – one two-finger KitKat and a family packet of Minstrels. The Minstrels it was.

'I don't have cakes, or even oatcakes, so these will have to do. Well done, we got him.' She ripped the top open and propped up the bag in between Sam and Perry's desks.

No one moved for them.

'Where have the chocolate gremlins gone?' She sat down with a thump. 'Okay, okay. I'm trying to make light of the situation, but it's got to you guys too?'

Sam and Perry nodded.

'We can't let it,' Allie warned. 'We have to be compassionate because he's terminally ill, but Michael Benedict has murdered three people and, if we can, we need to get some answers for their families.'

'Can I sit in with you?' Perry asked.

'Of course. I need to jot down some questions and I'm ready. Shall we say twenty minutes, time to snaffle a sandwich beforehand?'

'Absolutely.'

Half an hour later, they were sitting across from Michael Benedict in interview room one. Benedict had refused legal counsel, which hadn't surprised anyone.

Allie stared at the man before her. Close up, and in the light, she could see how his illness was affecting him. Pale skin with eyes like dark sockets, huge bags underneath them. His hair was thinning, untidy and in need of a good cut. He had the overall look of a person who had given up.

She would definitely have a challenge with her emotions during this talk.

Perry began the recording, and they introduced themselves before starting their questioning. But once that was done, Michael surprised them both by speaking first.

'I'm going to tell you everything you want to know,' he said. 'I killed all three of them.'

Allie sat upright, a little shocked momentarily by the business-like attitude and the coldness of the man. Then she settled into her seat again.

'Okay, why don't you run us through it all, beginning with Billy Whitmore?' she said.

'I've known his mum, Gladys, since I started doing my rounds. I was a binman, but I guess you already know that.'

'We do.'

'I used to be an accountant, but I was made redundant.' He chuckled. 'I was devastated when I lost my job and all I could get was that, but it turned out to be a good move.

'Gladys used to live in Forest Avenue until that bastard of a son forced her out and into a bungalow. Well, I knew she wasn't happy there. Sure, she used to put on a brave face, yet I could tell she hated it. But she's a lovely woman and too nice to say anything to... Billy.' He almost spat out the name. 'Not that he ever visited her. Out of sight, out of mind.'

'So you set out to kill him. Why was that, Michael?' Allie asked.

'I couldn't see her suffering, and no one else was going to do it. She used to tell me about how he was as a boy. How she missed him being around. And then when I started following him and found out what he was doing, well, I saw red.'

'What he was up to?' Allie didn't want to interrupt his flow, preferring to keep him talking. But there was so much she had to get through before she could charge him.

'Dealing drugs and messing around with that young lad across the road from the pub.'

Allie's senses heightened. 'Which lad?'

'Him in flat seven. Billy went in there all the time. Lord knows what he did, but that man has learning difficulties, and it isn't fair.'

'What are you getting at exactly?'

'I'm not saying anything because I've never been in the flat. But it's something you should be keeping an eye on. He has groups of lads around there, taking advantage too.'

'And you know this because...?'

'I'd been watching Billy for a few weeks before I killed him. I studied them all. I wanted to be sure that when it came down to it, I was *able* to go through with my plan. You might know I'm not in the best of health so I'm quite weak at times. I needed to have some advantage.

'So I'd wait outside his house, hidden away, and follow him. I spent a fair bit of time in the shadows behind the old Red Lion watching him go into the flat and then stay there for anything up to an hour. Then he'd go off dealing.'

'Okay, so what happened on the night you killed him?'

'I was across the road when he came out of the flat. I approached him and said I was after a fix and had been told he would sell me something.' He coughed slightly before continuing. 'It didn't take much persuading to get him around to the back of the pub where it was quiet. And then I stabbed him.'

CHAPTER FIFTY-NINE

Michael Benedict's words were so devoid of emotion that Allie's earlier pity dissolved. She said nothing, waiting for him to continue.

'I stabbed him in the stomach first,' Michael went on. 'I had to catch him unawares or else he could have turned the knife on me. I must admit, I surprised myself how hard I hit him.

'It was like a punch really, not that I've had much experience of that. I've never been a fighter. Anyway, I must have got him good and proper because he gave one hell of a grunt. And then I had to fight him off as he came at me.

'I couldn't see anything. It was dark back there, but I pulled out the knife and went at him again.' He paused to swallow. 'After a while, he stopped fighting and dropped to the floor. I waited for a couple of minutes and then I put my hand in front of his mouth, like I've seen them doing on the TV. I couldn't feel any breath.'

'Why did you steal his mum's scarf and push it in his pocket?'

'I thought I might not have been able to stab them all so I

wanted you to have a clue to link the three of them in case I couldn't stop. I found a notebook and some money in one of his pockets, but I left it there. I'm not a thief.'

Allie glanced at Perry who was stony-faced beside her. Benedict was making out he'd left the money behind because he had morals. They were going to need some time out once this interview was over.

'I forgot to leave something when I visited Debbie, so there didn't seem any point when I killed Carlton.' Michael coughed again.

Allie noticed his plastic cup was half empty. 'Would you like some more water?'

'No, I'm good with this, thank you.'

'Okay, we'll move on to victim number two. Debbie Mayhew.'

Michael sat forward to take another sip. He cleared his throat and began again.

'She was a nasty piece of work. I used to chat to Irene on my round, as I do a lot of people. Irene wanted a couple of odd jobs doing, and I offered to help. I didn't take any money.

'I was there for a couple of hours, and we got chatting past the usual small talk. She told me that Debbie was abusive to her. She said she hit out when she was drunk, and she would steal anything to sell on so she could get a fix. Irene was close to tears when she was explaining it to me. I hated how she was feeling.'

'So you found out she was living with Irene?'

'You'd be surprised what a binman knows about a neighbourhood. You get to see the outside of people's lives, and quite often a glimpse of what goes on behind closed doors. I saw funerals, removal vans, new cars, one car in the drive instead of two, caravans missing when people went on holiday.

'I could often tell if someone was happy or sad. Lonely,

perhaps. Irene is quite a well-liked woman; she has a lot of friends. I can't understand why they did nothing to help her with Debbie.'

'Back to my question, please, Michael,' Allie moved him along.

'Yes, I knew she wasn't living there when I'd visited. But I learned by chance that she'd moved in. I bumped into them both at the supermarket. Irene introduced me to Debbie. She said hello but then walked off.

'In the conversation I had afterwards with Irene, she mentioned she was going away for the night. I had planned to follow Debbie one evening and attack her away from home, but this was an opportunity I couldn't turn down, which is why everything happened so quickly.'

'How did you manage to get in so easily?' Allie wanted to know.

'There was no resistance. I followed her to the pub, saw her score, and waited until later that evening to call around. She was so drunk when I knocked on the door. I made her a drink and popped in a little Rohypnol.

'Once that had taken its effect, I was able to stab her. I did think an overdose might have been poetic justice, but I needed you to know it wasn't accidental. So I decided not to do that.'

Allie sat there, a little dumbfounded.

Michael wiped his brow with the back of his hand. 'I will have a little more water, please.'

Perry refilled his cup, and Michael continued.

'Sorry about that.' He pointed to himself. 'Dry chest. Where was I?'

Allie realised she hadn't asked any of the questions she'd written out before the interview. Now there seemed no point to them.

Was Michael Benedict confessing to clear his conscience?

'Shall we move on to Carlton Stewart?' she asked.

'Oh, yes. I left him until last because I knew he'd be the hardest, and the most dangerous, to do. I was putting myself at risk by killing someone so young in my condition. But my luck was in that night.' He chuckled. 'The front door was open when I got to him.'

'I'm sorry?' Allie frowned.

'I was going to knock and have it out with him, and if he got the better of me, then so be it. I'd had enough of life by then. My treatments were getting me down, and I wasn't bothered if I came out of the confrontation dead or alive. He'd end up in prison too, and that would be his comeuppance.' He sneered. 'My knife was in my pocket. But like I said, when I got there, the front door was open, and I found him lying unconscious. He'd been beaten bad. Obviously, someone else didn't like him.'

That chilling smile again. Allie grimaced inwardly.

'So I didn't have to do much,' Michael went on. 'I was in and out within a few minutes. I left the door as I found it, although I wasn't sure why it was open.'

Allie was.

Kenny Webb must have beaten Carlton, as she'd suspected, but then Michael had come along and finished him off.

Allie had collared some truly horrifying criminals during her time in the force, and yet nothing surprised her for long. No one would question this if it were in a film or a book. But in real life, it was too... unbelievable.

When the ghouls got the details of this case, this story would play out on true crime podcasts around the world for years. She could almost picture it on Netflix as a police drama.

Michael coughed again.

He was sweating profusely, Allie assumed nerves getting to him.

'Would you like to take a break?' she queried. 'I'm aware that you may need medication for your condition.'

Michael shook his head. 'I'd like to continue. I have a lot more to say. You've been asking about how they were killed. I want to tell you why now.'

CHAPTER SIXTY

'They were all thoughtless bastards,' Michael spat. 'Merely interested in looking after themselves, getting what they wanted, and stuff the consequences. They didn't understand how much they hurt the ones closest to them.

'Gladys dreaded Billy turning up. She had to hide her money from him because he'd search for it once her back was turned. Making excuses so he could leave the room and hunt around. Many times I caught her in tears because of what he'd done. She didn't have anyone else she could trust enough to tell. It was easy for her to offload to me – easy for all of them, really.'

'And Debbie Mayhew? Was it because she was violent towards her mother?'

'She showed no respect whatsoever. I loved my mum and would never speak to her the way any of those three did to their relatives. And I had to watch her suffer before...'

Michael's eyes welled with tears, the only emotion Allie had seen him show since he'd been arrested. She couldn't empathise with him now, though, not after listening to his confession.

'I'm dying, Detectives. I don't care what happens now. I didn't know when you would find me, but I wasn't going to stop until I was caught.' Michael looked first at Allie and then Perry. 'My mother was housebound towards the end. Can you imagine how that must have felt? And then I heard about Trudy Stewart having a stroke and moving into a residential home.

'Carlton was cruel to his nan. Trudy had taken him in since his mum moved on. Taking his life was amazing.' Michael looked at them. 'He was lying unconscious on the floor in the hall, unable to do anything for himself. Like my mum was in her final days. Her heart failed at the end, and she passed in her sleep. At least I had that to be grateful for, that she didn't suffer too long.'

He took a moment to control his temper, a hand curling into a fist.

'I think Trudy was taken ill because of his actions, a bit like what happened to my mum, really. Carlton put her under a lot of stress. He was evil, much worse than the Billys and Debbies of this world.' He stared at them. 'So you see, they were all heartless and deserved to die. *They* fucked up those women's lives, causing them suffering and pain.'

Allie saw him perspiring now as he wiped a hand across his brow. 'Let's take a break, Mr Benedict, and we can –'

'No!'

She visibly jumped. Beside her, Perry did the same.

'Are you sure?' she wanted to know. 'Because my next question may be hard to swallow.'

'Oh, I'm ready for anything.' Michael grinned.

'Did you murder your brother, Mr Benedict?'

CHAPTER SIXTY-ONE

Earlier, it had been a hunch, but the more Allie had listened to the anger in Michael Benedict's voice, the more she realised it could be the only outcome. The trigger that had happened six months ago.

Michael chuckled. 'You got me, Detective. I'm guilty as charged.'

'So that's yes?' she wanted him to confirm for the recording.

'Yes, I killed my brother too.'

'Why did you do that?'

'Because I was tired of all the promises that never materialised. From everyone, as well as him. People saying they would do one thing and then doing nothing. It was appalling.'

'You mean regarding your mum?'

'Graham washed his hands of any responsibility. He'd always be far too busy supporting his family to lower himself to sit with Mum for an hour if I needed to go out. His visits became less and less until they were non-existent. A text message had sufficed for his contact.' Michael banged a fist on the table. 'Except I found out eventually that Graham *had* been visiting when I'd been at work. Somehow, he'd managed to steal Mum's savings book and cleaned her out of twenty-seven thousand pounds over the space of a year. When I'd sold my own property to move in and support Mum, I found the evidence in her spare room. He'd put the savings book back, empty.'

'That must have been hard to stomach,' Allie remarked.

'It was. And then he had the audacity to come and see me after the funeral. His depot was a few streets away, off the main road, so he walked round during his lunch break. He said I'd have to move out because he was entitled to half the value of the bungalow and was going to sell it. Well, after *all* he'd stolen from Mum beforehand, I lost it. I hit out at him, and he punched me back.

'We started fighting, and then somehow, I don't know how, but I grabbed him around the neck and started to squeeze. And I took great pleasure in the look of fear in his eyes as he clawed at me to loosen my grip. I *wanted* him to feel the same pain I was in.' Michael lifted his hands out in front, miming his actions. A tear rolled down his face, and he flicked it away. 'I couldn't stop. Before I knew it, he went limp and dropped to the kitchen floor.'

'What happened next? Allie urged him to continue.

'I panicked, of course. I wasn't sure if anyone had seen him arrive and might notice that he hadn't left and I didn't know if he'd told his wife or anyone at work that he was coming to see me, and it was risky. So I pulled him into the bedroom and covered him with a duvet. Sarah called me later that week, and I said I hadn't seen him.'

'So where is Graham now?'

'I buried him in the garden, the same night.'

Allie sat forwards. 'At the bungalow?'

Michael nodded. There's a couple of metres of ground between the shed and the fence so I was well hidden. And so was he.' His laughter turned into more coughing, and he held up a hand before he continued, his face turning a puce colour with the effort. 'You look angry, Detective.'

'I'm just shocked that you never spared a thought for the relatives of the people you'd murdered. You might have been angry with Billy and Debbie and Carlton, but you left their loved ones grieving for them. It still doesn't make what you did right.'

'No one could love those parasites.'

'You don't know that.'

'I can see with these!' Michael pointed at his eyes. 'They all deserved to die! At the least they needed sorting out.'

He coughed again, and Allie realised he'd told them enough to be charged. Although Michael didn't want to stop, as police officers, she and Perry had a duty of care to look after him. His illness was against him today.

'I'm going to pause the interview, Michael.' Allie leaned over to stop the recording.

There was a screeching noise as the legs of Michael's chair scraped across the floor. He pushed against the back of it, his eyes widening as if he was in pain, and then he shook uncontrollably.

'He's having a seizure.' Allie jumped to her feet, pressing the alarm button on the wall. 'Help me get him to the floor, Perry.'

They managed to lay Michael in the recovery position.

'Michael?' she cried. 'Michael, it's okay. Help is coming.'

Perry was on his phone to the emergency services.

The door to the room opened, and another officer dropped to the floor to assist.

Michael's limbs were flopping. Thankfully, he was coming out of whatever had happened to him.

But then he was foaming from his mouth, and Allie knew. He was slowing down because life was leaving him.

'Come on, Michael,' she said. 'Stay with us. Help will be here soon.'

More and more bubbles of saliva escaped his mouth. Gently, she moved round so she could place his head in her lap. Then she held him until he stopped moving altogether.

CHAPTER SIXTY-TWO

ONE WEEK LATER

Allie was battling with a second oatcake crammed with bacon and cheese. Simon wasn't around to complain about her adding sauce to them and, despite feeling full, she was determined to snaffle the lot.

It was eight a.m., and all that could be heard from her team were sighs of delight as they tucked in. An oatcake breakfast had been her treat, to say thank you for the hard work on Operation Moorcroft.

Because Michael Benedict had died in custody, there was due to be an enquiry. But once the post-mortem had been carried out, Christian had called to say initial findings had concluded that Michael had taken several doses of his medication shortly before he'd been arrested. He couldn't be clear whether any of them solely would have ended his life, nor how soon they might have worked, if at all. Benedict had gambled that his life would end, and it had paid off.

They'd blamed themselves for it at first. Allie said she should have pushed more for Michael to take a break but equally knew no matter what, he wouldn't have survived because they hadn't known what he'd set out to do.

It wasn't good to witness, but it hadn't been their fault. Yet Allie felt as if she'd let down the victims' families. They didn't receive justice for the killing of their loved ones. Benedict never went to prison for what he'd done.

Jenny had gone with her to inform the relatives of the news. She didn't tell them everything that had happened, the whys and wherefores would remain in the station, but she had given them enough to gain closure.

Graham Benedict's body had been exhumed from the rear garden of the bungalow. The hole had been extremely deep. A team of forensics were still at the scene. Allie imagined details to come for days yet.

Yesterday, on her own, Allie had visited Gladys, Irene, and Trudy, taking flowers for each of them. She would do anything to soften the blow for them.

The four people in her team wouldn't forget Michael Benedict either, nor would she and Perry banish from their thoughts what they had witnessed in the interview room. But in time, the memories would fade, not forgotten but more distant.

Allie wiped her mouth with a napkin and threw it in the bin.

'That's me riding in the car like a beached whale.' She rubbed at her tummy. 'I'm off out this morning. I have a few loose ends. Be good, people, until I return.'

'We always are, boss,' Frankie insisted.

'Want me to come with you?' Perry looked at her, his hands full of mugs.

'Absolutely not. There's no way I'm stopping you from

making a brew.' She laughed. 'You don't do it often, so someone needs to write down the date.'

Perry feigned hurt. 'I'll have you know I make my fair share of drinks.'

'Yeah, but you make sure they're so awful that we hardly ever ask you,' Sam noted.

'There's a method in my madness. And I could say the same about you.' Perry smirked as he walked away. 'You can't kid a kidder, so they say.'

Allie's first visit was to Car Wash City to see Kenny Webb. There was no need to call unannounced this time, so she'd rung ahead to ensure he was in. She strode across the fore-court, aware all eyes were on her this time, but she passed right through the workers.

Although she had given them the glare.

She rapped on the door and went into Kenny's office.

'Allie!' he cried, as if happy to see her. 'How the devil are you?'

'It's better you know this devil at the moment, Kenny.'

He laughed and pointed to the empty seat across his desk.

Allie chose to stand.

'You have something to tell me?' he asked, leaning back in his chair.

'I wanted to reiterate that even though I can't get you for the assault on Carlton Stewart –'

'I told you that had nothing to do with me.'

'– it doesn't mean that we don't know it was you who carried it out.'

'Did someone see me doing it?'

Allie sighed. 'Sadly not. But I also wanted to make sure that nothing happens to Fiona Abbott again.'

'That didn't have anything to do with me either.'

'It never does, does it?' She glared at him. 'I think Fiona is staying loyal to you by not telling me the truth. But now that Billy's no longer around, perhaps you'll keep away from her?'

'*If* I'd visited her in the past, of course...'

'Of course.'

He stared at her now. Allie didn't drop her eyes from his until he gave a slight nod.

It would have to do. Kenny knew there was no real proof, so it was a truce of sorts. She hoped he'd stick to his word. Even though Fiona was easily led, she and her girls had been through enough. Maybe she'd come clean in time.

She made for the door; was halfway out of it when Kenny spoke again.

'Until next time, Allie.'

She smirked, but he couldn't see. Keeping her back to him was childish, but she wouldn't allow him the satisfaction of turning around again.

And there would be a next time. There was definitely some link to the notebook they'd found on Billy.

The boys washing the cars gave her the look this time as she marched past them, and she laughed inwardly. She wondered how many of them were doing the dealing for Kenny. Had any of them been asked to take Carlton's or Billy's places? Milo Watson, perhaps? She'd have to keep an eye on him.

Because only time would tell.

CHAPTER SIXTY-THREE

Allie parked in Redmond Street, opposite the old Red Lion. Grace stood on the pavement waiting for her. She locked her car and glanced across at the pub. You could almost be forgiven for not knowing there had been a murder on that very spot just over a week ago.

The crime scene tape had been removed and the temporary fencing renewed so that no one could get around the back. The metal shutters at the windows had been strengthened too, ensuring no way of getting into the building itself. A lone bunch of flowers stood propped against a corner, holding its own in the weather.

A gust of wind took her quicker than she'd expected, and she almost knocked Grace over when she reached her.

'Nasty weather,' Grace said, holding on to her arm before she flew off any further.

'I should have tied my hair back.' Allie grappled to keep it out of her eyes. 'I hope it's more settled for you next Saturday.' It was Grace and Simon's wedding the weekend after.

'It'll be fine.' Grace crossed her fingers and held them up in the air. 'As long as I get some decent photos, I don't mind.'

'Speak for yourself. All I'm interested in is the cake!'

Together they went down the steps towards flat number seven. Allie had arranged a meeting with Andrew. She wanted to introduce him to Grace, so that he had someone to turn to. She wasn't certain he would ever speak directly to her, and they needed to find out what was going on in Redmond Street. Kenny Webb was behind something, and Andrew may be the key.

'I really appreciate this.'

Grace waved her comment away. 'It's fine. I'm happy to be of assistance. Besides, I'm returning the favour for all the things you helped me with.'

The door opened.

'Hi, Andrew,' Allie greeted him. 'Can we come in and have a quick chat with you?'

Andrew nodded, and they followed him upstairs.

Allie noted the room was clean and tidy again, but also there were what looked like several new games lined up in a row ready to play. She wasn't going to make small talk this time, though. Perhaps Grace could ask him about them when she next visited. Because there was a worrying selection of violent ones.

They sat on the settee while Andrew dropped into the nearest armchair, his eyes to the carpet.

'Andrew, this is Grace,' Allie introduced. 'She's my colleague and she works on the estate.'

'Hello, Andrew.' Grace smiled. 'I'm someone who you can talk to whenever you feel the need.'

'About what?'

'Anything really. If you have a problem, if something is bothering you, I want to reassure you that you can tell me about it in the strictest of confidence.'

'I said I didn't see what happened to Billy.'

'Yes, we know that. But see me as a friend you can call at

any time.' Grace got a contact card out and handed it to him. 'Can you keep this safe somewhere?'

Andrew shook his head vehemently.

'You don't want it?'

'I am fine on my own.'

'I'm sure, but I want you to have it.'

'I said I'm fine!'

Andrew's reaction wasn't what Allie had expected, and even if they couldn't force him to get in touch, it seemed either he wasn't in need of help, or he was telling them he didn't dare ask for it. Whatever, it was time to leave. He'd clearly stopped communicating with them.

'What do you think?' Allie asked Grace once they were out of hearing range.

'I get the same feeling as you,' she said. 'He's definitely spooked about something. Do you think he might be a cuckoo?'

'From the amount of gaming stuff in there? I do.'

'I'll try and find out more, have a chat with some of the neighbours. Perhaps now the murders are solved, and not linked to drugs, they might be more likely to come forward with information for us. Names of his visitors, hopefully.'

'Thanks, Grace. I appreciate it. He seems like a nice lad, and he doesn't deserve to be used.'

Andrew watched the ladies walk back to their cars. They stayed for a few minutes, talking together, before driving away.

He paced the room. He was in big trouble if it got back to Milo that they'd been here. Milo didn't like the police, and he'd think he was a grass.

Andrew wasn't a grass. He didn't dare to tell tales.

The front door opened, and footsteps thundered up the

stairs. Andrew froze, knowing who it would be because there was only one person with a key to let themselves in.

Kenny Webb walked into the room.

Fear coursed through Andrew when he realised he must have seen the police.

'I didn't tell them anything,' he cried, his arms rising up to protect his face.

'It's okay, Andy.' Kenny smiled, pulling them down for him. 'What did they want?'

'Nothing.'

'You sure?'

'Yes.'

'How's the TV? Still enjoying it?'

'Yes, thank you. It's a good gift.'

Kenny nodded. 'Why don't you sit down for a moment?'

Andrew did as he was told, perching on the edge of the settee. Kenny's glare made him feel uncomfortable as he stood in front of the fire with folded arms.

Then Kenny moved to sit next to him.

Andrew froze. He wasn't sure whether Kenny would be nice to him or not. He had been horrid to him before.

'I wanted to come and see you to say that now Billy and Carlton are gone, you'll be working for me.'

'What will I have to do?'

'Don't worry. I'll look after you.' Kenny placed a hand on his shoulder, giving it a firm squeeze. 'As long as you do as you're told, you'll be safe with me.'

Andrew didn't like the sound of that. But he wasn't going to say anything about it. He wasn't in a position to say no.

CHAPTER SIXTY-FOUR

SATURDAY

Grace and Simon's wedding was held in a barn on the outskirts of the city, at a venue that catered for the ceremony as well as the reception. It had been a pleasure to celebrate the union of two of her friends. Allie wasn't sure which one she valued the most.

Grace was a friend she could say anything to, keep a secret, have a laugh with over a glass of wine or three.

Simon was a colleague who she hoped to work with for many years to come. His scruples were impeccable, his demeanour a credit to him. Who cared if he thought oatcakes should be naked?

Finally, the speeches were over, the cake had been cut and shared out, and the music was playing low before the first dance in an hour heralded the start of the evening disco.

Allie and Mark sat quietly with the rest of her team, Lisa with Perry, Frankie with his wife, Lyla. Sam with Craig, her

daughter, Emily, nowhere to be seen but in the building somewhere. They all giggled as they watched Alfie and Ben sliding
across the dance floor on their knees.

'You should try that at work, Frankie,' Perry teased,
pointing at the boys. 'Just your level of fun.'

'No need, old man,' Frankie replied. 'I often slide across
the kitchen floor at home. I'm a dab hand at it now. And
you're only jealous because your ancient knees mean you can't
bend that far.'

'Ha ha, mic drop!' Allie cried.

Perry joined in the laughter. 'Even I have to admit that
was pretty quick, lad.'

Frankie grinned. 'Sometimes I am way too good.'

As the banter continued between the two of them, Allie
blew air over her face, feeling the effects of the drink she'd
been consuming throughout the day taking its toll.

She looked at Mark with a goofy grin. How she loved the
man who'd walked into her life so many years ago, becoming
her best friend as well as soulmate, and even loved her with
all her faults.

Looks wise, he hadn't changed much, his dark hair only
now beginning to grey at its roots. Laughter lines were
heavier as he'd matured, and she was glad his smile could still
warm her heart the way it used to.

She nudged him. 'I'm so drunk.'

He laughed, and for some reason, they couldn't stop until
there were tears in their eyes. Then, he hugged her tightly.

'We're okay, you and me,' he told her.

'Yeah, after twenty-five years, we can just about tolerate
each other.'

He stuck out his tongue and crossed his eyes. 'I wonder
what the next twenty-five will bring.'

'I'll be seventy-one!' Allie gasped.

'I'll be seventy-five. That's even worse.'

'It is. But you'll always be my old man.'

'I bet you'll still have that stubborn streak.'

'Oi.' She prodded him in the shoulder. 'I bet you'll snore even louder than you do now.'

'So will you.'

Allie gasped, feigning disgust. 'I do not snore.'

'No, come to think of it, you barely sleep.'

They grinned and then went quiet for a moment. Allie reached for his hand, linking her fingers through his.

'Let's do it,' she said. 'Let's look into fostering.'

'Really?' Mark's eyes widened.

'Really.'

'You're sure?'

'I'm sure! I've been checking out the website, and that leaflet you gave me, and there are lots of options. We could even work with a family to give them respite a few times a year. I might fancy doing that, getting to know a child like an aunty does.'

Mark's mouth dropped open. 'Wow, you have done your homework.'

'I said I would.'

He nodded, his eyes watering a little. 'We could move my office into the smaller bedroom, so a child has more space. Somewhere to call their own.'

'Somewhere they might feel safe, even if it's only needed for a short while.'

They shared a smile and, as the music moved from fast to slow, he looked into her eyes. 'Shall we dance, Mrs Shenton?'

She nodded, slipping her arm through his as he led her to the dancefloor. His love still protected her from most of her demons. And that was all she needed right now.

A LETTER FROM MEL

First of all, I'd like to say a huge thank you for choosing to read Broken Promises. I hope you enjoyed my fourth outing with Allie Shenton and the team.

If you did enjoy Broken Promises, I would be grateful if you would leave a small review or a star rating on your Kindle. I'd love to hear what you think. It's always good to hear from you.

The next book in the series, Hidden Secrets, is on preorder for May 27th.

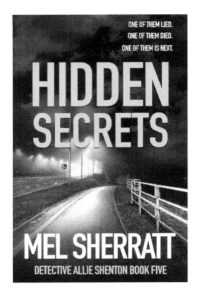

Could you stay quiet about a murder?

Killed on his way home from a night out, Kit Harper had lots of secrets. At the opposite end of the city, another man is found smothered in his bed. Jack Carter had secrets too.

A photo of a young woman reveals a clue and with dual cases to run, Detective Allie Shenton and her team are pushed to their limits. As attacks on a close group of friends continue, a link to a cold case twenty years ago is unveiled.

Can Allie figure out who is telling the truth about what happened on that fateful night? And who is lying through their teeth, to get away with murder?

Set within the gritty streets of Stoke-on-Trent, this fast-paced British detective novel is a dark murder mystery with an emotional pull.

Preorder now

***

Before you go, would you like to join my reader group? I love to keep in touch with my readers, and send a newsletter every few weeks. I also reveal covers, titles and blurbs exclusively to you first.

Join Team Sherratt

ALL BOOKS BY MEL SHERRATT

These books are continually added to so please
Click here for details about all my books on one page

DS Allie Shenton Trilogy

Taunting the Dead

Follow the Leader

Only the Brave

Broken Promises

The Estate Series (4 book series)

Somewhere to Hide

Behind a Closed Door

Fighting for Survival

Written in the Scars

DS Eden Berrisford Series (2 book series)

The Girls Next Door

Don't Look Behind You

DS Grace Allendale Series (4 book series)

Hush Hush

Tick Tock

Liar Liar

Good Girl

Standalone Psychological Thrillers

Watching over You

The Lies You Tell

ACKNOWLEDGMENTS

To all my fellow Stokies, my apologies if you don't gel with any of the Stoke references that I've changed throughout the book. Obviously writing about local things such as *The Sentinel* and Hanley Police Station would make it seem a little too close to home, and I wasn't comfortable leaving everything authentic. So, I took a leaf out of Arnold Bennett's 'book' and changed some things slightly. However, there were no oatcakes harmed in the process.

Thanks to my amazing fella, Chris, who looks out for me so that I can do the writing. I wish I could take credit for all the twists in my books but he's actually more devious than I am when it comes down to it – in the nicest possible way. We're a great team – a perfect combination.

Thanks to Alison Niebieszczanski, Caroline Mitchell, Louise Ross, Sharon Sant and Talli Roland, who give me far more friendship, support and encouragement than I deserve.

Finally, thanks to all my readers who keep in touch with me via Twitter and Facebook. Your kind words always make me smile – and get out my laptop. Long may it continue.

ABOUT THE AUTHOR

Ever since I can remember, I've been a meddler of words. Born and raised in Stoke-on-Trent, Staffordshire, I used the city as a backdrop for my first novel, TAUNTING THE DEAD, and it went on to be a Kindle #1 bestseller. I couldn't believe my eyes when it became the number 8 UK Kindle KDP bestselling books of 2012.

Since then, I've sold over 1.8 million books. My writing has come under a few different headings - grit-lit, thriller, whydunnit, police procedural, emotional thriller to name a few. I like writing about fear and emotion – the cause and effect of crime – what makes a character do something. I also like to add a mixture of topics to each book. Working as a housing officer for eight years gave me the background to create a fictional estate with good and bad characters, and they are all perfect for murder and mayhem.

But I'm a romantic at heart and have always wanted to write about characters that are not necessarily involved in the darker side of life. Coffee, cakes and friends are three of my favourite things, hence I write women's fiction under the pen name of Marcie Steele.

Printed in Great Britain
by Amazon